To my friend
Ginny - come by
and visit Alicia and
Me in Tampa. Enjoy
Implied Consent and
tell me what you think.

Your friend,
Cody
Dove

IMPLIED
CONSENT

A NOVEL

by Cody Fowler Davis

palari
Publishing

Palari Books is a division of:
Palari Publishing LLP
1113 W. Main St.
Richmond, VA 23220
www.palaribooks.com

Library of Congress Cataloging-in-Publication Data

Davis, Cody Fowler, 1959-
 Implied consent : a novel / Cody Fowler Davis.
   p. cm.
 ISBN 978-1-928662-13-6
 1. Trial practice--Fiction. I. Title.
 PS3604.A9563I46 2008
 813'.6--dc22
                2008008559

Interior by Brian Bear
Cover by Ted Randler

This book is dedicated to my grandfather, Cody Fowler. Big Cody, as we called him, was President of the American Bar Association and the American College of Trial Lawyers. He was a lawyer's lawyer who sought justice for all, not just those who could afford it.

"Revenge is a kind of wild justice, which the more a man's nature runs to, the more ought law to weed it out."

- FRANCIS BACON (1561-1626)

CHAPTER 1

S tanding before the Florida Supreme Court was usually an adrenaline rush for Justin Cartwright III. He was a win-at-all-costs trial lawyer who thrived on the challenge of fabricating a defense and then hearing that his client was absolved by a jury of paying money which was rightfully owed. Justin was used to the Supreme Court denying appeals when out-smarted lawyers asked the justices to grant a new trial as a result of Justin's tactics. Of course, he wanted his clients to be victorious, but Justin was always focused on his professional track record and his reputation among his peers. He was determined to be known as a winner. Unfortunately for Justin, he now faced a very different kind of decision.

"Therefore," Chief Justice Ed Soriero—a friend and occasional tennis buddy of Justin's—and a judge who had decided many appellate cases in favor of Justin's clients, said, "in consideration of the outrageous disregard Mr. Cartwright displayed for the ethical canons of the Bar of the State of Florida, we feel compelled to uphold the decision of the trial court and the recommendation of the Florida Bar Association, suspending Mr. Cartwright's license to practice law in the State of Florida for a period of two months."

Justin stared in amazement at the chief justice. He had been sure his relationship with Ed would have insulated him from losing his ability to handle cases.

"Mr. Cartwright has ten days to turn over his current caseload to associates or other firms. In the event that Mr. Cartwright can bring evidence within seven days that this Court has acted in error, we will reopen the matter. We offer this proviso as a courtesy to Mr. Cartwright, who has argued eminently and with great distinction before this Court for a period of many years."

The chief justice paused, shaking his head slowly. The packed courtroom, including the six other justices, all leaned slightly forward in their chairs, wondering what the pause was all about.

"Mr. Cartwright," the chief justice said, trying to restrain his emotions, "I had intended to recuse myself because of our long-standing friendship. Indeed, we went to law school together, and I've had the privilege of serving with you on committees of the Florida Bar trial section.

"But the evidence against you is so overwhelming that despite our friendship, I had no choice but to vote with the rest of the Court in its unanimous decision to issue this sanction against you. On a personal level, I could not be more embarrassed by what you have done."

He brought the gavel down hard on his raised desk.

"Court is adjourned."

As reporters rushed out of the majestic courthouse to jump on their cell phones and dictate stories, one of the most celebrated defense trial lawyers in the State of Florida stood shamefaced, aghast, shocked at the severity of the sentence and at the personal rebuke the chief justice had delivered to him in open court. His wife, Catherine, looked away, too embarrassed to meet her husband's pleading gaze for support. Justin's attorney, an appellate specialist whom Justin had met—and defeated— in the Florida Supreme Court on at least half a dozen occasions, busied himself packing his yellow pads and law books into an oversized attaché case, also avoiding eye contact. Justin spun around to take in the full measure of the response in the galleries to the punishment he had just received. To his further shame, a group of schoolchildren from a Tallahassee middle school were looking down upon him, the teacher vigorously explaining what he had done and the nature of his punishment. A few of the children caught Justin's eye, and the disapproval they displayed caused his face to turn bright red.

It seemed as though everyone in the courtroom wanted to hurry away from the scene as quickly as possible. Few things were more painful to watch than the professional reputation of a successful man being torn away from him in public. Justin felt like a prominent military commander being relieved of his duties during a court martial from the U.S. military for conduct unbecoming an officer and a gentleman. He tried to hide his mortification by maintaining a cold, stern façade.

And then, suddenly, Justin saw him.

In the last row of the balcony sat Anderson Parker, Justin's one-time protégé, and more recently, his nemesis and one of the reasons why he found himself in this situation, embarrassed before his most important peers.

"I can't believe Anderson had the gall to show up here," Justin murmured, not loud enough for his wife or his lawyer to hear. He could see Anderson looking down at him with the grim expression of a man who has come to see justice done. Justin turned back to the front of the courtroom, stiffening in humiliation as he felt Anderson's eyes boring into the back of his neck. He couldn't believe the man he felt was solely responsible for his degradation had the audacity to witness it in person.

All of the justices and spectators had filed out of the courtroom already; only Justin, his attorney, and Catherine remained. Justin's rage was directed not at the Court, for temporarily removing his license, or at himself, because he was comfortable with the choices he had made in the courtroom during the case the Florida media had dubbed Green 61. His anger and resentment centered on Anderson Parker.

Justin was not a violent man, but he knew the vindictiveness he felt toward Anderson would never diminish—not as long as Anderson could practice law and he could not. And not as long as Anderson was around to serve as a reminder of his defeat.

Justin ignored the outstretched hand and apologies of his attorney for having failed to overturn the verdict against him, glared at his wife, and stormed through the courtroom. Just before he reached the door, he looked up at the gallery and stared at Anderson with a hatred so fierce that anyone who noticed it would have thought Justin might run up the stairs into the gallery at any moment, wrap his hands around Anderson's neck and strangle him right there in the middle of the courtroom.

"You might think you've won, Mr. Parker," Justin announced, pointing a long finger at Anderson, "but you'll be sorry. I don't easily forget those who betray me."

CHAPTER 2

T he next day, Anderson was back at work in the firm he'd built after leaving Justin's practice. In the middle of his desk lay a DVD that Anderson was not eager to watch. He gingerly picked up the case as if he were handling a three-day-old dead fish. He turned the cover over and studied the party scenes displayed on the front and back—one in a bar and one on a beach. He knew exactly what he would see once he played the movie. It was easy enough to guess just by looking at the provocative pictures. Once upon a time, he probably would have laughed if someone had shown him one of these movies. But now that he was married and had girls of his own, it was different. His stomach churned at the thought of his own daughters ever being involved in something as vulgar and coarse as the wild parties depicted on the case.

Unfortunately, this particular DVD was not just any ordinary dirty movie. Anderson happened to know one of the girls involved. Dana Estes had babysat for his girls since she'd been a young teen and had hung out at their pool many times during previous summers. She had been too busy to babysit the last few years so he hadn't seen as much of her since she'd entered high school. But she was still a neighbor and the daughter of one of his good friends.

Last winter, Dana had gone on a Caribbean cruise with her parents and some of her friends to celebrate her nineteenth birthday.

According to her father, the girls had been approached by one of the crew members to come to a party down in their cabin. Once at the party, the crew had convinced Dana to try a couple of shots of tequila and then they'd encouraged her to sign a release, a document of which she had no memory when confronted with it by her father six months later.

It turned out that she had gotten very drunk and had begun dancing and going crazy with the rest of crowd. The wilder she'd danced, the louder the guys had cheered. In the spirit of the moment, she'd begun to strip, dancing for the camera.

Anderson knew this was not the first time that a young girl experienced remorse for a drunken escapade. The difference was that Dana's antics had been captured digitally forever, and was now available in ten-second clips on the Internet and in a movie, sales of which, industry experts estimated, ran into the tens of thousands of copies.

Dana's father, James Estes, had turned to Anderson for legal relief when a friend mentioned to him self-consciously that he thought he'd seen a girl that looked just like Dana on one of the *Florida Dreamz* Internet clips. James had not believed him, but once he saw the video, he called his daughter immediately to get her explanation. Dana admitted to sneaking out with the boys, but denied knowing anything about the video.

Anderson intended to bring suit against both *Florida Dreamz* and the owners of the ship for creating a situation in which something like this could happen. The only problem was that Anderson now had to watch the movie. And he was dreading it. Carefully, he opened the case and popped out the offensive disk. He glanced into the hallway to make sure no one was looking and reluctantly slid the DVD into his laptop.

Anderson was disgusted by the blatant sexuality of the entire performance he was forced to view, but even more so by the fact that all the girls were obviously drunk and ready to do just about anything. Scene after scene of girls in all shapes and sizes flashed before his eyes.

Suddenly the video cut away to a party on board a ship, the Sun Lines *SS Martland*, and Anderson leaned forward expectantly. Dana and her family had taken their cruise on this ship. And sure enough, within moments, she jiggled into view, smiling drunkenly at the camera. As she began to perform for her audience, Anderson closed his eyes. He'd already had enough and the show had just begun.

That's when he realized he wasn't alone.

One of the young attorneys in his office, Doug Ellison, was standing alongside his desk, peering over his shoulder at the screen. Anderson had been so wrapped up in the video that he hadn't noticed Doug's arrival.

"So this is what you do when we all think you're working so hard! You dog, Anderson!" Doug exclaimed.

"Actually, Doug, I'm working, believe it or not, while you're clearly screwing off—wandering the halls and socializing. I wish this were for fun."

Doug nodded knowingly. "Sure you do! Watching *Florida Dreamz* is definitely what I call hard work. I wish I had your job."

Anderson wearily waved him to a chair.

"Then maybe I'll let you help me with this one since you obviously have free time. I'm sad to say, but this really is a case I'm handling for a neighbor. One of the girls in this particular video is the daughter of my good friend, and I know her as well. For Christ's sake, she used to babysit my kids. This one hits a little too close to home for me. According to her father, they got her drunk and had her sign a waiver, and now this—" Anderson paused as if looking for a word to categorize what he'd been viewing "—is all over the Internet. I've told them I will handle the case, but watching the film clips is a little more than I can take. I must be getting old because I truly feel like a dirty old man. It's disgusting."

"It really is a client," Doug said, taking a seat opposite Anderson and shaking his head slowly. "I thought you were just—"

"Never mind what you thought," Anderson said wearily. "I can't believe this stuff goes on."

"What stuff?" Doug asked. He knew that his boss had a reputation for being a straight arrow, but this seemed a little bit over the top. "Everybody's heard of *Florida Dreamz.*"

"Not me," Anderson admitted. "I feel like I'm living in a bubble. Doesn't anybody care about ... decency anymore?"

"I think people are a lot more interested in indecency," Doug grinned. "I know I am." Doug had a reputation at the firm for seducing a different woman practically every weekend. Anderson marveled at his co-worker's ability to spend so much time hopping in and out of beds and still managing to work seventy solid hours a week at the office, weekends included.

"I feel so naive," Anderson admitted. "There's this whole world out there I know nothing about."

Doug smirked. "Anytime you want a tutorial, I'm the man to ask. There are a lot of girls out there, and fortunately for me, they all like to play just like those girls on the video."

Anderson replaced the disc in its case and tossed it to Doug. "I'll tell you what," Anderson said. "From now on, you're in charge of reviewing the evidence in this case. I can't look at that stuff."

"Gee, boss!" Doug said. "Now you don't have to give me a Christmas bonus this year! This is even better!"

"Just research the law on the validity of waivers," Anderson said. "And find out where that cruise line is registered. There may be some maritime law issues as well."

"Aye, aye, Captain!" Doug retorted, snapping off a mock salute as he headed for the office door. "I'll get to the bottom of this, even if I have to watch all fifty volumes of *Florida Dreamz*!"

"You do just that," Anderson said, watching him go. "Better you than me."

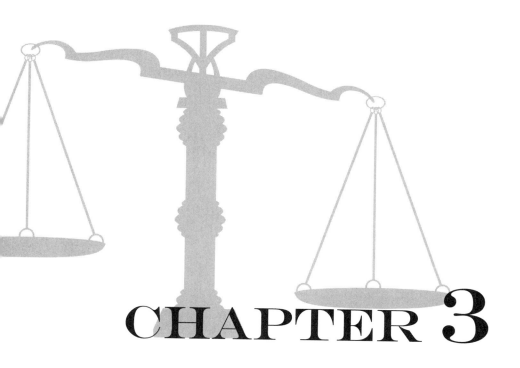

CHAPTER 3

The following Sunday evening found Anderson working late in his home office, where he had been for much of the weekend, preparing the *Florida Dreamz* injunction motion. Just after 10:30, his wife, Ruth, came into his study, placed her hands on his shoulders, and started to massage his back.

"Anderson," she said softly as he put his pen down on his yellow pad and closed his eyes, "you worked through dinner and you didn't even tuck the kids into bed. On Thursday, you missed Emily's first soccer game, and yesterday, you didn't find the time to kick the ball with either of them like you usually do. I'm beginning to feel like your clients are more important to you than your family. What's going on?"

Anderson turned and looked up at her. "Sorry, darling," he said, sounding distracted. "We've got to get some filings in tomorrow morning, and I just want everything to be perfect."

Ruth nodded and bit her lip. "Honey, do you remember what you told me when you left Justin's firm? We decided that you would start your own practice, not only because it was your only option at the time," she laughingly reminded him. "But even more important, you didn't want to have to work day and night like you'd been doing ever since we've been married. You wanted to spend more time with us, and we decided to make the sacrifice so that could happen. Now it seems like you're getting back on that old treadmill. This is not what we planned, not at all."

Ruth moved her hands down from his shoulders to his chest. "Don't get me wrong," she said, as she leaned against his back, wrapping her arms around him. "I love the money you're making. The girls and I have a lot of fun spending it..." Anderson smiled. He enjoyed his role as a successful provider for his family.

"But it's certainly not worth losing you to the office again." Ruth said firmly. She straightened and came around in front of her husband, sitting in the chair opposite him. "Let's talk," she said. "You can tell me what this case is about and why it's so important that it's kept you in the office all weekend. Maybe that will help you get focused, and then you can come on upstairs with me. It's been a while since we've had some quiet time alone." She squeezed his hand gently, implying all sorts of warm promises if he did as she requested.

"If you like," Anderson said. "I've got to warn you, though. It's kind of embarrassing."

"For you or for the client?" Ruth asked, grinning.

"Probably for both of us," Anderson said. "And you have to promise not to talk about it to anyone else because it involves people we both know."

"Now I'm really curious. What in the world is it about?"

Anderson looked at Ruth, trying to decide whether telling her would be a good idea or not. He knew he wouldn't be able to keep his shock about Dana's activities to himself so he justified his disclosure by the fact that Ruth absolutely never revealed anything he had told her involving any of his cases. Besides, he always appreciated Ruth's candid advice and relied on her as a sounding board.

"Okay, I'll tell you, but be prepared because it's not pretty," Anderson said, settling back into his chair.

"Last December, four freshman girls from the University of Tampa took a cruise on the *S.S. Martland*. The ship sailed out of Channelside and made ports of call in Key West and Cozumel."

"Sounds lovely so far," Ruth commented.

"During the cruise," Anderson continued, "the girls were befriended by an employee named Eric who worked in food service. On the return leg from Cozumel to Tampa, Eric approached one of the students—who just happened to be Dana Estes."

"Dana Estes?" Ruth face expressed her shock. "Our Dana?"

Anderson nodded. "Yeah, little Dana. That's why I'm not too proud of this case. Just listen to what happened and you'll see," he said with a small sigh. "Okay, so according to her father, Eric asked her if she and her friends wanted to come to a party in his cabin after he got off duty. The girls thought it would be fun to be a little daring so they agreed."

Ruth looked thoughtful. "Teenagers never think anything bad will happen to them, do they? They think they're invincible," she said, shaking her head slowly.

"It gets worse," Anderson said. "Later that night, Dana and her friends went to the crew's quarters to party with Eric and his buddies. The liquor was flowing and Dana says one of the crew persuaded her to take shots of tequila. According to her dad, she isn't a drinker so it went straight to her head."

"Sounds like things got a little out of hand." Ruth rolled her eyes.

"It does sound that way," Anderson agreed. "So first Eric had Dana sign a waiver, which should have raised her suspicions, but she was probably too wasted to have any idea what she was doing. And then he videotaped her dancing without her shirt."

"He did what?" Ruth was astounded. "And even if she'd been drinking, how in the world did Dana get talked into taking off her shirt? That's just unbelievable!"

"Wait. It gets even more complicated," Anderson replied. "Eric then sold the video to the producers of *Florida Dreamz*."

"What's that?" Ruth asked.

Anderson grinned. "I'm glad I'm not the only totally naive person left on the planet," he said. "Apparently, it's a series of videos of girls on spring break or at resorts, dancing, stripping, and doing whatever lewd acts they can entice them to perform while under the influence. From what I hear, Dana's video is one of the milder ones. But I'm sure that doesn't make her feel any better because now Dana's video is on the Internet, and it's part of one of the *Florida Dreamz* compilation videos that you can buy from their website."

Ruth was appalled. "That's horrible!" she exclaimed. "How could she have done that?"

Anderson shrugged. "She obviously didn't know what she was getting herself into," he said. "I mean, if she had known that by signing that waiver, he could take her video and put it on the Internet and then sell it, I'm sure she'd never have done it."

Ruth looked doubtful. "I don't know about that, Anderson. We love Dana, but from what I've heard through the neighborhood rumor mill, she's gotten a lot wilder since her babysitting days," she said with an air of disapproval. "I wouldn't be surprised if she knew exactly what she was doing."

"You really believe that?" Anderson asked, surprised.

Ruth nodded knowingly. "Like I said, there's been a lot of talk among the mothers on this block about Dana," she said. "So what are you doing, attacking the waiver?"

Anderson blushed slightly. "Of course," he said, with a wave of his hand. "It's the most logical step. She was under the influence of alcohol when she signed it. It's not valid. We're going into court in two weeks to try to enjoin *Florida Dreamz* from using her video, either on the Internet or in their compilation package."

"This is a bad case," Ruth said, "but not for the reason you think it is."

"What are you talking about?" Anderson leaned forward in his chair.

"Dana's wild," Ruth said matter-of-factly. "Everybody in the neighborhood knows that. She's been in trouble before. And attacking the waiver? It just sounds like a girl who sleeps with a guy on the first date and then wakes up in the morning and decides to press rape charges, even though she consented. And there's always a lawyer to take that case."

Anderson looked wide-eyed at his wife. "I beg your pardon?" he asked, stunned. "Is that how you see me? Is that how you see this case?"

Ruth shrugged. "I know attorneys can't always be choosy about their cases," she said. "But if you want my opinion, she knew exactly what she was doing. Her parents probably heard about the video and they're the ones who are behind the case. I'm sure she couldn't care less about the whole thing. Am I right?"

Anderson blushed again. "Well, to be honest, it was her father who contacted me," he admitted. "And I haven't even been able to get Dana on her cell phone."

"That's because her father's only interested in his reputation," Ruth said. "Not hers. It's a dumb case. I wish you didn't have to do it."

"It's a perfectly fine case!" Anderson said, raising his voice slightly louder than he would have wished. "I can't believe you're questioning this! That kid Eric tricked her. Now she's all over the Internet! How would you feel if that happened to one of our kids?"

"Our kids are not like Dana Estes," Ruth said. "Honestly, Anderson, I wish you had a little more discretion about the cases you took on. This is going to be nothing but an embarrassment for you and the firm. I bet Dana knew exactly what she was doing. And the fact that it's been on the Internet for months and she never lifted a finger to do anything about it—what does that tell you?"

"But, but—" Anderson stammered. As much as he wanted to defend his choice of case, he had to admit that his wife had a point. He had gone into this whole sleazy matter with the understanding that he was upholding Dana's honor. But if she didn't care, if it was strictly to salvage her father's reputation, then why should Anderson care so much? He remembered James's face as he'd pleaded with him to take the case. He couldn't desert his friend now—there was too much at stake and he truly believed that Dana had been wronged.

"I've got to get these pleadings drafted," he said curtly, his tone suggesting that the conversation was over. "Regardless of how you may feel about the case."

"*Florida Dreamz*," Ruth said, standing now and looking disapprovingly at Anderson. She headed for the doorway. "I think you're dreaming for taking this one."

CHAPTER 4

Justin Cartwright III, sentenced to 60 days away from his office and his beloved law practice, paced back and forth on the deck at his Cabbage Key Island home, barely glancing at the sunlight sparkling on the Intercoastal Waterway as he tried to think of a time when he had spent even 60 hours away from his office. In all the years since he had started work, he could barely think of any such moments. Catherine had tried, on several frustrating occasions, to get Justin to take a real, live vacation, one where they go to the beach somewhere other than Cabbage Key, two hours south of their home in Tampa, somewhere they might drink daiquiris, maybe go to a casino at night, and just hang around and spend time together as a couple. Justin was the wrong man for sitting around or hanging out in casinos. Constantly checking his BlackBerry for any updates on his current cases or a potential new case arriving was much more thrilling to him than any winning hand at a blackjack table. He was a slave to his work, but a slave who had no desire for liberation.

The Florida Supreme Court, therefore, could not have devised a more powerful or effective punishment for the attorney than to sentence him to 60 days away from his oversized leather chair, his massive desk, and his team of underlings—attorneys and staff—whom he ordered about with imperial ease.

It wasn't fair to say that Justin had spent no time at all in the office during his suspension. His attorney had told him that he was allowed to pop in "once in a while" to handle personnel issues, to raise the morale of the troops, or to make clear to his clients that his absence was only temporary. Justin made liberal use of that "once in a while" clause and contrived an excuse that brought him into the office at least once a week. He was punctilious nonetheless about avoiding any action—verbal, written, or otherwise—that could even roughly be construed as "practicing law." Were he to do so, and worse, were he to be caught doing so, he would face the lawyerly equivalent of the death penalty—a revocation with possibility of appeal of his Bar membership. As in most things legal, when it came to his own career, Justin was content to approach the line, but he wasn't willing entirely to cross it.

Catherine should not have been surprised by the fact that Justin had spent the first 45 of the 60 days of his banishment either pacing the deck of the house on Cabbage Key like a caged animal or seated behind his desk reading case law, mulling over client files, and otherwise preparing himself for the moment when these longest 60 days of his life would be over. There was nothing restful about this unsought vacation, either for Justin or Catherine, whose repeated entreaties to her husband to come fishing or sailing or even to the restaurant across the channel over on Useppa fell on deaf ears. Justin took the same workaholic approach to his undesired vacation that he did to every day of his life—he got up early, was at his desk and computer before the sun rose, and remained there, all but unreachable, until the clock struck five and it was time to come down for a drink.

On the 46th evening of his banishment, he and Catherine were sipping martinis on the deck, Catherine watching the sun preparing to take its nightly dip into the Gulf of Mexico while Justin read the *Fort Myers News-Press*, squinting unhappily in the failing early evening light.

Catherine sighed. The high hopes she had brought to this unexpected family vacation had long since been dashed by Justin's inability to slow down and smell, if not the roses, then the salty brine from the waters of the Intercoastal. Worse, from Catherine's perspective, was the fact that Justin's mental energy, normally completely consumed by the end of the day due to his prodigious appetite for work at his law practice, had little release, which meant that on this long vacation, Justin was even slightly edgier company than at home. Still, time with Justin, even under these circumstances, was better than nothing, and Catherine strove to make the best of it.

"I'll give you some hot news that you won't find in that paper," Catherine offered as a conversational gambit.

"What's that?" Justin asked, not lifting his eyes from the newspaper to see the setting sun or his wife.

"The O'Briens are getting a divorce," she said with a confidential tone in her voice.

That caught Justin's attention. Joey O'Brien had been the dean of the defense personal injury bar in the Tampa area for decades. A highly respected attorney, he had little use for Justin, especially after the local newspaper had written that Justin was making roughly three times more money a year than O'Brien, who commanded a firm five times the size of Justin's.

"Really and truly," Catherine said, delighted she had finally found something with which to capture her husband's attention, even if it was somewhat sordid. "It's not a happy story," she continued.

"Do tell," Justin said, unconsciously folding the newspaper with meticulous care and placing it on the side table. "Why didn't you tell me the sun was setting?" he added impatiently, glancing at the horizon.

Catherine just shook her head. "Kathy just got sick of his fooling around," she explained.

Justin looked surprised. "Joey fools around?" he asked.

"Are you kidding?" Catherine asked, equally surprised. "You never heard the rumors? Well, they weren't exactly rumors. It was practically in the society column in the Tribune, it was so widespread."

Justin shook his head slowly. "I had no idea," he said. He thought about Joey O'Brien—a former fullback for Florida State University, a tall, ruddy, good-looking guy. He should have guessed that Joey's appeal to the ladies would have been too hard for him to resist forever.

"The only time you care about people is beating them in court," Catherine surmised.

"Or at the bank," Justin admitted.

"I hear Kathy's going to try to take him to the cleaners."

"Why?" Justin asked, and Catherine just rolled her eyes. "Oh, of course. The philandering. He really did all that?"

She nodded. "All that and more. You're not even going to believe how Kathy caught him."

"How's that?" Justin asked, reaching again for his newspaper, which he slowly unfolded to the sports page. It was clear to Catherine that he was losing interest in the story. "Did she hire a private investigator to follow him around?"

Catherine shook her head. "Even better. You're going to love this. She actually hired a model. Well, the girl called herself a model. I think she was nothing but a glorified stripper. Anyway, she hired this model to come to his office as if she were applying for a job. She had one of those mini-cams built into her handbag! Joey put the moves on her, and she got the whole thing on video. Isn't that wild?"

"Unbelievable!" Justin exclaimed. "Would that be admissible?"

"You're the lawyer. You tell me."

Justin thought for a moment. "I'd love to be his lawyer," he said. "They set him up. It was entrapment. She was putting the moves on him, no doubt. I could have that whole video tossed out of court in a New York minute. I hope he's got a good divorce lawyer, for his own sake."

"It's unbelievable how you men stick up for each other. Or maybe it's just you attorneys."

Justin grinned as he studied the sports page. "Both," he said. "I can't believe she did something like that to him. I mean, imagine. What a way to take a guy down."

"According to the video," Catherine said, as if revealing a secret that she wasn't supposed to mention, "it looked like he didn't put up too much of a fight."

"Really? Wow, that sounds like the case Anderson took on, the girl who got videoed on a cruise ship. Some people have no scruples. Or maybe just no common sense."

"Who are you talking about?" Catherine asked. "Anderson or the girl?"

Justin was about to answer, when suddenly an idea came to him. "I was about to say both," he admitted, "but I have to say this. You've just given me the best idea I've ever had."

"I did?" Catherine asked.

"I think if you send a beautiful woman to any man's office," Justin mused, "he'd have a hard time resisting her. Don't you think?"

"I'd like to think you could," Catherine huffed. "We're married, remember?"

"I'm not talking about me," Justin said, thinking. He stared off into the sunset. "That was really pretty," he said, surprised. "We ought to come out here more often."

Catherine rolled her eyes. "I've only been saying that all summer long. So what's your brilliant idea?"

"Anderson. He's everybody's hero, ever since he beat me in the Green 61 case." Justin was referring to the case in which Justin's legal tactics had triggered the forced vacation.

"What about Anderson?" Catherine asked, trying to figure out where Justin was going with this.

Justin grinned, and for the first time since his suspension, he actually looked happy. "I think you've given me a way to deal with Anderson," he said slyly. "Maybe he's everybody's hero, but that doesn't mean he's a saint."

"What are you talking about, Justin?" Catherine asked impatiently. "Who cares if he's a saint or not? What does that have to do with you?"

"Everything," Justin said, a Cheshire-cat smile on his face. "Absolutely everything."

CHAPTER 5

A couple of weeks later, Justin was finally back at his desk, reveling in the feeling of control that he was so comfortable with. To be sitting in his oversized leather swivel chair, the command center of his own personal ship, The Law Offices of Justin Cartwright, felt better than anything he could imagine. How he had missed being here, barking out orders, developing strategy, hammering opposing counsel. It was just so sweet to be back.

The only thing that marred his pleasure was the headline on the morning's *Tampa Bay Business Journal*. As always, Justin's long-suffering assistant had placed the week's issue, along with the *Tampa Tribune*, in a neat stack on his desk. And as if out of a bad dream, there was Anderson's smiling face on the front page of the *Journal* with an article praising his most recent successes as a plaintiff's attorney. Justin felt as if there were no escaping Anderson.

He quickly pushed the *Journal* to the side of his desk, flipping it over so that he wouldn't have to stare at Anderson's grinning mug. He buzzed Eleanor, his office manager. "I need to see you," he said.

When she entered the office, seconds later—she never kept Justin waiting—she had barely gotten out an "It's so nice to see you back" before Justin ended all pleasantries with a wave of his hand, which turned into a gesture motioning Eleanor to take a seat in front of him.

"Anderson," he said, skipping even a greeting. It was his nature to get right to the point. "What do you know about him?"

Eleanor blinked a couple of times. "What do I know about him?" she repeated. "In what sense?"

"As a man," Justin replied. "I know what kind of lawyer he is. I'm wondering what kind of human being he is."

"He always seemed like a decent guy to me," Eleanor said, knowing that the words were most likely not what her boss wanted to hear.

"Don't tell me about him being decent," Justin said, seeking to contain his temper. He had promised himself that he would try to control his temper with Eleanor upon his return to the office, but he didn't exactly see how he was going to keep that promise. He was too impatient and wanted everything done yesterday—and he had no tolerance for questions or hesitation of any sort when he issued a command. "I want to know about his social life. Did you ever know him to fraternize with women?"

"'Fraternize,'" Eleanor repeated. "Doesn't that mean to spend time socially with other men?"

Justin looked skyward. Eleanor had the wonderful ability to take all of his instructions exactly as dictated, without any argument or discussion, but that same tendency could make her maddeningly precise about language, as was the case here.

"Eleanor," Justin began, working extremely hard to keep himself in check, "perhaps fraternize' wasn't the best word choice. Understood. Did you ever know Anderson to have any inappropriate contact with women, either in our firm or out of it? Clients, witnesses, anything like that?"

Eleanor thought for a moment and shook her head. "If he did," she replied, "he did it without my noticing it. But I think you're barking up the wrong tree. I know that Anderson isn't exactly your favorite person, but I don't think he's ever crossed the line in his marriage. And if he did, he was certainly discreet enough not to let any of us know about it. He's never been a topic of conversation at the water cooler, if that's what you're driving at."

"That's exactly what I'm driving at," Justin said, not even bothering to mask his disappointment. "Well, if he didn't step out on his wife, what was he like as a bachelor? Do we know anything about that?"

Eleanor shrugged. "Not all that much," she admitted. "I think he was married by the time he came to the firm."

"He was," Justin said. "I went to his wedding when we worked together at the old firm. By then, he was settled and the quiet, staid Anderson that we all know. But I have this feeling that surely he has some wild history back from his college days—you must have heard him refer to something..."

Eleanor shrugged again. "Beats me," she said. "I wasn't exactly privy to his lifestyle before he got married. Or even after it, for that matter. He's a pretty private kind of guy."

"He never talked to you once about his social life?" Justin asked. "I mean, the two of you were always pretty chummy."

"Not really," she said. "Although there was that one time…" she added, her voice drifting off.

"What are you talking about?" Justin asked sharply.

"Well, do you remember when that girl, Paige something, was killed? She was about 18 or 19. He represented her parents in one of the few plaintiff cases our firm handled."

"Wasn't it something bizarre?" Justin asked, thinking back. It was a case that Anderson had handled for the firm, and Justin was only mildly conversant with the facts.

"It was a terrible case," Eleanor said. "She was a beautiful girl—she was a prom queen or something like that. She and a couple of her friends were down at the Ice Palace. They were rushing to cross the street and her shoe got caught in the track just as the trolley—"

"I remember now," Justin said, grimacing at the memory. "She was killed, wasn't she?"

Eleanor nodded. "That was a very disturbing case for Anderson. For all of us, but especially for Anderson. He really took that one hard."

"How come?"

"I'm trying to remember," Eleanor said, rubbing her forehead in an effort to jog her memory. "Oh, I know. It was because the girl who got killed—Paige—Paige … Paige Jacobs…."

"That's right." Justin was impatient. "What about her?" he prodded.

"I seem to remember that Anderson said she had an absolutely uncanny resemblance to this girl he had dated in college."

"Oh, really!" Justin exclaimed, fascinated. He began to rub his hands together. "Tell me more."

"Her name was Alice," Eleanor said as the memories returned. "Apparently, Alice and Paige were dead ringers for each other." She grimaced. "I guess that's not the best choice of expression under the circumstances. The fact is, according to Anderson, they looked absolutely identical from the photographs. At one point, he and I were working late getting some filings together and he seemed extremely disturbed. I asked him what was wrong, and he told me the whole story of what had happened with him and Alice."

"So tell me! This is exactly what I was asking for," Justin said.

"Well, it's not exactly about how wild he was or anything like that but I'll tell you what he told me," Eleanor said, somewhat reluctantly. "He said he was a sophomore at Chapel Hill when he met Alice at the student center. She had put up a sign indicating she was selling two tickets to a concert, which was part of the homecoming activities. Anderson said that the attraction was mutual from that very first moment. She was petite—about 5'3" with brown hair that she wore in a ponytail. She had green eyes and, Anderson said, she had the cutest figure in the whole school."

Amazed, Justin stared at Eleanor.

"How do you remember all this?"

"It's the only time Anderson ever spoke to me at all about his private life," Eleanor said. "It stuck with me."

Justin nodded. "Go on," he said enthusiastically. "What happened next?"

"They dated for a year," Eleanor recounted. "The relationship ended suddenly, and it was Alice's decision. Anderson said he thought they made a perfect couple, in every way."

Justin raised an eyebrow.

"In every way," Eleanor replied. "It was during the fall of his junior year that she told Anderson that she had talked with her family and friends and decided that the relationship was not moving forward and that it had no future. Her rejection took him totally by surprise. He was devastated. He said he couldn't think about any other girl and that he tried to bury himself in his studies, but his heartbreak never eased up until he met Ruth his senior year."

Justin found himself confused by the story. How could Anderson be such an accomplished trial lawyer? In his opinion, love and caring were two emotions that had no place in a top-notch defense lawyer.

Justin took out a pristine yellow pad from his top desk drawer. Eleanor knew that he liked to keep stacks and stacks of yellow pads in the office, because he would start a fresh yellow pad with every new case. It was a ritual of Justin's that gave him great delight, because virtually every file he opened ended in a settlement or verdict favoring his client and a large paycheck in his wallet. At this moment, after being away from his desk and his treasured stack of yellow pads, opening up a new "case"—one he was building against Anderson—was a sweet moment, indeed.

"Tell me more about this girl," Justin said. "Brown hair, 5'3", good figure. Anything else?"

"I could get a picture of Paige from the files," Eleanor offered.

Justin nodded quickly. "Do that immediately," he said. "Anything else?"

"I got the impression from what Anderson said that she had that whole Southern belle aura, the prom queen thing," Eleanor said. "I think that was the key to her personality."

"Ruth isn't like that at all," Justin said, thinking about Anderson's wife. "I mean, she's attractive and everything, but she's more of the natural type. Somehow, I can't see Ruth ever wanting to be a homecoming queen, even though she's certainly hot enough. I think she'd see herself as above that sort of thing."

"He was probably looking for something that was as completely opposite to Alice as he could find." Eleanor's voice had a wistful note. "Is there anything else, Mr. Cartwright?" The whole conversation had made her extremely uncomfortable. She still felt like she had violated Anderson's privacy by sharing with Justin what she had been told in confidence. She justified it by reminding herself that Justin was the one who paid her salary, and that anything Anderson had told her, he had done so on Justin's time. It wasn't much of a justification, but it was the best she could come up with at the moment.

"Actually, there is one more thing," Justin said. He could tell that Eleanor was anxious to get away.

"I want you to find a new paralegal for the firm."

Eleanor looked surprised.

"But why?" she blurted out.

"Because I think it's a good idea," Justin said.

"But...billing's down because you've been away, and even if you hired somebody new, we still don't have enough work for all the paralegals currently on the team."

"I don't care," Justin said. "Having a new person around here will be exactly the kind of spur I need to go out there and sign up some more cases. It'll be an incentive, if you follow my drift."

"Okay," Eleanor said, sounding uncertain. "You're the boss. Anything particular you're looking for in the new paralegal? Any particular experience? Any kinds of cases that you think you'll be signing up? I mean, I don't exactly know who to look for."

Justin took the yellow pad on which he had written copious notes about Alice—her physical description and her relationship with Anderson.

"I don't care what kind of cases she's handled in the past," he said, sliding the yellow pad across the desk to Eleanor. "If I see that she looks like Alice, that'll make me happy. Am I clear enough?"

Eleanor swallowed hard. "Yes, sir," she said.

"Good," Justin replied, smiling to himself. "That's all, Eleanor," he added. And he watched as she got up, shaking her head, and walked quickly toward the door.

"And Eleanor," he barked.

"Yes, sir?"

"I want to be involved in reviewing the resumes and interviewing the girls you find. Understand?"

"Absolutely, sir."

CHAPTER 6

Justin made notes on the resumes, forwarded by the placement agency, as he reviewed them. Five looked like possibilities. The sixth candidate was a waste of time—her extracurricular activities included her church and the Fellowship of Christian Legal Workers. Justin threw her resume in the wastebasket.

He picked up his phone to page Eleanor. She didn't even have the opportunity to say anything before he barked his orders. "I want three interviews set up tomorrow and two the next day. I'm not interested in the O'Connor girl so drop her from the list."

Eleanor wondered why this particularly qualified candidate was being discarded before Justin even talked with her, but then she decided she really didn't want to know. Justin's requirement that the interviews had to take place in the next two days didn't surprise her. Justin was of the opinion that nobody's schedule mattered but his own.

The first young lady arrived promptly at 1:00 for her interview and exited Justin's office at 1:18. The candidate for the 2:00 interview arrived on time and left at 2:20. The last possibility arrived at five minutes after 3:00 and at 3:40 entered the elevator to take her back to the lobby.

An email appeared on Eleanor's screen just as the elevator doors closed. "Come to my office immediately and bring the two resumes for tomorrow's interviews."

Holding the three resumes in his hand, he leaned forward. "What the hell are you doing?" he began in a disdainful voice. "Don't you know how important this paralegal thing is to me? My time is valuable and it was totally wasted today on all three interviews. The first girl had a fat ass and the second was obviously too tall, not to mention her figure was much too bony. Number three looked promising—until I found out she has lived with the same guy for three years and is now engaged. Just great! Can't you follow simple directions?"

She didn't know what to say so she just handed him the two resumes for the next day.

As Justin began to review them, he waved his hand in the air. Eleanor, knowing this was his signal ordering her dismissal, returned to her office.

"This gal looks like she has serious potential. Maybe Nicole Babson will be the answer to my prayers," Justin said out loud.

CHAPTER 7

Doug's eyes popped open and he immediately turned toward the clock on his nightstand. Eleven-thirty—still plenty of time to shower, dress, eat, and meet Anderson at the office to prepare for the Estes trial, which was starting on Monday. Doug didn't mind working on Saturdays as he knew the requirement came with the territory. He was the associate of a hard-charging boss who always made sure he gave the best for his clients.

But it was difficult to balance his very active social life with the weekend requirements. Back during his college days at Georgetown it had been easy to stay out late on M Street, take care of his lady friends, and then drag his ass out of bed for early-morning classes. Now, as he rapidly approached 30, it was more challenging to keep everybody happy.

As he swung his legs over the side of the bed, he saw the note tucked under the phone. "Thanks for the great time! Don't forget to call me for a follow-up. Katie." Doug closed his eyes and tried to activate his memory bank. She was an attractive blonde who had kept him up most of the night. He had met her at one of the bars on South Howard Avenue. She had fallen for his line about being a lonely workaholic who was looking for a classy gal to spend quality time with. It still amazed him that these somewhat intelligent women fell for his bullshit. To him, the only quality time he thought worth pursuing was the kind conducted under the sheets, or on top of the covers, depending upon preference, and there was no need for further communication after the first, and only, quality time was consummated.

Doug's mind started to clear as he pulled his 325i into the employee parking lot of Anderson's recently renovated redbrick office building. As the Beamer pulled alongside Anderson's Durango, he again wondered why his wealthy boss didn't buy a Mercedes or a seven series. Anderson had told him that his SUV was the perfect car for taking his two daughters to school and soccer games. He was oblivious to the fact that his car reflected poorly on his status as a powerful attorney, at least in Doug's opinion.

Juggling his briefcase and Starbucks coffee, Doug pressed the elevator button for the second floor. When the doors opened, he turned toward the conference room. He was spreading out his papers just as Anderson entered the room.

"I see you're ready to get going on this trial, Doug. Good job. I like a man who's prepared to work."

"Yes, sir. I believe in giving my best to the firm and our clients,"

"Okay, then. Let's go over what we've got so far." Anderson looked down at his notes. "When Judge Abrunzo did not grant our request for a temporary injunction as to the publication of the video, he indicated this matter would be expedited so he could make a decision as soon as possible as to whether or not a permanent injunction would be entered. He further ruled that a jury would decide the plaintiff's negligence claim against Sun Lines and the action to invalidate *Florida Dreamz's* consent form since Dana was intoxicated. Finally, he indicated that after the jury returned its verdict, he would rule on the permanent injunction request as that issue was a matter of law for the court."

"I like the fast track the case has taken because Mr. Estes wants to get that video off the Internet quickly, but at the same time we haven't had time to depose all the possible witnesses," Doug replied.

"You're right... This will be trial by surprise. We really won't know what all the witnesses will say. We took the deposition of Captain Sheldon and defense counsel deposed Dana. Other than that, what witnesses will say is surmise."

Four hours later, the trial plan was completed. Anderson would put on two witnesses to prove Dana's case—Eric and Dana. Doug was to prepare a detailed memorandum of law setting forth the standard for entering a permanent injunction. Lastly, Anderson was going to meet with and prepare Dana for her testimony the next day.

Doug was worried about the case. The two of them had never lost a trial together and he didn't want this to be the first. He had this gut feeling that the jury wouldn't sympathize with Dana—although he liked her. Or to be more accurate, he liked what he'd seen of her body on the video he had reviewed at least ten times over the last few days.

CHAPTER 8

T he deafening music filled her ears and her body swayed to the insistent beat of the drums. The louder, the better, Nicole thought, as she made her way across the room, aware of every male eye following her progress. Nicole made the most of the attention as she approached the bar. She knew she looked good and she enjoyed the feeling of being desired. She'd arrived early enough to claim a seat at the bar, where she could watch the newcomers entering and decide whom she'd target that evening.

"Charlie, what's new?" Nicole smiled at the bartender who was cleaning glasses before the evening rush began. "What's a girl gotta do to get a drink around here?" She rested her elbows on the countertop so her breasts spilled out of her tiny tank top, on full display.

"Now, Nicole. You know I'm always there for you. All you have to do is ask. So what can I do for you this lovely evening?" Charlie said as he walked over to her. His eyes were riveted on her chest.

"Oh my, you're such a charmer, Charlie. You got anything in the back that could make a girl happy?"

"I am here to please. I need to grab more stock to get ready for the evening. Why don't you step into my office and let's see what we can find?" Charlie was already turning toward the storage room behind the bar.

Nicole casually walked around the bar and pushed the storage room door open, letting it swing closed behind her. When she emerged a few minutes later, her face was flushed and her eyes glittered brightly with excitement.

Nicole's eyes struggled to focus. The steering wheel seemed to have a mind of its own and her car kept swaying across the road. She leaned closer to the windshield trying to see more clearly, but the damn lights kept flashing in front of her eyes. How could anyone expect her to drive safely with those lights? One of these days she was going to have to write a letter to the Highway Department telling them about this. What morons.

The stereo system blasted Britney Spears's latest hit as she sang along. The stop sign was there and gone before she even saw it.

The judge stared sternly over his glasses at Nicole. "Young lady, you are very lucky no one was hurt and that you are here in my courtroom in one piece. I hope you realize that." Nicole slid farther down into her seat. She knew he was right.

"Since this is your first offense, I am going to require you to perform 80 hours of community service. I hope you use this as an opportunity to reevaluate your life and make some big changes. Most people don't have a second chance when they see me in here, did you know that? Their lives are changed forever, with no going back. But this time, you do have a chance. Next time, you probably won't be so lucky. And unless you do something drastic, I can promise you there will be a next time. My advice, for what it's worth, is that you get help now before it's too late."

Nicole lay sprawled across her bed with the sheets rumpled and twisted around her legs. She'd slept fitfully, trying to decide what to do, and as a result, had hardly slept the entire night. Toward morning, she'd fallen into a light sleep, which was now being interrupted by the playful antics of her sleeping companion. She pulled her pillow over her head to shut out the morning light and moaned.

"Not now, Sebastian," she grumbled as she pushed away the wriggling ball of fur. "Not now," she repeated even more adamantly as the kitten approached from the opposite direction, continuing his licking and purring. "I can't move. I just can't. You're going to have to wait." But Sebastian was having none of that and continued his persuasive ways until Nicole peeked one eye out from under her pillow to glance at her clock.

"Oh, crap," she cried, jumping out of bed. "I've gotta be at work in 30 minutes. Why didn't you wake me sooner, you little lazybones? If I get fired from this firm, we're both in trouble. I'm already in deep enough shit as it is."

Nicole threw off her covers and stumbled into the bathroom, grabbing clothes from the pile on the chair as she ran. She splashed cold water on her face and glanced briefly at herself in the mirror. "Oh, God. What a mess..."

Nicole stared at her computer screen in a daze, wondering how everything around her had fallen apart so quickly. Yesterday, she had been determined to have a quiet night at home and make an attempt at getting her mess of a life into some semblance of order. Despite the warning from the judge, somehow she'd ended up back in her usual haunts, trying to silence the noises in her head with music, alcohol, and sex. She was still recovering from the night before and felt as if a monster had her head between his massive hands and was squeezing as hard as he could. The chime of an incoming email got her attention.

"Good morning! Last night was fantastic. Let's do it again, wild woman! How about we meet at Shenanigans? I hear there's a big party tonight."

Oh my God. I gave him my email? What was I thinking? I must have been totally out of it.

Quickly, she typed back. "Sorry. Not tonight. Too much work." Maybe that will shut him up. I hope.

"Come on, Nicole. I bet that's never stopped you before."

"Well, it is this time. I have more important things to do than mess around with you. Leave me alone. Now."

At least he doesn't know about my arrest. Thank God for small favors—very small favors. It's time to shut this life down and get out of here before it's too late.

And she turned off her computer so she wouldn't be tempted to respond further. He didn't know her last name, she was pretty sure. Or where she worked. She should be safe, at least for now.

She had to get her life together first. God, even after her arrest and the warnings from the judge, she'd still ended up drunk and in someone else's bed. Tonight, she was going straight home after work. No night on the town. She promised herself tonight was the night she was beginning a new life and getting her shit together.

Several hours later, she looked at the clock and realized it was that time already. Turning off her desk light, she gathered her purse and briefcase and headed down the hallway.

Nicole opened her dresser drawer and pushed aside the pile of shirts. Buried underneath was a picture frame turned over on its face. She gently lifted the frame from its hiding place and carried it over to her bed where she sat holding it in her lap. Tears welled up in her eyes as she looked at the photograph. A wistful smile crept across her mouth, but was replaced suddenly by a thunderstorm of emotion. Her forehead wrinkled up in anger and the veins in her hands popped out as the tension tightened throughout her body. She stood up determinedly and, carrying the frame, marched straight into the kitchen. Nicole jerked open drawer after drawer until finally she found what she was looking for. She flipped the frame over and pulled off the back. She pulled out the picture and held it over the sink, clicking the lighter and holding it to the corner of the paper. Watching the edges curl and the smoke rise in the air, she felt a small sense of satisfaction and release. Maybe she would be able to move on. Rick was part of her past and she had to let him go. She would never let herself fall for the false promises of love again. Men only wanted one thing, and as long as she never forgot that, she would be fine.

Another sunny day in California. Wonderful. Just what I need, Nicole thought, as she pulled her robe tighter around her waist. Sebastian meowed mournfully until she picked him up and carried him with her into the kitchen. Scooping some kitty food into a bowl for him, she prepared herself a cup of coffee, then sat down at the table. Resting her head in her hands, she glanced at the notes she'd written the night before. Call Meredith, she'd scribbled. Maybe that wasn't such a bad idea after all. She hadn't talked to her cousin in years, and they'd always been close—at least when they were kids. It couldn't hurt to try. She didn't have many other options.

She dug through her purse and found a crumpled piece of paper wedged into the back of her Day-Timer. For once, luck was going her way. She pressed the paper against the table, smoothing out the wrinkles, and thought about Meredith and what she could say to justify her silence for so many years. Nothing. She had no excuse. Just call, she thought. Get over your pride and just pick up the phone.

Her hands began to sweat as she heard the phone ringing. She was just about to hang up when a breathless voice answered, "Hello?"

"Meredith? It's me. Nicole."

Silence.

"Nicole? Is that really you? Why haven't you ever called me back? I've been so worried about you. I haven't heard anything from you in years. And now suddenly, here you are. Are you okay?"

"I know, Meredith. I've been a jerk, but I had so much going on in my head, I just couldn't deal with family. I'm sorry. I've had some bad things happening here lately and I was hoping to start somewhere new. I thought maybe you might help me. Could I come stay with you for a while? I know this is out of the blue and you've got your own life to live, but I thought maybe if I could just get on my feet again, I'd be ok—"

Meredith interrupted. "You've got to be kidding. Of course you're welcome. I'd love to have you stay with me. I've got an extra bedroom and everything. You'll love it here in Tampa. And we'll have the best time together! Oh, please come. I miss you!"

Nicole smiled and felt the tension easing out of her neck and shoulders. Meredith had always been there for her. She'd be okay. She just needed to get away from the place where everything had gone wrong and start new. That's what she had to do.

"You're the best, Meredith."

CHAPTER 9

W hen Anderson, Doug, Dana, and her father, James Estes, arrived in the courtroom, Anderson was surprised to find Charles Towler, defense counsel for the cruise ship, seated at the counsel table closest to the jury box, the table Anderson preferred, the one the bailiff usually reserved for him. Anderson glanced over at Fredrick, the bailiff assigned to the case, with a look of disapproval. Fredrick shrugged his shoulders.

Anderson placed his briefcase on the middle table, leaving the third table farthest from the jury box to Lloyd Greenwald, defense counsel for *Florida Dreamz*. He felt out of sorts, not arriving first and especially not getting his usual table. Anderson squared his shoulders and began to arrange his papers.

Charles walked over to Anderson as his team started to unpack their bags and exhibits. "I'd like to talk to you alone. No clients. No other lawyers. Just you and me. The witness room in the hallway. Two minutes, okay?"

Anderson kept his head down and continued to work on the organization of his legal pads, as if ignoring Charles's presence. Once Charles had left the room, Anderson turned to Doug. "I need to take care of this. Be right back."

The conference room was dark and cramped. Four straight-backed and extremely uncomfortable-looking chairs surrounded a small table. Charles was standing on the opposite side of the room as Anderson entered. He glared across the table where Anderson waited to hear what he had to say.

Charles spoke first. "Although we have never before been on opposite sides of a case, I have known of you and your reputation for many years. Honestly, you now disappoint me. To be more accurate, you disgust me. You symbolize what is wrong with the jury trial system today." Anderson almost turned on his heel and left the room without saying a word, but he decided that out of respect for his fellow member of the Bar he would let Charles vent.

"You will do anything for money," Charles continued. "You know damn well that Sun Lines had no knowledge of Eric's actions. Additionally, your client signed that waiver and decided to dance knowing full well what she was doing. But you smell money and file a bullshit claim. Sham lawsuits like this one have to be stopped. So take your best shot, because my client is not offering one red cent to settle this matter."

"I suppose you think it's acceptable that your client's employee got my client drunk, tricked her into signing a consent form, and then had her dance practically naked! That's what I see as the injustice in this case. That a big company with lots of money can come in here and push around a naive young girl as if she doesn't even matter."

"Then we obviously disagree. Let's see what the jury thinks." Charles stormed out of the room without giving Anderson a chance to say another word.

Anderson's legs were shaking, he was so mad. He dropped into a chair and looked down at his trembling hands. Charles's words reminded him of Ruth's comment. *I think you're dreaming for taking this one.* He realized his anger was directed at his wife for not supporting him in Dana's case and making him feel like a schmuck. He had to win this one.

Anderson took a deep breath to regain his composure. As he walked back into the courtroom, Doug looked up at him. "What happened in there, sir? You look like you saw a ghost. You okay?"

Anderson patted Doug on the shoulder. "Everything's fine, Doug. Just fine."

Judge Abrunzo instructed the prospective jurors as to the basic facts of the case and then advised them that the lawyers would ask them questions in the voir dire process.

In picking the jury, Anderson asked numerous questions that stressed his theme in the case—the cruise line was responsible for the inappropriate actions of Eric and *Florida Dreamz* was wrong for enticing Eric to trick Dana into signing an invalid waiver when she was intoxicated. He made his inquiries in such a manner as to make the potential jurors feel that the production company was earning a large sum of money at the expense of extreme embarrassment to an innocent young woman.

Toward the end of his voir dire, Anderson tried to have the jurors acknowledge that the cruise line should always be held responsible for the actions of its employees when they take place during a cruise, but he ran into problems with juror number twelve. The gentleman, a middle-age white post office employee, responded to Anderson's question in a firm voice. "I don't buy your suggestions. It's ridiculous to suggest the employer would always be liable. What if the worker does something crazy on his own?"

Anderson tried to act like the juror's answer didn't hurt, but he was upset the man had made his speech in front of the entire panel.

"I assume your statement would be different if the evidence showed the officers of the ship didn't take reasonable measures to determine if their crew was engaging in activities that endangered the paying passengers who could not leave the vessel?"

"Wrong assumption. That would not be enough," the man said, holding his ground.

Anderson realized he was never going to get him to help his position so he moved on with the questions, attempting to identify jurors who would sympathize with Dana's case. Finally, and as always, he tried to befriend the jurors so they would like him personally and find his arguments persuasive.

Overall, Anderson did not think the panel of potential jurors was going to make a good selection for his client's trial. His concerns escalated when the jurors responded positively to the excellently crafted questions asked by Charles.

Anderson did the best he could with his three preemptory strikes to end up with six jurors and an alternate who could possibly understand Dana's position, but he was still worried that this was not the best jury to hear her case.

After lunch, Anderson presented his opening statement, stressing Dana's humiliation and embarrassment in having her almost naked image on the Internet while *Florida Dreamz* made significant sums of money at her expense as well as any other girls who had been caught in the same trap. He also emphasized that the Sun Lines' employee was only able to recruit Dana and other victims because of the confined environment of the cruise ship.

The courtroom was silent as Anderson moved behind Dana at counsel table, placed his hands on her chair, and pointed out, "Sexual exploitation of America's youth will continue unless you send a financial message to *Florida Dreamz* and Eric's employer, Sun Lines Cruise Ships."

Charles, dressed in a snappy dark gray suit and blue button-down shirt with a red and light blue-striped power tie, positioned himself behind the podium facing the jury and addressed the jury in his most sincere voice.

"Mr. Parker ended his opening statement trying to evoke sympathy and anger on your part. Plaintiff's counsel's claim for money should be judged on facts, not emotion. Why did he stress sympathy? Because he can't prove facts indicating liability on behalf of Sun Lines, which would justify you allowing counsel to win the lottery."

Charles discussed the facts of the case, suggesting that the management of the vessel had no knowledge about what took place between Eric and Dana.

Next, Lloyd Greenwald, a First Amendment lawyer turned litigator, stood to address the jury on behalf of *Florida Dreamz*. Lloyd's long gray hair, tweed jacket, and wrinkled khaki pants did not convey the traditional image of a defense lawyer, but more like a stodgy college professor. Doug leaned over and whispered to Anderson, "I believe this boy smoked too much dope during his undergraduate days at Yale."

Anderson pretended to be taking copious notes as Lloyd spoke, but he was writing out a note to his associate. Don't underestimate him. He's brilliant. And the jury may like his unorthodox style.

After Lloyd had completed his opening statement about how all Americans should be free to enter into contracts as they see fit, Judge Abrunzo instructed Anderson to call his first witness. Anderson stood and began to question Eric. On direct examination, the employee of the cruise ship testified about how a man had approached him during a two-day layover in Tampa. It had been a Saturday, two weeks before the incident with Dana. Eric testified that he had been having lunch at the Bennigan's located next to the Channelside docks when a man, who identified himself as Jay, asked to join him for lunch. Jay then asked him if he wanted to make some easy money. Eric admitted that he had been eager to supplement his income since he was trying to save enough money to go to college. When he expressed interest, Jay proceeded to set out the deal—if Eric could obtain video clips of young girls dancing topless, he would be paid $500 per clip; if he could get action shots of naked girls, he would be paid $1,000. Of course, all video had to be approved, and unused footage would remain in the custody of *Florida Dreamz*.

Jay gave Eric a business card with the company's address for mailing any film he might think worthy of consideration. He also left waivers and told Eric that all video had to be accompanied by a form signed by each featured girl.

"What happened the night of the incident?" Anderson began. "How did the two of you actually meet?"

"Well," Eric began, "I saw her hanging around the pool, and she was pretty attractive, so I just asked her if she wanted to come to a party later. And she said yes."

"Where was the party?"

"In the crew quarters," Eric said, glancing around the courtroom for the first time. He had kept his eyes cast downward from the moment he had been sworn in.

"Are guests on the ship supposed to be in the employee quarters?" Anderson asked. His tone was professional but courteous. He didn't want to push Eric too hard or spook him out of wanting to tell the truth.

"Not really," Eric admitted.

"Go on," Anderson said, glancing at the jury and noting their apparent high level of interest in the discourse.

"It was a pretty mellow party," Eric said. "A few guys from the crew and a few girls who were guests. Just some music on."

"Any drugs?" Anderson asked.

Eric shook his head vehemently. "No drugs," he said firmly. "If they caught you with drugs on the ship, they'd practically throw you overboard. They'd actually send out a smaller boat or even a helicopter to pick you up and take you off, and then you'd be prosecuted. Nobody messed with drugs."

Anderson nodded. "What about alcohol?" he asked. Alcohol had been his main subject of interest, not drugs.

"There was drinking," Eric admitted sheepishly. "A few people were having something to drink."

"What about Dana?" Anderson asked, studying Eric. "Was she drunk?"

"She wasn't drunk," Eric insisted.

"But she had something to drink," Anderson countered.

"Sure she did," Eric said. "Pretty much everybody did. But she wasn't drunk."

"How can you tell?" Anderson asked.

"I can tell," Eric said. "Anyone can tell. She had maybe one shot. You don't get drunk on one shot. Or at least she didn't."

"So when she signed the consent form," Anderson asked, his tone implying great doubt, "she was stone-cold sober?"

"I didn't say she was stone-cold sober," Eric replied defensively.

"What I'm saying is, she wasn't drunk. I guarantee you, there's no way on earth she was drunk. I've been around drunk people in my time, and she wasn't one of them."

Anderson glanced at the jury and then turned to the judge. "No further questions."

On cross-examination, Charles had Eric testify that nobody on the cruise ship, with the exception of his roommate, knew about his deal with *Florida Dreamz* or the first and last "video" party held in his cabin.

Lloyd stood confidently, "I have no questions for the witness." He obviously felt that no damage had been done to his client by Eric's testimony.

Judge Abrunzo announced there would be no more witnesses that day and court would reconvene the next morning at nine o'clock sharp.

That night, Anderson, Doug, Dana, and her father met in the firm's main conference room. As Anderson and Dana practiced their direct examination one last time, Anderson told her, "Remember to stress to the jurors that you would not have signed the form if Eric's friend had not talked you into the two tequila shots first."

Dana seemed uncomfortable with her father sitting next to her. Anderson wondered if something was going on that he didn't know about. Somehow, the situation didn't seem right and Anderson didn't like that at all.

Anderson pressed on. "As we discussed yesterday, I am going to complete your direct by playing a portion of the video to the jury. They will be shocked and I want them to see tears from you. Can you do that?"

Dana nodded as her father placed his arm around her shoulders. "Tomorrow, the jury will see the travesty of what this slimy organization did—putting our family through all this embarrassment. Anderson will restore your reputation, honey. Don't you worry."

CHAPTER 10

The U-Haul did not always cooperate and the move to Florida was difficult. But Nicole was pleased she made the change. Life was looking better every day.

She squinted and held up her hand to block the noonday sun as she lounged by the pool at the Harbour Island apartments. She walked into the cool water and sat down on the steps next to Meredith. She splashed water on her face and arms as she turned to her cousin. "I really needed this, Meredith. Thanks for letting me come."

"Of course! I'm so excited to have you here." Meredith's smile was a mile wide. "Tampa is great, but I work so much that it's not easy to find the time to get out and meet friends—and it gets lonely." She could hardly contain herself; she was so thrilled by the prospect of having Nicole in town. "Now we can go out together. It'll be great. We're going to have so much fun together." Meredith leaned over and gave Nicole a big hug. "I've missed you since you moved away. You just disappeared!"

Nicole looked down into the water. "I know, but after Mom and Dad divorced, I sort of fell to pieces, to put it mildly. I'm sure your mom's told you all the sordid details so I won't bore you. But when Dad decided to hook up with that bimbo and leave Mom, I couldn't take it. I was too mad and humiliated about what he'd done to our family. I figured the best thing to do was get out of town."

"Yeah, I know." Meredith grimaced. "We couldn't believe it either.

He'd always seemed so in love with your mom. And how could he do that to you? What a jerk! Have you even seen him since he left?"

"No way. I refuse to talk to him or Eileen. They ruined my life, not to mention Mom's, and that's not something I'll easily forgive."

"I heard they'd moved to Nashville—that he'd taken a job teaching at Vanderbilt?"

"Well, I don't know and I certainly don't care. The farther, the better. I definitely need a change and Tampa seems as good a place as any, especially since you're here. All I know is that it is time for me to get over these two-faced men and get a new life for myself."

Meredith looked over at Nicole in surprise. "So what happened with you and Rick then? Last I'd heard from your mom, you two were almost married. I wondered why you left him behind."

"What do you think happened? Same old story. And with that bitch lawyer just down the hall. I guess a paralegal wasn't good enough for him. He wanted the real thing. He just doesn't realize she's going to eat him alive. Oh well, he deserves it."

Meredith wrapped her arm around Nicole's shoulder. "Well, as I said, I'm certainly glad you're here. It'll be like old times."

"I promise I won't be a pain. Right before I left California, I sent my resume to some local agencies and I've got a few interviews lined up already. Tampa seems to have a lot going on in the legal community so I don't think I'm going to have any problem getting hired."

"Definitely. You'll find something right away. And who wouldn't want to hire you? You're smart and beautiful. Can't beat that!"

Nicole grinned and slipped down into the water, leaning her head back to wet her hair. "Maybe I'll meet some young thing who just can't resist me. You never know. Wednesday I've got my first interview with a firm downtown. Have you heard of them? The Law Offices of Justin Cartwright? They seemed like a good fit for me—I really don't want to work for a big firm anymore so I thought I'd try this one and see what it was like."

Meredith wrinkled her nose in disgust. "They've got quite a reputation, as a matter of fact. I've even heard of them and you know, I don't know much about the law. But that Justin Cartwright is quite a character. I know of him from the Yacht Club. I hope you're tough because he's known for being ruthless."

"Sounds like my type! I bet I can handle him just fine." Nicole smiled to herself as she submerged her body.

CHAPTER 11

Tuesday started with Dana being sworn in as a witness. As Anderson had instructed, she dressed extremely conservatively. In fact, Dana looked like she was going to a church event, with her knee-length black skirt and white ruffled blouse buttoned to her collarbone. She'd even worn her hair in a low ponytail, emphasizing her youth. The final touch was the tiny gold cross resting in the soft skin at the base of her throat.

Anderson began by asking Dana to describe the cruise. He let her talk at length about how much fun she'd had in planning the trip with her parents and inviting her friends to go with them. He had her tell about their outings at the various island stops, snorkeling and shopping. After Anderson skillfully guided her through her memories of the trip, there was no doubt that he had left the jury with an image of a young girl, thrilled to be with her family and friends, enjoying the innocent joys of beautiful waters and bright sunshine. Once he had set the scene he wanted in their minds, he led Dana to the day of the incident.

Dana bowed her head and spoke in a quiet voice. "When Eric asked me to the party, he seemed like a nice, trustworthy guy. I felt safe with him mainly because he wore a Sun Lines uniform. But when I got to his room, he was different." Her voice cracked on her last words.

"How?" Anderson pressed on, "Could you describe for us why you felt this way?" Anderson turned his body toward the jury as if he were one of them, wondering how things had taken such a nasty turn for such a pretty, young lady.

"He was pushy. He hadn't been like that at all when we were upstairs. But as soon as we got down to his room, he started acting crazy. Real hyper, you know? I started to worry a bit and I wasn't sure I could find my way back to my room since my friends had decided to leave the party earlier. The crew's quarters are way down in the bottom of the ship and I didn't want to be wandering around down there by myself. It's scary. I figured I better stay and try to deal with it. They were playing music and everyone there was dancing and acting pretty wild. Eric's buddy—I think his name was Scott—started flirting with me and wanted me to drink a shot of tequila. When I told him no, he made fun of me—telling me I was a wimp, a wuss, stuff like that."

Anderson raised his eyebrows in shock. "Really? So then what happened?"

Dana looked embarrassed. "I hate to admit, but I gave in—I took a shot. I didn't want to draw attention to myself. I thought if I did what he said and didn't make a scene, he'd get bored and leave me alone."

"So he pressured you into it?" Anderson asked her.

"Yes, and then he made me drink another. I started feeling pretty woozy and had to sit down for a second. That's when Eric appeared with a piece of paper and told me I needed to sign it if I wanted to stay."

"Did Eric explain what it was you were signing?"

"No, he just handed me a pen."

"What happened next?"

"I think there were five girls in the room, maybe six. One of the girls grabbed my hand and pulled me into the center of the room. We all started dancing in a circle and Scott started grinding on me. My head was spinning and I guess I lost control. We started making out and—I guess things got a little out of hand. He told me how beautiful I was—that I should show off my body." She paused.

"Go on, Dana. It's okay..."

"Well, he pulled my shirt up over my head and began cheering for me. I vaguely remember Eric with his video camera, but not much. The next thing I knew, my bra was off. I can't remember how it happened. Just that it did. All the guys were clapping and hooting. They started yelling, 'Take 'em off. Take 'em off.' That's when I realized they wanted me to take off my pants...and woke up to what was going on. I grabbed my shirt and pulled it on as I ran out of the cabin."

Anderson walked over to the witness stand, a sympathetic look on his face. "Do you need a break, Dana?"

"No. It's just that I have never been through anything like this and it's very embarrassing to talk about."

"Okay. Let's continue then." Anderson walked back over towards the jury, looking directly at them as he asked, "When did you learn about the video being shown on the Internet?"

"Someone told my dad about it. He called me to find out what was going on. I couldn't imagine that what he said could be true so I went online to see for myself. I couldn't believe it—it was me, really me. I was mortified.

"I told Daddy what had happened as best as I knew—that Eric and Scott had gotten me drunk. I vaguely recalled signing a piece of paper, but had no idea what it was. I knew Daddy would know whom to call and get them to take my pictures off the Internet. The next day, he called the corporate offices of *Florida Dreamz* demanding that the video be taken off their website. He told me that he eventually spoke to a Mr. Gallagher who told him the organization had a signed consent form that allowed publication of the video and there was nothing we could do about it." Dana looked over at her father as she spoke. "As you can imagine, Daddy was furious. That's when he called you to see if you could stop this from happening."

Anderson asked the court for a five-minute recess so his video equipment could be set up.

The jury looked disturbed as the two minute clip played. In the background, male voices could be heard encouraging Dana to keep going. Dana looked briefly at the images and then put her hands over her eyes and began to cry.

Anderson patted her hand and told the judge, "I'm finished, Your Honor."

Charles Towler's cross-examination was brief and courteous. He established that Dana could not say that any other employees of Sun Lines knew about the party or the filming besides the boys in the cabin.

Then it was Lloyd Greenwald's turn. He stood beside the podium, placed his hand on his chin, and asked inquisitively, "Nice costume... I mean, outfit. Is it new?"

Dana looked down at her skirt and blouse as if she'd never noticed them before. "Yes," she said.

"Have you ever worn this outfit before today?" Lloyd asked.

Dana looked puzzled. "No."

Lloyd appeared to switch the direction of his questioning. "Did you meet with Mr. Anderson Parker this last weekend?"

"Yes, I did. He's my attorney," she said curtly.

"Did you buy your outfit after that meeting?"

"I bought it on Sunday afternoon with my father."

"I take it that is a yes to my question?" Lloyd persisted.

"Yes," Dana answered glumly as she realized what he was implying. Lloyd shrugged his shoulders and returned to counsel table.

Sun Lines' first and, as it turned out, only witness was Captain Sam Sheldon. He was a lumbering bear of man, white-haired with a ruddy complexion. He looked like a friendly grandfather—not a man who would permit anyone to take advantage of young women on his ship. As expected, he testified he had no knowledge of the filming. He swore under oath that he would have stopped it immediately if he had known anything about it. But with a slight twinkle in his eye he added that he considered ship employees to be under his watch only during their eight-hour shift—what they did on their own time was their business, not his.

Anderson's cross exam focused on what was done—or not done, as the case may be—by the ship's officers to monitor crew activities. He stressed that the Sun Lines employee handbook dictated that employees were not to socialize with the paying passengers. Captain Sheldon maintained his cheerful dignity throughout the questioning and could not be swayed from his testimony.

Lloyd called Brian Gallagher as *Florida Dreamz*'s first witness. To the surprise of everyone in the courtroom, Brian was a well-dressed and well-spoken corporate businessman. He testified that he personally reviewed all video used by his company and confirmed none of it was pornographic in nature. Brian also discussed how he made sure there was a valid, signed consent form for each and every person appearing in any of their videos.

Charles passed on questioning but Anderson jumped up immediately. "Do the naked girls receive any money for the videos you sell?"

Brian replied calmly, "Not all females in our videos are naked. Some of them are fully clothed. But to answer your question, our video clips are available online for free. Anyone can watch them. Only the full-length movies are sold as DVDs or as downloads."

"But do the girls receive any type of compensation?"

"No, they do not."

Anderson continued to ask questions about the waiver and Brian consistently responded with his answers—the waiver was drafted by a team of lawyers to make sure it complied with all legal requirements.

For his final question, Anderson turned toward the jury again, as if asking for them the question that everyone in the room wanted to know.

"Sir, how do you live with yourself?"

Brian paused as if pondering the question before he replied, "Our country is made up of diverse people who have different tastes and interests. Lucky for all of us, our founders drafted the First Amendment so people can enjoy those interests without persecution from others. My company provides entertainment, and just because it may not be your cup of tea, does not make it wrong."

"Even if it hurts an innocent person? Does that still make it okay? No need to respond, sir. We already know your answer." Anderson glanced over at the jury to see if he'd scored any points. "No more questions, Your Honor."

CHAPTER 12

Back at their house, Ruth furiously ripped the weeds from her flower beds. As she jerked out each offending plant, she pictured Anderson. Sometimes he made her so angry she could scream. So she retreated to her garden to escape the feelings that would overcome her at those moments. Other times she felt an overwhelming sense of despondency when she thought about her marriage. Anderson was such an idealist, such a perfectionist. It's what had attracted her to him in the first place. But no matter how many times he promised to give her and the girls more attention, Anderson's passion for the law and drive to help those who needed him always won out. And he never even realized he was doing it. His heart was in the right place. He was a good man. But he could be so oblivious to what was going on right under his nose.

Ruth knelt in the grass and rested her hands on her knees. She longed for the old days, before Anderson was so successful. Even though they hadn't had much money back then, life had seemed simpler. She knew she was also being idealistic in remembering back and thinking things were better then. But right now, in the midst of her troubles with Anderson, she'd give anything to go back to the days when he wasn't so wrapped up in his law practice.

In some ways, even working for Justin had been better. Justin had been a cruel taskmaster, but at least the firm had been Justin's responsibility, not Anderson's. Now everything fell on Anderson's shoulders. Which affected her—and their girls.

She remembered when they'd first met. They'd both been seniors at Chapel Hill. On this particular day, she'd been heading to the library to study, as was her usual schedule. The air was crisp and cool, the colored leaves swirling around her feet as she rushed up the sidewalk. She tripped over a raised brick buried under the leaves and her books and papers scattered across the pathway. As she bent to gather them up, she realized someone had stopped to help her. And that was how she met Anderson.

From that moment on, they spent every day together. Ruth felt an immediate bond with him, one she'd never felt with anyone else before. She knew he was the one and she was more than willing to go wherever he wanted to go. But her one requirement, even though it had been unspoken, was that she came first, that their relationship came first. And Anderson had always made that happen, all through law school, the painful years of working for Justin Cartwright and especially during the years when she was pregnant and their children were young. They'd gone through a lot together and survived. But something was changing.

Ruth heard voices coming down the sidewalk. She quickly brushed the tears from her cheeks and plastered a smile upon her face. She sure didn't want the neighbors spreading rumors. That's how it worked in this tight-knit community. Everyone was friends and cared about each other, but that also meant they talked a lot. The good with the bad. All part of the package. She just wasn't up to it right now.

"Ruth! I haven't you seen you in ages." Sarah pushed a jog stroller up the sidewalk with three-year-old Michael in tow, riding his tricycle. "How are the girls? We've missed them at the Yacht Club. We haven't seen y'all at the pool as much this summer. But your garden looks gorgeous, despite this drought. You've been working on it like crazy, haven't you? I can tell!"

Ruth stood up and stretched. "Hey, Sarah! Hey, William!" She reached into the stroller and tickled the infant's feet. He grinned and wriggled his legs in response to her voice. "What's up, Michael? You sure are fast on that tricycle."

"Watch me, Miss Ruth! I go fast!" He began pedaling as fast as his plump little legs could go, wobbling down the sidewalk.

"Whoa, young man," shouted Sarah. "That's great, but wait on me, okay?"

Michael swerved to a stop in the grassy lawn next door and turned back to make sure they were both watching. Sarah looked at

Ruth. "Some days I don't know how I'll survive until the next morning. These guys have so much energy. I love them to death, but girls seem so much easier."

Ruth laughed. "Only because you don't have any. Never forget that the grass is always greener and that whole cliché, you know. Girls have their own unique way of getting under your skin. They're just different from boys."

"Well, whatever. We're lucky to have great kids, aren't we? Even if they do keep us on our toes all the time! So, how's Anderson? We don't see him much either. I saw that article about him in the Business Journal. Sounds like his new firm is doing great. Tom's just been promoted at Raymond James so he should be getting a bonus soon. I'm so excited—we've been hoping for this for a long time. We're thinking of adding on that family room we've been talking about." Sarah rambled on.

Ruth listened but mostly she observed Sarah's expression as she talked. Sarah looked absolutely content with her life. Ruth remembered feeling exactly the same way a few years ago.

CHAPTER 13

"Nicole Babson to see you."

At the sound of Eleanor's voice, Justin looked up quickly from a brief he was revising on his laptop. Without thinking, he checked to make sure that his tie was properly knotted and he glanced at his reflection on the computer screen to make sure his hair was neat. He stood and watched expectantly as Nicole Babson stepped into his office.

She was perfect. She was gorgeous, and she could tell that he thought that she was gorgeous just from the way he was appraising her appearance. Nicole had gotten used to this over the years—the quick glance at various aspects of her physique.

"Won't you...come in?" Justin said, motioning to a small round table with four chairs opposite his desk.

"I'd be delighted to," Nicole said coolly.

After Meredith's comments about Justin and his reputation, Nicole had done her homework and found out as much as she could about the man who sat before her. She knew of his reputation for ferocity in the courtroom and rectitude with female employees. She had the strong feeling, from the way Justin was studying her, that he was the sort of man who might study the menu but would never actually order. That observation made her feel more at home, as she seated herself at the round table.

Justin quickly took a seat opposite her, continuing to assess her looks, her hair, her eyes, her physique. She was definitely similar in appearance to the woman Anderson had loved so much back in college. The resemblance between the description Anderson had provided and this young woman's appearance was eerie, almost uncanny. And then Justin had to ask himself whether he was simply indulging in wishful thinking—that he wanted her to look so much like Anderson's ex. But no, he told himself. She really and truly looked just like Alice, slightly older, a little more mature. This was indeed promising.

"Thank you for taking the time to come in," Justin said with all the charm he could muster.

Nicole flashed a winning smile. "Thank you for taking the time to see me," she said in a voice exuding familiarity from the get-go. She might not have been a true Southern belle, but she knew enough about the art of seduction in the workplace to know just how to speak to this man.

"You have a most impressive...resume," Justin said.

"I hope I'm not just another pretty face," Nicole parried.

Justin gave a slight grin. "You're far more than that," he said, "although I have to admit that you really are a very attractive woman."

"Why, thank you, sir," Nicole replied, flashing her million-dollar smile once again. "And everybody I've talked to in Tampa tells me that you're the most powerful trial lawyer in town."

Justin felt himself blushing, something he rarely did and just for a moment, he thought about veering from the contours of his plan and hiring Nicole just to keep her around. But everything Eleanor had said was true—the firm's diminished workload did not in any way suggest the need for an additional paralegal. If anything, they should have been having serious thoughts about whether to keep their current roster of employees intact. But somehow there would always be a place for a Nicole Babson, that is, as long as a man was in charge of hiring decisions.

"I'd like to ask you a few questions," Justin began. "Some of them may be a little bit...unorthodox."

"Go right ahead," Nicole said, hoping she appeared nonplussed by this unusual interview.

Justin nodded quickly, and a change came over him. Any sexual charge he had been experiencing from the presence of Nicole vanished in a heartbeat. He was suddenly all business.

"Are you married?" he asked, studying her in a different way, a way that Nicole could not quickly identify.

"N-no," she replied. "I never have."

Justin nodded quickly. "Seeing someone?"

"Uh, no—I'm new to town," Nicole said, startled by the directness of his questions.

"No kids, no ties to the community, no history in Florida?"

Nicole, baffled, shook her head.

"Ever been arrested?"

"Nope."

"Are your parents still married?"

"No," Nicole said, wondering what that had to do with anything.

Just what he was looking for, thought Justin.

As an undergraduate at Princeton, Justin had majored in psychology, so he considered himself to be somewhat of an expert on human nature especially after his years of observing people in the courtroom. Nicole's answers excited him. She appeared to have the characteristics of a woman who might consider engaging in his scheme—if the money was right. He really liked the fact that her parents were divorced, and she apparently wasn't capable of maintaining a relationship for an extended period of time. Maybe her opinion of men wasn't that wonderful. So far, so good.

Before her arrival, Justin had investigated her background and was encouraged by what he'd found. First, he'd gone online to the California Official Court Records and found she had pled guilty to a crime. She had lied about that. Perfect, Justin thought, lying is definitely a prerequisite for this job. Don't know how she thought she'd get away with it, though.

Next, he had called the office manager at the Santa Barbara firm where Nicole had been employed. He'd been told confidentially that Nicole had been dating one of the lawyers in the firm. When he broke up with her and began dating one of the female attorneys in the firm, she'd lost it. She'd still been able to do her work, but everyone at the firm knew it wouldn't be long before she left.

Without apologizing, Justin turned in his seat and typed a quick email to Eleanor. "Cancel second interview today. I want to spend more time with this gal. I think she might work out, and if she doesn't, we will reschedule the other candidate."

The interrogation continued for another 45 minutes, until Nicole finally tried to ask a few questions of her own regarding benefits. Before she could even finish her first sentence, Justin interrupted.

"These are all minor issues that can be resolved if I decide you are the right person for this position."

These weren't minor issues to Nicole, but she went along with Justin, waiting to see what he was up to and what salary he offered before she made a decision.

He cleared his throat. "How do you feel about men who take advantage of women?" he asked, watching her carefully.

Startled, Nicole shifted somewhat uneasily in her chair. Justin could see the confusion in her eyes—what was it that he wanted from her? And then her true feelings won out. "I hate them, if you want my honest opinion," she said firmly. "I've got absolutely no use for any man that mistreats a woman in any form or fashion. No excuses."

Justin nodded. "I feel the same way," he said. "How do you feel about...undercover work?"

Nicole blinked several times. "As a paralegal? Working for you?" she asked, utterly bewildered by the turn the conversation had taken. This was unlike any job interview she had ever experienced. "Sure, I'm game."

At that moment Justin knew Nicole was the perfect candidate. He would do whatever was necessary to retain her for his plan. Justin had practiced his speech because he knew his content and delivery had to be perfect. Leaning forward, he began. "First I want you to know I am a good person who firmly believes all people should be treated fairly and equally, irrespective of whether they are male or female. Unfortunately, in the course of my legal work, I've run into a man who believes he can do whatever he wants, especially with regard to women. I don't know if you've ever had any problems with self-centered lawyers who think only of themselves no matter what the consequences are, but trust me, it's a bad situation."

Justin didn't wait for a response from Nicole. He didn't need an answer. By the look on her face, he could tell he was connecting with her emotional issues.

He continued. "I have a plan to seek justice upon an arrogant lawyer and I want your assistance. It will be a win-win for you. You will be standing up for the rights of women and at the same time you'll make a lot of money. Just think, you could use your tax-free compensation to reestablish your life in California."

Nicole put her hand to her chin and responded, "I'm confused. What do you want me to do?"

"I know you must think I'm nuts," Justin said. "But I'm sure you're familiar with the fact that there are people in our society who do wrong things and never get punished for their actions. A lot of men wreak havoc in the lives of others, and they just somehow get away with it."

A flash of anger was triggered deep inside Nicole. That's exactly how she felt about her father. And about Rick.

"I'm well aware of that," Nicole told Justin in an even tone.

"I thought you might be," Justin said. "There's a trial attorney here in Tampa," Justin explained, his voice low, "who is, shall we say, notorious for the way he takes advantage of situations and people. Especially women. Do you catch my drift?"

"Not entirely," Nicole admitted. "But I've got a vague sense of where you're going."

"Let me be a little more specific," Justin said, his eyes resting briefly on her breasts, which were peeking out of her top.

"This guy has been setting himself up as some sort of moral beacon," Justin said quietly, an edgy tone to his voice. "He's created nothing but trouble for a lot of people I know, myself included, with this whole holier-than-thou thing. But I'll tell you what—he may be talking the talk, but he sure isn't walking the walk. I wouldn't be surprised if one day that halo over his head slipped a little and started to choke him."

"And my job," Nicole surmised, "is to get that halo from on top of his head to around his neck?"

Justin smiled. "You catch on fast," he said with a self-satisfied grin.

"And how am I to get close enough to this man to grab a hold of his...halo?"

"Great question," Justin said, amused by her play on words. "It's pretty simple. I want you to get a job working for him."

Nicole looked confused. "How am I supposed to do that?" she asked. "He doesn't know who I am."

"He will," Justin replied, "the moment you walk into the door of his office and tell them you're looking for a job. I have another motive for picking you for this job—you look like his ex-college girlfriend. The one that got away. The one he wanted to marry."

"Wow, that's devious, Mr. Cartwright."

"If you don't accept the job, I will deny I ever talked to you about this whole thing. But if I might say so, with a history like his, and a body and face like yours, there's no way he won't give you the job."

Nicole bit her lip. "All I'm supposed to do," she began, "is to turn up on the doorstep of his office and get hired? Then what?"

"Let nature take its course," Justin replied. "How you do it is none of my business. But what I'm looking for from you—are pictures with the two you in an explicitly compromising position. Am I clear?"

"What do I get out of this?" Nicole asked, cocking her head and studying Justin.

"My undying gratitude?" Justin asked, grinning. He knew he had her. Once the conversation had turned to money, there was no doubt in his mind that she had already bought in. "I'll pay you $50,000,"

Justin said, "in cash. Also, $10,000 to get started, another $10,000 after you get the job with Anderson—" Justin stopped mid-sentence. He had not intended to spill the name of the person for whom she would be working. But it was too late now. "And another $30,000 when you get me the pictures. At that point, you can stay in Tampa, go back to California, or do anything you want to do. But that's what I'm looking for. And that's what I'm paying for."

She shook her head.

"A hundred," Justin said. "That's $25,000 to start, $25,000 when he hires you, and $50,000 when you get the pictures."

Nicole studied Justin's face as if they were sitting opposite each other in a poker tournament. "You really don't like this guy," she said.

"You got that right," Justin replied. "And neither will you."

"Well, if he's going to be so unpleasant to work for," Nicole said, pressing her advantage, "it's gonna take $200,000. Make it $50,000 to start, $50,000 when I get the job, and another $100,000 when I bring you the pictures. I'm not going to be able to stick around Tampa very long after this whole thing comes out. I'm gonna need some real money so I can disappear."

Justin's smile went thin. That was considerably more than he had intended to pay for Anderson's downfall. But, as he reflected quickly, the money meant nothing to him.

"Deal," he said tersely. It was too good to be true—the perfect woman, with the perfect plot for bringing down Anderson.

"Deal," Nicole said, reaching across the table to shake Justin's hand. "You get me the cash, and I'll get that job."

"I know you will," Justin said with a slight quiver in his voice. The enormity of what he had done dawned on him. He realized, as he shook Nicole's hand, that he had sealed Anderson's doom.

Or his own.

CHAPTER 14

After the lunch break, Lloyd advised Judge Abrunzo that his client was going to call one more witness. Sally Holmes was an attractive, slightly heavy-set, college girl.

Lloyd approached the witness stand. "Sally, do you know Dana Estes?"

"Yes, we're both students at the University of Tampa."

"Are you good friends with Dana?"

"I wouldn't say we're close friends, but I'm a little sister at one of the fraternity houses and she comes there to party, too."

"So you and Dana party together then?"

"Oh yeah, she's definitely a party girl."

"Is alcohol served at any of these parties?"

"Well, officially students under 21 aren't supposed to drink at the houses, but in reality, we all do."

"Okay, thank you, Sally. I appreciate your honesty."

Sally gave a slight smile and nodded her head.

"Let's talk about Dana. That's why we're here today, yes? Have you ever seen her drink before—say, at one of these parties?"

"Oh, she's one of the best at holding her alcohol. One night I made the mistake of matching shots with her. She won—I threw up all night. Does that answer your question?"

"What about dancing? Do you dance at these parties?"

"Of course."

"What about Dana?"

"She's good. I think she used to dance for her high school dance team. Whatever. She's got what it takes."

"Could you describe what you mean by that? How does Dana dance?"

"Let's just say she gets pretty wild. The guys love it when Dana gets going."

James Estes looked over at his daughter with a look of disapproval. A couple of jurors noticed his expression.

Lloyd continued. "Sally, have you ever seen Dana take off any of her clothing when she was dancing?"

"Sure. That's what the guys loved about her."

"Could you tell of us of a specific incident that you personally observed?"

"Last year at the Kentucky Derby party. I remember that one specifically because we were all doing shots. Dana was wasted. We were dancing next to each other and she reached over and began tugging on my shirt. I asked her what the hell she was doing and she dared me to dance topless with her."

"Did you?"

"No way. If I had her body, I might have. But I wasn't about to get into a comparison contest with Dana Estes."

"What happened next?"

"She told me to stop being a prude. She said she'd done it before and it really turned the guys on."

"Did Dana take her shirt off?"

"Of course. I went back to the bar to get away from her, but I could hear everyone cheering her on. She was the talk of the crowd for weeks. But that's the way she likes it."

The wheels were turning in Anderson's brain as he tried to figure out what to ask on his cross-examination. Even though he did his best, there wasn't anything he could do to get Sally to change her story or to discredit her testimony.

After Lloyd rested his case, Judge Abrunzo told counsel that he wanted to go straight into closing arguments since it was early in the afternoon and there was plenty of time to finish the trial that day. Anderson tried diligently to persuade the jury in his closing, but it was clear they were not going to accept Dana as a victim.

Charles's argument was brief. He focused on the testimony that Eric was not on duty at the time of the filming. He also stressed the testimony of Captain Sheldon for the proposition that the people in charge of the vessel acted reasonably in monitoring the ship's employees. Judge Abrunzo became impatient when Lloyd did not say or do anything after

Charles was finished.

"Mr. Greenwald, do you plan on presenting a final argument on behalf of your client?" he snapped.

Lloyd stood up and rested his fingertips on the top of the counselor's table. "Oh yes, I certainly do," he said as he walked to the podium without any notes.

"This claim for money is really about contract law. A contract is a writing about promises. One party agrees to do something in exchange for another party promising also to do something. If one party to a contract does not fulfill his or her promise, a contract is broken. Mr. Parker wants you to find that my client, *Florida Dreamz*, acted unreasonably so he can obtain damages and then cry to Judge Abrunzo, asking that Ms. Estes be allowed to break her contract. The issue is not whether you approve of what Dana was doing. The real question is whether she signed the consent form. And we all know she did."

Lloyd moved toward the jury until he was directly in front of them. "But this case should be decided because of a breach of an implied contract involving Ms. Estes, Anderson Parker, and you. What do I mean? Here it is—you, the jury, made a promise to all of us in this courtroom. You agreed to take time from your busy lives, miss work and time with your families so a jury trial could be held. In exchange for your sacrifices, the lawyers and clients promised to be straight with you, not lie, and not try to mislead you."

Lloyd turned and pointed directly at plaintiff's counsel table where Anderson and Dana were seated. Raising his voice another decibel, he said, "Breach of contract by Mr. Parker and Ms. Estes. Anderson Parker tried to mislead you by having Ms. Estes dress as conservatively as a nun. And Ms. Estes, well, she tried to persuade you that she normally didn't drink and do those wild things like you saw on the video. Shame on them, but lucky for our system of justice, you will not be fooled. Maintain your implied contract to dispense proper justice by answering the first two questions the judge will ask you at the end of these closing arguments with an emphatic 'No.'"

Lloyd's argument shocked Anderson. It was totally off the cuff, or at least seemed to be, and would either anger the jury or convince them to issue a defense verdict. Within 30 minutes, Anderson had his answer. The jury published a unanimous verdict absolving both Sun Lines and *Florida Dreamz* of any liability. Judge Abrunzo discharged the jury and thanked them for their services. Once they had left the courtroom, he turned to the attorneys and their clients. "Based upon the evidence presented this week in trial, and considering the jury's verdict, I am declining to enter any form of injunction on behalf of Ms. Estes."

The trial was a complete and total loss for Dana Estes. The production company was free to use her image as it saw fit, as allowed by the signed consent form.

Anderson sat in his car, parked in the driveway of his house, and listened to the ticking of the engine as the motor cooled down. He was in no hurry to walk in the front door. He knew what Ruth's response was going to be. He had wanted to be the knight in shining armor that rescued Dana and her father from the abuse of the money-grubbing slimeballs. But instead, he'd found out that everything Ruth had warned him about—about Dana and her reputation, about how the jury would respond—had come true. She'd been right and he hadn't listened to her.

CHAPTER 15

As Anderson walked up the path to his porch, he paused to look at the gardening Ruth had been doing. He'd been so busy these last few weeks, he hadn't even noticed all the changes. Last few weeks? Who was he kidding? How about the last few months! Ever since he'd won the case against Justin, he had been swamped with phone calls from people asking him to represent them. Digging through the cases, determining which ones to take, and then, of course, following through on all the work had been more than a full-time job. He'd been so busy that he had hired more people to work for him. But then he had to train and monitor their work, too. He could never escape the constant ringing of the phone, the knocking on his door, the barrage of emails and letters.

It was all up to him—the firm depended on him to survive. His family counted on him to make money. It was a vicious cycle. And to make matters worse, Ruth was getting up in arms about how much he was working. He'd hoped when he first started his own firm that he would be able to juggle his time better and make more time for his family. Instead, he'd been overwhelmed with the increasing responsibility and demands on his time that a thriving and prosperous law firm created.

Anderson let out a deep sigh as he pushed open the front door and gently closed it behind him. Maybe he could have a few moments of silence before he had to break the news to Ruth about today's trial. He set his briefcase on the floor and dropped his keys on the silver tray resting on the antique chest of drawers in the front hall. The house seemed quiet without the normal rambunctious noise his two girls made running and giggling through the rooms. He glanced at his watch and realized that it was 9:00. No wonder the house was quiet. The girls were already tucked into bed and probably even asleep. He'd missed bedtime. Again.

Anderson walked toward the kitchen where he could now hear Ruth rinsing dishes and putting away the remainders of the evening's dinner. He stopped in the doorway to watch her at the sink. She'd pulled her hair up into a knot on top of her head and he could see the curve of her neck as she bent over the pot she was scrubbing. He wanted to tiptoe over and surprise her by kissing her right there in that spot where she was so ticklish....but he wasn't sure anymore what her response would be. Irritated, probably. She used to love it when he did that—although she'd act like she didn't. She would laugh and turn, trying to hit him, but he'd hold her in his arms and they would kiss. They hadn't done that in a long time.

Ruth turned. She pushed her hair out of her face with the back of her wet hand. "Ah, the hero is finally home! So? How'd it go?" she asked.

He pulled out one of the chairs at the table and slumped down into it. His entire body felt as if it had been in a battle—and definitely not on the winning side. How he wished Ruth would sympathize. Maybe even just give him a hug. He was so tired all the time, but she never seemed to notice anymore.

"Today was not one of my best, if you really want to know. We didn't win, just like you predicted."

"And how much did you lose on your costs? I wish you could make James pay. He's so clueless about that daughter of his. I told you she was bad news, didn't I? I just knew this would happen. The jury found out that she's a tramp, right? That she drinks like a madwoman and will drop her clothes for just about anyone?"

Anderson didn't answer. What more was there to say? Ruth was absolutely right. So why did he feel so angry? If he didn't leave the room now, he was going to blow up at her. He couldn't take it anymore. For once, he wanted someone to be on his side—to see what it was like trying to handle all the things that came through his door every day and to be on top of things and always ready with the answers for his employees and his clients.

He grabbed a bottle of water from the refrigerator and a couple of cookies from the jar Ruth always kept filled for the kids before heading up to the bedroom where he hoped to escape Ruth's glare for just a few minutes.

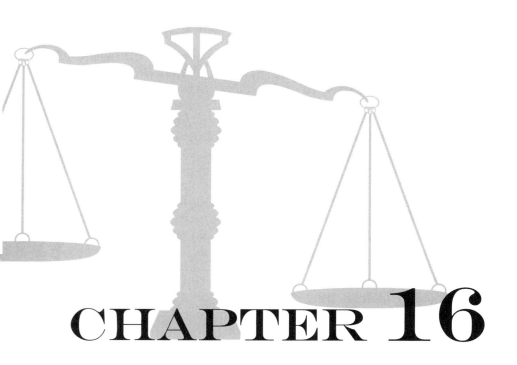

CHAPTER 16

The week after the Estes trial, Anderson began driving home after a tough day at work. It was a longer day than usual simply because he didn't want to go home, face his wife, and hear from her again "I told you so," about the *Florida Dreamz* case. Anderson sensed, accurately, that Ruth was peeved on a number of levels. First, she was unhappy about the fact that he had completely disregarded her advice, and that she had been proven correct. Second, Anderson's most valuable asset was his time, and if he was picking dogs for cases, he was effectively throwing his most valuable asset out the window. If he didn't win, he didn't get paid, and then on top of that, there were all the expenses the case entailed. So Anderson's payday wasn't just a zero. He—and therefore Ruth—actually lost money because the case was handled on a contingency basis.

Ruth grew up in a working-class home where money had been scarce, and although she was now more comfortable with the amount of money she was spending on the house, on clothes, on her family, and, to Anderson's mind, on everything under the sun, there was a still of part of her that planned for the worse. No matter how much money they had—and they had plenty—she had never completely gotten over the fear that the money would run out. So Anderson realized her concerns had little to do with the case or where they were financially. It had to do with where she came from and who she was beneath her apparent comfort level with affluence.

But maybe most important of all, to Ruth and to Anderson himself, was the fact that this case had consistently taken him away from his family—and with no positive result either financially or professionally. Anderson knew Ruth was right about the amount of time he had been spending at work but he didn't know what he could do to change it for now. And her nagging didn't help at all.

So Anderson was in no hurry to get home. When he did arrive around 7:30, Ruth, as he had expected, was frosty. Not mean, not overtly angry, but definitely cool. After the kids had gone to bed, Anderson tried to talk with her, but Ruth expressed little interest in making conversation. She kept busy with her projects around the house and managed to avoid him for most of the evening.

Anderson had prepared for this possibility by bringing work home with him. He went to his office, cracked open his briefcase, and got busy with a file he was handling, a wrongful death case that required a huge amount of time and effort on his part. If anything, working on the case gave Anderson some measure of relief from the tension at home and his sense of failure at having lost at trial. He could focus on this case and put off thinking about what was going on in his own home.

He heard Ruth putting the dishes in the dishwasher and straightening up the house, but he did not interrupt his work to attempt further conversation with her. And she, for her part, did not venture anywhere near his study.

By the time Anderson had finished his work and gone upstairs to shower and get ready for bed, Ruth had already fallen asleep.

CHAPTER 17

Nicole felt like she had hit the jackpot with her assignment from Justin. Here was a chance to make serious money—tax-free. With that amount of cash, she could do whatever she pleased. Go back to California, go to the Caribbean; she could do just about anything that struck her fancy. And if instead of spending her money, she was careful with it, she wouldn't have to work for years.

But first things first. She needed to find a way to convince Anderson's firm to hire her for a paralegal position. She immediately went to work researching anything she could find out about Anderson Parker, P.A. She went to an Internet café—she didn't want to do any research from home just in case Meredith noticed her Google history and wondered what was going on. She learned that the firm presently had four lawyers, four secretaries, two paralegals, an office manager, an investigator and a runner. The firm represented plaintiffs exclusively, and apparently successfully, based upon published jury verdicts.

Nicole was especially interested in finding out whatever she could about Anderson's office manager, Gwen Hughes. Gwen would be Nicole's key to the kingdom and the treasure that lay within. If only she could find something about Gwen that she could use...and then Nicole noticed the dress Gwen was wearing in the office staff picture. She printed out the photo, folded it in half, and put it in her purse.

Two days later, Nicole Babson appeared at the renovated redbrick warehouse where Anderson maintained his offices. She walked up to the receptionist at the front desk and asked to speak with the office manager. Within a few minutes, Gwen appeared, wearing an outfit quite similar to the one Nicole was wearing. She looked extremely distracted and clearly in no mood to deal with a walk-in interviewee until Nicole exercised her opening gambit.

"Is your dress a Diane von Furstenberg?" Nicole asked.

"Why, yes it is!" exclaimed a somewhat startled Gwen. "You're wearing one, too, aren't you?"

"She's my favorite designer," Nicole confessed. Anything to build rapport.

"It looks great on you," Gwen gushed. "I don't really have the figure to carry it off, like you do, but her clothes are so stylish and comfortable that I just can't resist. They're my one splurge."

Nicole rolled her eyes. "You're kidding, aren't you? You look fantastic! I think her clothes look great on everyone. That's what I love about her designs—they're so versatile. And not a splurge at all. I'd say they are essential. When I can afford it, this is the only kind of clothing I like to wear—she makes me feel so sophisticated and classy," Nicole admitted. "Anything else and I feel kind of trashy, you know?"

"Oh, I do know!" Gwen exclaimed. "I've never been into this whole 'office casual' thing. I never know what to wear on those days. I just always feel so professional in this." Then she quickly glanced at her watch. "Oh, my God, I've got a meeting in ten minutes. Were you here to see me? Did we...have an appointment?"

"Honestly? No," Nicole admitted. "But I'm actually looking for work as a paralegal." And she added quickly, "And before you say no, I have seven years of experience working in litigation, I've got an incredibly good work ethic, I'm single and I'm not dating, and I'll bust my butt for you because I just moved down here and I'm trying to get established. And I'll take $38,000 a year to start."

Nicole could see that she had struck her target. Especially with her willingness to take a starting salary that was $6,000 to $8,000 below the going rate for paralegals with her level of experience in the Tampa area. Nicole then placed her resume in Gwen's hand.

"It's funny that you should be coming along right now," Gwen said. "I was about to put an ad in the Hillsborough County Bar Bulletin for a new paralegal, because we've got this really huge wrongful death case coming up. And I have to admit that if you're okay with those numbers, the price is right."

Nicole shrugged. "I'm kind of a simple girl," she said. "I'm just try-ing to get my life established here in Tampa. I had a pretty bad breakup with my fiancé back in California. So I'm really just looking to get on my feet, pay off some credit cards, and start over."

"I understand," Gwen said warmly. "I've been there myself. Who hasn't? Look, here's the deal. Most of the time, you'd be working di-rectly with my boss, Anderson Parker. It's his firm, and so it's really up to him. But I know he'd be thrilled if we had somebody to step into the gap, because it's a really big case and he's been distracted with this other crazy case. I don't know if you saw anything about it in the paper. The *Florida Dreamz* case."

"I did," Nicole said. "I wasn't going to bring it up, because I know it must have been a big blow for your firm to lose that case. Personally, I think that girl was kind of slutty to begin with." She paused. "I hope that's okay for me to say."

Gwen looked both ways before she gave Nicole a conspiratorial nod. "I feel the same way," she said, relieved to find someone who shared her opinions. Nicole actually had no idea how Gwen felt about the case, but given the conservative nature of her attire, it stood to reason that she would not have had any sympathy for the plaintiff, even though she had been the law firm's client.

"She knew what she was doing. I can't stand girls like that."

"I agree," Nicole confided.

"Anyway," Gwen said, looking at Nicole as if she had just found not only a new hire, but a new best friend, "I'm sure Anderson will be very happy to meet you. I'll tell him I've got a good feeling about you. You certainly come across as very professional. I'm sure your references are great, too. And I hate to say this, but everybody loves a bargain."

"That's just a start," Nicole cautioned with a smile. "If I do well for your firm, I hope you'll think about paying me what I'm worth later on down the road!"

Gwen gave her a warm smile. "You can count on that," she said. "Um, let me talk to Anderson. I was supposed to meet with him five minutes ago—"

"I hope I didn't make you late," Nicole said.

"Not at all," Gwen said. "As it happens, we were going to talk about writing the ad for the new paralegal. But you may just have solved that problem. Why don't you just hang out here for a couple of minutes and I'll see if he can meet you right now?"

"Would he do that?" Nicole asked, thinking, this was just too easy.

"If I tell him to," Gwen grinned. "Just sit down and wait a

minute. I'll be right back."

Gwen rushed into Anderson's office and jumped straight to the point. "I've found the perfect new paralegal. She's just what we're looking for. She's nice looking and appears to be extremely professional. She talks a good story about her work ethic and the best news is her salary demand is low. We need to hire her right away before someone else snatches her up."

"Maybe we got lucky here," Anderson said. "Set up an interview for me, call her last firm for a reference, and then we will decide."

"She's actually here right now," Gwen said, a measure of urgency in her voice. "I think you should meet her. I would think she's got interviews at other firms."

"Right now?"

"Right now."

"Then send her in."

Gwen handed Anderson Nicole's resume as she left to retrieve Nicole.

CHAPTER 18

Nicole's first impression of Anderson was very different from what Justin had led her to expect. He was a tall, good-looking man, with the kind of broad, rangy physique she favored, but he didn't seem like the smooth operator Justin had implied that he was. She was always suspicious of men who were too suave and self-confident – but Anderson didn't seem to be especially arrogant. She wondered whether Justin really knew who he was talking about. On the other hand, she thought, I'm not exactly who I appear to be either—obviously appearances can be pretty deceiving.

"Gwen tells me that you're looking for work as a paralegal," Anderson said, ushering her over to a pair of couches in his office.

Nicole nodded, glancing around the office as she took a seat on the couch and smoothed her skirt. "You have a beautiful office," she said. "Is that yours?" She nodded toward the huge fish mounted behind Anderson's desk.

Anderson gave an embarrassed grin. "Actually, I needed a little bit of help reeling that guy into the boat," he said. "I'd never caught anything that big before. Or since, for that matter. Thanks for noticing it—that boating trip was a great day on the water so it's a nice memory to have here in the office when I'm working day and night!"

Bull's-eye! She thought. One way to a man that always seemed to work was through his pride—and Anderson was no different. "Well, it's stunning. You should be quite proud. I couldn't help but notice it," Nicole said. She was also sure that he was aware of her resemblance to his old college girlfriend—she could tell by that starstruck look he had. Plus, she had her own way with men and she'd already begun to reel him in. Rare was the man who could resist Nicole once she'd focused her attention directly on him. She knew that Anderson was appraising her looks, but he did so in a much more subtle way than Justin's blunt, no-nonsense style. She had the sense that Anderson was admiring her rather than simply sizing her up for the kill, as so many men typically did.

"I haven't had time to review your resume in detail," Anderson admitted. "Gwen tells me you have substantial experience in litigation?"

Nicole gave a businesslike nod, her demeanor shifting into a more serious expression. "Yes, in California I worked quite closely with the lawyers in my firm on many of their difficult cases. I loved the challenge and hope to find something similar, if not more challenging, in Tampa," she said.

"Well," Anderson said, "we may be able to offer you just that here at my firm. However, it would mean that you'd be working pretty closely with me. Actually, very closely, because I'm going to need help on a huge case with a massive amount of documents, depositions, and all the rest that comes with the territory. It's too much for me to handle on my own, and everyone else here is tied up with other projects. It's a wrongful death case, but it's exceptionally complex, given the circumstances. We'll pretty much be going night and day on it. It's going to require a lot of evenings and weekends, especially once the trial gets started. Will that be a problem for you?"

Aha, Nicole thought. Evenings and weekends. No telling what could happen when they'll be spending all that time together, much of it alone. Perfect.

"That's not a problem at all," Nicole said. "I'm new to the area, and I don't have a lot really going on in my life right now. Since I've just moved to town, I've been trying to get a job and organize my apartment over on Harbour Island. At the end of the day, I run over to the Athletic Club to work out and head on home. I live a pretty quiet life, to tell the truth, so I'm available whatever hours you might need me." Nicole had every intention of letting Anderson know that she had no steady boyfriend and was available for whatever he might want, business-related or not. But Anderson took her remark a different way.

"So you aren't working now?" he asked.

"No, but I'm planning on taking on temp work until I get a permanent job. I don't like to have too much free time on my hands. You know what they say about that—the devil's playground and all!

I sure don't want to get into any trouble. Besides, I love what I do and I already miss my job. I thought it might be nice to have some time off, but I'm bored already and ready to get back to work."

"It's kind of a tough time around the firm here," Anderson said. "We just took a major hit on that *Florida Dreamz* case. I'm sure you saw something about it in the news."

"I actually followed that case pretty closely," Nicole said. "I thought it was outrageous that you guys lost. I mean, how could a jury believe that trashy girl they brought in to testify against your client? I didn't think she had any credibility at all, based on what I saw in the news."

Anderson looked not just flattered but delighted that she had taken the time to follow the case, and more importantly, to side with him. Nicole had seen nothing about the case in the news, but she had certainly done her homework when she Googled Anderson's firm, and the loss was the first article that came up. She had then found out as much as she could about the case so she could use it as another tool to butter up Anderson. She'd hoped he'd bring it up first, so she didn't have to. Losing a trial is not something that lawyers like to remember.

Anderson gave a chuckle. "That's not how my wife sees it," he admitted ruefully. "She said I should never have taken the case."

Nicole was surprised that Anderson would already be confiding in her about a marital rift. But now that she knew, she would do everything in her power to exploit the situation once they were working together.

"I'm sure your wife is an amazing woman," Nicole said diplomatically. "But personally, I think this was a perfect case to take. If people get in a situation where they can be taken advantage of and then find their picture is all over the Internet the next day, well, what's this world coming to?"

Anderson nodded excitedly. "That's exactly what I thought!" he exclaimed. "It's good to find someone who thinks the same way I do!"

"I guess you'll want to check my references first," Nicole said, sensing that this was the perfect moment to close the deal. She checked her watch, a new Rolex that she had bought for herself with some of Justin's money. "I've actually got to be going. I was just stopping by to drop off a resume, and I've got a couple of interviews with other law firms this afternoon."

"Cancel them," Anderson said firmly. "You've got the job. We'll check out your references, and I'm sure they'll be fine, so there's no need to worry about that. And I heard that you were offering to start below market. That's very generous of you, but our other paralegal with your level of experience gets $45,000, so I wouldn't feel right paying you any less. Will you take the job?"

"It would be my honor," Nicole said, extending her hand and giving Anderson a warm, inviting smile.

"No," Anderson replied, shaking her hand and holding on to it for perhaps a millisecond longer than office etiquette and decorum dictated. "I think the honor will be all mine."

That night, Anderson was in a considerably better mood than the night before. He was actually whistling, something he generally only did after he won a large verdict. Ruth wondered why he was so happy, but was certainly not about to ask.

CHAPTER 19

G wen Hughes pulled up in front of the building at 7:30 and found Nicole at the door waiting for her. "I didn't expect you to be here already," Gwen said with surprise. "You must be an early riser!"

"I believe in working long hours," Nicole answered. "I plan on being the first one here and the last one to leave. Besides, I love the law and want to learn from the best."

"Wow," said Gwen, impressed and, at the same time, slightly suspicious. Nicole seemed almost too good to be true. "Well, I know you'll be a great asset to the firm."

"I'll do my best," Nicole promised as the two went up in the elevator and crossed the lobby toward Gwen's office. After handling her start-up paperwork, Gwen took Nicole to the cubicle that would now be hers so that she could settle in and arrange her things.

"I'm assigning you to Doug, one of our junior attorneys, first. He's handling a standard automobile case right now. Let's see how you do with this before we move you on to the bigger stuff, okay?" Gwen told her.

Nicole was disappointed she wouldn't be working with Anderson right away. But she knew she'd be able to prove her worth quickly and that Anderson would be asking for her soon. She could bide her time.

✧ ✧ ✧

Once on the job, Nicole was always the earliest to arrive and the last to clock out, just as she had promised, not to mention she worked many evenings and even on the weekends. Her fellow workers noticed and reacted with a mixture of admiration and resentment. The new paralegal was setting the bar higher for all of them, and they weren't completely pleased.

After a few weeks, Anderson stopped by Nicole's desk and asked her to join him in his office. He motioned for her to sit on his couch and then sat down across from her.

"Nicole, you did an excellent job of putting together the demand package in the Patton automobile case. The firm is very appreciative of the long hours you're working, but we want to make sure you don't burn out. Are you okay?"

Crossing her legs, Nicole said, "Mr. Parker, I appreciate your concern—"

Anderson interrupted. "Please. Call me Anderson."

"Thank you. Anderson, I enjoy my job. My goal is to work as many hours as possible so I can continue to develop my skills as a paralegal. As I told you in my interview, my life is really pretty simple. I work hard, go home to my apartment which I share with my cousin, exercise and swim at the Athletic Club, and then go to bed. I have no other involvements right now so my life is the law and keeping my body in shape."

"You sure seem to be doing a good job with both." Anderson chuckled appreciatively.

She studied him, and he immediately tensed. This was the first time he had ever paid such a personal compliment to a woman who was not his wife. He had surprised himself—the comment had come out of his mouth before he realized it. Things had not improved much at home, and here was a beautiful young woman who reminded him in so many ways of Alice. And just as quickly, Anderson thought, What am I doing here?

"Anyway, back to the case," Anderson said, hoping to reel in the conversation before it went in a direction over which he would have no control.

Nicole decided it was time to plant one of her seeds. "You're sweet to worry about me but I'm fine and ready for more assignments. You know, now that you mention it...there is one thing I miss."

"What's that?" Anderson asked.

"I really miss having someone to hang around with. I haven't been involved with anyone since I left California. Truthfully, I'm a little lonely sometimes."

Anderson swallowed hard. She was unmistakably signaling her

availability, a fact that Anderson had no idea how to handle. He was flattered and terrified, all at the same time. Best to stick to work and change the subject quickly.

"Yeah, I guess being so far from home is tough," he said. He cleared his throat uncomfortably as he tried to purge all thoughts of his young paralegal working out at the gym and then going home all alone. "The main reason I wanted to talk with you is because I need your help on a death case that is going to trial in six weeks. The accident, which serves as the basis for the litigation, is a tragedy in every sense of the word. Let me give you the facts first and then I'll tell you about the work I need done."

Nicole, noting the transformation in Anderson's tone, quickly switched to business mode. He was not quite ripe for the picking. But she could wait. She was a patient woman and knew she could get what she wanted, given the time and the proper setting. Nicole sat up straighter and nodded her head for him to begin. Anderson looked relieved.

"Approximately two years ago," he said, "it was the day before the 18th birthday of Charlie Smith, a senior at the elite Hillsborough Preparatory School. Charlie was a good student who excelled in the drama department there. He'd been accepted early to New York University, where he planned to major in theater. His girlfriend, Caroline, decided to surprise him with a pre-birthday celebration, so she called her two best friends, Jana and Angela, and asked them to meet her at Charlie's house in Hyde Park.

"Before Jana left her house she took a bottle of Bacardi rum out of her parents' liquor cabinet and concealed it in her purse. Once the three of them arrived at the house, they said hello to Charlie's parents, ran up the stairs to grab Charlie from his bedroom, and then headed out to the pool house in the backyard. Apparently, as part of their little get-together, they consumed quite a bit of rum. We know that on at least one occasion Charlie's mother went to check in on the group and she admitted in deposition she saw a liquor bottle." Nicole reached for a notepad and started writing as quickly as Anderson spoke.

"After about two hours," Anderson continued, "Jana and Angela decided they had to leave. It was a Thursday night and their parents expected them to be home at a decent hour. The two of them had driven to Charlie's house together in Jana's car since they lived near each other. They left Hyde Park by way of Dakota Avenue and turned right onto Bayshore Boulevard. After traveling approximately a quarter of a mile, Jana lost control of the vehicle. The Toyota went over the curb and hit a concrete pole located four feet off the road. Unfortunately, Jana didn't have her seatbelt fastened. Upon impact she went through the windshield and struck the pole with her head and chest. Angela fractured her right arm when her upper body was thrown against the passenger's door. Angela took her seatbelt off, got out of the car, and staggered over to Jana who was lying faceup in the grass. It was not a pretty scene."

"My God!" Nicole exclaimed.

"It gets pretty graphic at this point," Anderson cautioned.

"Go on," Nicole replied.

"Jana's face was sliced open from her ear to lips and blood flowed from her cheek with every heartbeat. Angela attempted to stop the bleeding by holding the two sides of her face together. But Angela couldn't see the true crisis. The blunt impact to Jana's chest had caused an aortic tear. Slowly and painfully, Jana was bleeding to death internally.

"Angela didn't think the injuries were life-threatening and she didn't want her friend to get into trouble for drinking, so she called Jana's mother instead of 911. Jana's mother raced to the accident scene and arrived shortly before the fire rescue unit, which had been contacted by a neighbor who had heard the noise. Jana's father was out of town on a business trip so he wasn't involved in any of the events that night.

"It was a parent's worst nightmare. Her mother tried to hold her face together as Jana bled all over her. Jana's mouth was filling with blood and her words came out as foaming crimson bubbles. Just as the rescue crew rushed over to her, Jana's heart stopped beating. Jana's mother was holding her only child as she died in her arms."

"How awful," Nicole exclaimed.

"Yes, but this is the real world of a trial lawyer," Anderson said. "This is what we deal with. Are you sure this is a case you want to work on?"

"Is it your case?" Nicole asked.

Anderson nodded.

"I'll be fine," she insisted.

"Good," Anderson said, and the relief he felt—that she had not been scared away by the blood and the gore—flooded him. There was something about this attractive, attentive young woman, something even more than her resemblance to Alice that made him want to work closely with her. Of course, he would do nothing more than work with her—but the idea of being in her presence on a regular basis satisfied some unfulfilled need. He did not want to admit this to himself, but he knew it was true.

"Okay, going on," Anderson said, attempting to corral his runaway thoughts. "After the funeral, Jana's father contacted me to find out if there was any basis for civil litigation. He was totally devastated by the loss of his daughter and he was worried about his wife who woke up almost every night screaming from the visions of Jana's bloodied dying face.

"The case presented some problems. First, Jana brought the Bacardi to the party and she had a history of drinking and taking liquor out of her parents' house. Next, Jana was not wearing her seatbelt, and it's common sense that a restraint would have kept her from being ejected from the car.

"It was clear from the toxicology studies that Jana was impaired and legally intoxicated. In fact, her blood alcohol level was 0.14. But the question is, who should be responsible for the drinking?

"After legal research I determined a lawsuit could be brought against Charlie Smith's parents for violation of Florida's Open Party Statute."

Nicole looked up from her legal pad. "I'm not familiar with that ordinance."

"Very few people are aware of this law until it bites them in the ass." Anderson stopped abruptly. "Oh, my apologies. That's wasn't exactly language fit for a lady."

"Don't mind me," Nicole said in a friendly way. "I've certainly heard the term before. I even have one of my own."

You sure do, Anderson thought, unable to make eye contact with her. He cleared his throat. "Um, let's see. Where was I? Okay, I remember—about ten years back, the members of our legislature decided that underage drinking had to stop, or possibly, they were trying to gain votes in light of the approaching election. Either way, a law was passed dictating that if minors are drinking in a house and the adults who own the house know of the consumption and don't immediately take action to stop it, the owners are responsible on a negligence basis for all injuries to the minors caused by impairment.

"Larry, our investigator, determined the Smiths had homeowner's insurance coverage in the amount of $5 million, so Jana's parents authorized the filing of a wrongful death lawsuit against Charlie Smith's parents. Thus: Joe Benson, as personal representative of the estate of Jana Benson v. Charlie Smith Sr. and Libby Smith.

"Defending a death case is a true art. Unfortunately, the Smiths were assigned an excellent defense lawyer by their insurance company. I know Tommy Guyton socially and know his court record even better. Tommy definitely knows how to neutralize sympathy. He decided early on to dig in on this one, and there's nothing worse than a talented defense lawyer who doesn't want to part with the insurance company's money.

"Tommy is going to stress to the jury what Jana did—bringing the rum to the house and driving without her seatbelt. He's also going to ask the jury to assign fault to Jana's mother for failing to secure the family's liquor cabinet that night when she knew Jana had a history of taking liquor from the house."

"Wow," Nicole exclaimed. "This is a fascinating case! What can I do to help you?"

"Well," Anderson said, impressed with her enthusiasm and excited about the idea of working so closely with her over the coming weeks, "I need you to review the entire file, including the homicide investigation report, which is lengthy. And then I want you to draft a memorandum setting out your trial strategy recommendations.

"Also, I want your thoughts as to additional investigation and discovery. The depositions of Charlie Smith, his father, his mother, and the investigating officer have been taken. I haven't set the depositions of the two minor girls yet because Larry's report indicated that they didn't offer any additional helpful information.

"This case needs immediate attention, so please consider this assignment your main priority. I'd like to meet with you on Monday, Wednesday, and Friday mornings at seven-thirty, until I say otherwise, to review the status of your work. I look forward to teaming up with you on this matter. I also want you to attend the trial with me. Any questions?"

"No. I understand. I will start immediately."

She gave him a professional nod and then the hint of a smile as she rose from her seat and headed out of his office. Anderson, intrigued, watched her go.

CHAPTER 20

Nicole's alarm rang at 5:30 the next morning. She pulled herself out of bed, missing the good-morning kisses from her little kitten that she'd had to leave behind in California. No excuses to linger in bed either with her kitten or a lover; she had work to do. Work she was truly enjoying. She pulled on a tailored black skirt and tucked in a rose-colored silk blouse, slipped her feet in her other big splurge—a pair of Manolo Blahnik black pumps. Twisting her hair into a knot at the back of her head, she ran out the door in time to be at her desk by 6:30. She again immersed herself into the details of Jana's accident.

By lunchtime, Nicole had put together the first draft of her investigation and discovery recommendations. She found it strange that Angela and Caroline had been consistently vague in their recollection of the facts surrounding that night. Almost as if the two girls had agreed to tell a similar story, as if they wanted to cover up something. It was understandable Charlie would try to protect his parents. But wouldn't the girls want to help the family of their dead friend?

Both the homicide officer and Larry had interviewed Angela and Caroline, but no one had taken their depositions. Nicole decided she needed to talk to the girls and get their stories directly.

Nicole quickly found the young women on MySpace and discovered where they went to college. Angela was attending George Washington University in D.C., and Caroline was studying at the

University of Pennsylvania in Philadelphia.

She called both girls several times throughout the afternoon, with no success. Finally, Nicole made contact with Angela, who was in her dorm room.

"Hi, Angela. I hope I didn't call at a bad time. My name is Nicole Babson and I'm calling from Tampa. I'm looking into the Jana Benson accident and would like to talk to you about it."

"How'd you get my number?" Angela said, surprised and defensive.

"I obtained it from the school's directory assistance. I appreciate you giving me a few minutes of your time. All I want is to talk to you about what happened at the Smith's house that night. I assure you I am not singling you out for information. I plan on talking to Caroline and Charlie also."

"Why are you bothering me?"

Trying not to scare her away, Nicole said, "Well, I work with the lawyer who represents Jana's family. Would you please talk to me about what happened at the party that night?"

"Look—I already told them everything I know. I don't have anything else to say. Read the police report. It's all there."

"Please think about my request. I'm sure you'd be willing to do anything you could to help Jana's family. Can't you tell me what you remember about that night?"

"I told you already—I have nothing else to say. Please, just leave me alone."

"Okay, but please think about what Jana's family is going through right now. I'll call you again later after you've had a chance to think about it." Nicole paused. "Maybe you could help by giving me Caroline's phone number? Or maybe Charlie's?"

"Caroline and I really haven't talked much lately. It's been painful enough for all of us and we don't want to have to keep living it over and over again. I do know she lives at the Alpha Chi sorority house at UPenn. Other than that, I just can't help you." Nicole could hear Angela holding back her tears over the phone, "But just so you know, if you do manage to get in touch with Caroline, and if she'll even talk to you, you definitely won't get Charlie's number from her. She hates Charlie. They've hardly talked for months. Charlie dumped her for some girl from Long Island."

Angela's refusal to talk about the night supported Nicole's hunch. She had to talk to these girls in person. Telephone calls obviously weren't going to work.

Friday morning was the first status meeting for Anderson and Nicole. After Nicole summarized her review and her telephone call with Angela, Anderson asked for her recommendations. Nicole realized he was truly interested in her opinions, which made her feel good about herself. Anderson was the first attorney who had ever wanted more from her than just organizing documents and scheduling depositions.

"It's crucial I talk to these girls face to face," Nicole said. "Most likely, Caroline will not want to talk about that night either. But I have an idea about how I might approach her. It shouldn't cost that much for me to fly up to meet them."

"Money isn't a concern," Anderson said. "If there's a chance it'll help us develop our evidence, go ahead and book the flights."

"I'll do that," Nicole said, as the meeting concluded. On the way back to her desk, Nicole reflected on how thoughtful and caring Anderson appeared. He must be just as good as I am at being an expert bullshit artist, she decided, as she went online to book her trips to Philadelphia and Washington.

Once she had arranged her flights, Nicole called Caroline's sorority house. A young lady answered the phone, "Alpha Chi!"

"Hi, I'm a senior at Hillsborough Prep in Tampa, and I'm interested in UPenn. I'm coming up to visit this Monday to look at the campus. I was hoping to talk to Caroline, since she also went to Hillsborough."

"Awesome! I'm one of Caroline's best friends! She's not here right now, but on Mondays she always eats lunch at the main school cafeteria, which isn't horrible, for your future reference. You can always get a good salad there. And then she studies at the science library from 1:00 to 3:00 before her chemistry lab starts at 3:15. You'll probably run into her there."

"Thanks, that's great. Oh, and don't tell Caroline one of her old schoolmates is coming. I'd like it to be a surprise."

"No problem! And stop by the sorority house if you have time. We're the best around! Good luck with your college applications. And hopefully we'll see you here next year!"

CHAPTER 21

On Monday, after a flight to Philadelphia by way of Atlanta, Nicole arrived at the main cafeteria a little after noon and scanned the crowd of students, comparing their faces to the picture of Caroline she had found in the high school yearbook. Nicole spotted her in the cafeteria line so she hurriedly purchased some yogurt and timed her payment so she would emerge into the sitting area at the same time Caroline did. When Caroline put her tray down on the table, Nicole sat down across from her. "Okay if I sit here?"

"Um, sure." Caroline's eyes were focused on her book.

Nicole tried to start up a conversation. "So, what're you studying?"

"Chemistry. I hope to go to vet school some day," Caroline said.

"That's great. Good luck." Nicole played with her yogurt, deciding how to broach the subject. "Um, Caroline, I wanna be straight with you. I'm also from Tampa and I was hoping to talk with you."

Caroline looked up in surprise. "How do you know my name? And what do you mean you want to talk to me? Is something wrong?"

Nicole knew this was the crucial moment where she could possibly alienate her. "No, nothing's wrong. I've just been trying to find you. I went to see Charlie Smith at NYU, but he told me you two weren't together anymore. He was with a blond girl, and when I first walked up, I heard them talking about spending the weekend at her family's house in the Hamptons. I assumed she was his new girlfriend. I hope I'm not telling you something you didn't already know."

"That asshole!" Caroline exclaimed, outraged. People at nearby tables glanced in their direction for a moment and then resumed their own conversations.

"I gave him three years of my life," Caroline continued, "and then I'm history. He made promises to me. I can't believe him! He is such a liar."

She glared at Nicole, twisting her napkin into a tangled mess.

"Yeah," Nicole said, commiserating. "Guys do that to get what they want—it just happened to me, too. I dated a guy for two years and then he dropped me for someone else, just like that. No reason at all. What a jerk." She stretched her hand out across the table as if to comfort Caroline.

"I know what you mean. Someone new comes along and they forget about the good thing they've got going. Guys just suck. That's my conclusion."

"Sounds like we have the same bad luck with men." Nicole took a spoonful of her yogurt, then carefully wiped her mouth with her napkin. "Well, I don't want to take much of your time because I know you're busy studying, but I did fly up here from Tampa for a reason."

She paused, evaluating Caroline's interest level, which was evidently quite high.

"I'm working for Jana's family," Nicole continued, "and, as you can imagine, they're devastated by her death. They've filed a lawsuit to recover fair compensation from an insurance company, and I'm helping with that. I'm suspicious that Charlie and his father haven't told the whole story. I think it's time for them to pay for Jana's death. It seems to me Charlie believes he can get away with anything and I don't think you should let him. I need to know the truth about what really happened that night."

Caroline stared at Nicole, as if trying to decide whether to break the agreement she had made with Charlie and Angela. The confirmation of Charlie's betrayal swayed her to Nicole's side.

Tears welled up in her eyes. "You know what? You're right. Why am I sticking by Charlie, when he isn't sticking around for me?" She sat up straighter and began to talk quickly. "Jana did bring alcohol to the birthday celebration, but it was just a small bottle of rum. Charlie's mom came out to the back house and saw the bottle, but she didn't say anything. About ten minutes later, Charlie's dad came out to say hi to everybody and he saw the empty bottle, too. He said Charlie would only turn 18 once.

"This calls for a real celebration!" Caroline added, mimicking a deep, booming voice. "His exact words. No lie. He went back inside and came back with a huge bottle of Bacardi. He put five glasses on the table, poured shots of rum for all of us and then proposed a toast to Charlie."

"Wow," Nicole said.

"Yeah, wow," Caroline agreed, and she continued. "Before he left the room, Mr. Smith planted the bottle back on the table with a loud thump. He told us to drink up and celebrate, we were only young once. So we did. We drank until that second bottle was empty and then Jana said she had to go home."

She paused. Nicole waited.

"Charlie and I should've never let her drive. What were we thinking? I guess the truth is we weren't...." Caroline's shoulders drooped, and she began to cry softly.

Nicole tried to look concerned as she fought to keep the smile off her face.

"I know this is difficult, and I respect you for doing the right thing. Charlie and his father both gave depositions testifying that Mr. Smith had no knowledge the group was drinking alcohol. Mr. Smith even went as far as to say that if he'd known, he would've immediately stopped the illegal behavior."

With her head down, Caroline said, "I know. After the accident that night, Charlie told Angela and me that nobody could ever know his father provided, or knew anything about, the alcohol. He told us there was nothing we could do to bring Jana back, but if the story ever got out about the alcohol, he and his father would go to prison. Charlie told me he loved me. He said we had a future together, but if we told, everything would change."

Nicole wanted to make sure she kept Caroline on her side, "Charlie was lying to you—even back then. He didn't care about your feelings then just as he doesn't think about you now."

By the look on Caroline's face, Nicole knew she was succeeding.

"The trial will take place in four weeks. If I provide you with an airplane ticket, will you come home to Tampa? I want you to make sure Charlie pays for all he's done and to assure Jana's family receives rightful justice. Will you do it?"

"I definitely will," Caroline said.

Nicole stood up to leave. She walked around the table and leaned over to give Caroline a gentle hug. Now that Caroline could no longer see her face, Nicole allowed her suppressed smile to spread across her face.

CHAPTER 22

Nicole took the late direct flight from Philadelphia to Tampa and was back at her desk early Tuesday morning.

"How did your work in the Liberty City turn out?" Anderson asked as he walked by her cubicle.

"Fantastic! My research really paid off. I'll bring you up to date tomorrow morning at our conference."

There was one more loose end to tie up. Nicole formed a plan to get Angela to talk to her on the phone. After lunch Nicole started calling Angela, and on her fourth attempt made contact.

"Angela, this is Nicole from Tampa. We spoke the other day." Nicole kept talking, not allowing Angela to have a chance to protest. "Thanks for telling me where to find Caroline. I flew to Philadelphia yesterday and had lunch with her."

"So, what do you want from me?" Angela asked impatiently.

"Please just listen to me for a few minutes," Nicole said. "Caroline realizes now the two of you were used by Charlie and his father. We talked about the night at the Smith's house, and she's coming down for the trial. She's decided she is going to tell the truth. That way, Jana's family can obtain the money they are owed by Mr. Smith's insurance company. She told me how Mr. Smith saw the group was drinking, brought out another bottle of Bacardi, and then proposed a toast."

"What? She really said all that?" Angela was shocked. "I can't believe her. We swore we wouldn't say anything. And Charlie is going to kill both of us. My God, what a mess."

"Do you really think Charlie and his father deserve your protection?" Nicole asked. "They're hoping their threats will keep you silent, but there's no reason for you to do that. Surely you'd rather help Jana's family than Charlie."

Angela sighed. "I guess you're right. I don't know whether to be mad at Caroline or what. God, I've been stressed about this for so long. I guess I'm glad Caroline told you what really happened. Maybe it's time we told the truth."

Caroline has agreed to tell the jury what happened," Nicole said, pressing her sudden advantage. I'm buying her an airplane ticket so she can come back to Tampa in four weeks for the trial. If I buy one for you, too, can Jana's mom and dad rely on you to do the same?"

"Okay. Count me in."

That night, Nicole worked on numerous memorandums for her meeting with Anderson in the morning. She cancelled her Washington flight and purchased tickets to Tampa for Caroline and Angela. Nicole was proud of what she had accomplished so far and wanted to impress him with her excellent trial preparation work.

Promptly at 7:30, the two of them met in the conference room. Nicole noticed that Anderson looked a little more polished than she'd seen him looking before. She was positive he was wearing a new suit. Definitely a tie she'd never seen before. She paid attention to details like that in a man. And did she smell cologne? Could this be for her? Her intuition said yes. And Nicole was rarely wrong about these things.

Nicole kept it professional. She told an extremely impressed Anderson about her meeting with Caroline, the phone conference with Angela, and their commitments to return to Tampa and testify at trial. Next, she handed Anderson her trial strategy memorandum.

"Defense counsel," she began, "is going to argue the accident was caused by Jana's negligence in bringing the rum to the Smith's house and by failing to wear her seatbelt. Additionally, he is going to argue that Jana's mother was partially at fault since Jana had a history of taking alcohol from the family liquor cabinet and she didn't take measures to stop the access.

"On behalf of the family, we should argue the accident was caused in total or at least in great part by Mr. and Mrs. Smith failing to stop the drinking when they saw the kids with alcohol in the first place and, even more important, by Mr. Smith providing a second bottle of rum.

"The key is we have the element of surprise because the defense will most likely not know about the two out of town witnesses. We want Mr. Smith to testify consistent with his deposition, and then he'll look like a liar and the jury will be angry."

She paused to see how well Anderson was accepting her approach. He was loving it—his admiration for her work (or for her) was etched all over his face.

"We also have sympathy on our side," Nicole continued, pretending not to notice how happy her boss looked with her work. "I recommend we try to put women on the jury and then with our first witness we go for their emotions. I suggest we slow down the first day of trial so we complete jury selection, opening arguments, and then end the day with the direct examination of Jana's mother. Mrs. Benson's story of holding her daughter as she died will bring tears to their eyes and hopefully nightmares to their sleep that night.

"I also have an idea on how to handle defense counsel's cross-examination of Mrs. Benson regarding her failure to secure the family liquor cabinet on the night of the death of her daughter. Monday night, I will condition Mrs. Benson to think about Jana's blood-filled mouth when questions are asked by defense counsel, so she will fall apart on the stand. That way, no meaningful answers will be received, and at the same time, the sympathy aspect of the case will be reemphasized.

"After her testimony, we should call Mrs. Smith briefly to prove she saw the drinking and didn't stop it. Then we call Mr. Smith and have him testify he did not know anything about drinking at his house. For icing on the cake we will have him confirm he would have immediately stopped the consumption of alcohol by minors if he had known about the drinking. There's nothing better than a self-righteous liar. Why can't men tell the truth?"

Nicole wished she hadn't made her last comment, but Anderson didn't react to it. He kept right on making notes on his legal pad.

"You should be an attorney," Anderson said admiringly. "I couldn't have put the case and the plan together better myself."

Nicole allowed herself a small, contented smile. "Thank you," she said humbly. "May I continue?"

"I wish you would," Anderson said, and for a moment he entertained the fantasy of helping Nicole through law school, coaching her while she studied for the bar exam, and then working with her. Then, just as quickly, he dismissed the whole idea.

"Next," Nicole was saying, "we shake up the courtroom with the testimony of Caroline and Angela. At that point the damage should be so severe, the defense will never recover."

Anderson leaned back in the reclining conference room chair, put his hand to his chin, and responded, "Absolutely masterful. Excellent work. I want you to sit at counsel table with me during the trial. During the next few weeks, please work on trial questions for all witnesses. One last thing."

Nicole waited expectantly.

"Nicole," Anderson began, choosing his words carefully, "your work on this file has been incredible. I appreciate your attention to detail, hard work, and professionalism. I look forward to our future collaboration on this case."

"Thank you, sir," she murmured as Anderson left the room.

After Anderson returned to his office, Nicole collected the file materials and returned to her work area. She was proud of herself. She thought of the honor of sitting at counsel table during the trial. And she tried to figure out what Anderson meant by "future collaboration on this case." If he meant sex, he sure had a lawyerly way of putting it.

Another thought entered Nicole's mind. Maybe he wasn't bullshitting her. Maybe he was the good guy he purported to be. Maybe Justin was wrong about him. To her surprise, and against her will, she realized she was really starting to like Anderson and she thought he might feel the same way. How could she betray him?

And then she reeled her errant thoughts back in. He was a man. Men lie. He was a liar. They all are. And he was going to pay for it.

CHAPTER 23

The Sunday before the trial Nicole and Anderson worked together for most of the day. Anderson wore khakis and a Polo shirt; Nicole wore jeans and a tight-fitting top chosen to catch Anderson's attention. It did.

Being at the office with Nicole's warmth and admiration was a nice respite from the cool distance Ruth projected at home. Despite the distraction of working in close proximity with Nicole in an otherwise empty office suite, Anderson got a lot accomplished. Anderson and Nicole, strategizing together, decided the key to victory was for the jury to decide that Charlie Smith, Sr. was intentionally trying to mislead them.

Anderson explained his theory on liars to Nicole while they took a break over a couple of sodas in the office kitchen.

"Almost everybody is capable of not telling the truth," Anderson began, "if the opportunity arises and they think they won't get caught. Through my years of observing witnesses in depositions and at trial, I've learned how to create a false sense of security so that people will bend the truth."

"A false sense of security?" Nicole asked, concerned. Was he on to her? Was that the subtext of his mini-lecture on liars?

"Yes, it's important that we appear unprepared so they don't have any idea we're setting them up. I want Charlie Smith to feel totally confident in his testimony so that he will continue to say he knew nothing. That's what I mean about a false sense of security. He will think everything's still on track and that he's safe—until we spring the girls on him," Anderson explained. "So we can't alert the defense that Caroline and Angela are coming to trial. Are we organized with those two witnesses? Do you have any reason to believe the Smiths know the girls are flying into town for the trial?"

Nicole spoke confidently. "We're all set. I spoke with both Caroline and Angela yesterday. They're both good to go. Their planes arrive early Tuesday morning and Larry is going to meet their flights at the gates. He isn't going to bring them to the courthouse until after Charlie Smith, Sr. testifies, or should I say lies. Neither of the girls has spoken to Charlie, Jr. and they don't think the Smiths have any reason to know they're coming to Tampa."

Anderson gave a nod of approval. "Good work. Now I've got to start to paint our façade. First, I will put defense counsel at ease by making him think our entire case is based upon evidence that Mrs. Smith saw the kids drinking in the pool house. I know Tommy will also be working the day before trial. Watch this."

Anderson placed the phone on speaker and called the large law firm where defense counsel worked. After the annoying recorded greeting played, Anderson punched in Tommy's extension number. As he expected, even though it was a Sunday afternoon, Tommy answered on the second ring.

"Tommy, it's Anderson. Glad to see you're billing some hours on a Sunday."

Tommy chuckled. "Without you, Anderson, it wouldn't be possible. Please keep filing lawsuits against my clients so I can pay the mortgage on my Colorado vacation home. Remember, some towns are too small for one lawyer, but no town is too small for two lawyers. You sue 'em, I'll bill 'em."

"Glad I can be of service to you, Tommy. Now it's time for you to help me with a little problem. My predicament is this—I'm representing two very nice parents who tragically lost their daughter. They are entitled to some significant settlement monies because Mrs. Smith saw the children drinking alcohol. So now it's time to pay up. Why don't you offer me a small fortune, we can settle, and then we can both get out of our offices and have Sunday dinner with our families. How's that?"

"Anderson," Tommy began, his tone sincere, "you know I would like to help you and your clients. But I have looked at this case from every angle and I don't see liability on behalf of the Smiths. If you're going to get money on this one, it will have to be by way of a jury verdict."

Anderson said, "Okay, if that's the way you want to play it. We'll see you in court tomorrow."

After Anderson hung up, he turned to Nicole. "Now I've put Tommy at ease. He feels sure that we have a weak argument so he's relaxed about tomorrow. In the morning I will give a 'soft' opening statement that won't discuss our smoking guns, and then we'll see if Charlie Smith, Sr. decides to tell the truth."

"I love it!" Nicole said admiringly. And again, the troubling thought crossed her mind: Is Anderson really a bad guy?

Anderson packed up his briefcase so he could complete his trial outline at home. "The preparation for this trial has been a joint effort," he told Nicole. "You've done a wonderful job. We make a great team."

Nicole was so excited about the trial she had a difficult time falling asleep that night. After her second Tylenol PM she started to doze off, her last thought being Anderson's words *we make a great team*.

CHAPTER 24

T he next morning, in keeping with their custom, Anderson and his team arrived in the courtroom first so they could secure the counsel table closest to the jury box and perpendicular to their seats. Anderson positioned the mother of the dead girl, a visibly traumatized Michelle Benson, in the seat closest to the jurors' box as he wanted the decision makers to focus on her. With Michelle was her husband, Joe, looking just as wan and bereft as his wife. Anderson was dressed in his usual courtroom attire: a conservative charcoal-gray suit, button-down dark blue shirt with a bold red tie. At the end of the table, Nicole's crisp white blouse was tucked tightly into her tailored navy-blue skirt. Her legs did not go unnoticed in the courtroom.

Tommy and his clients arrived and seated themselves at the defense table shortly before Judge Graham entered the courtroom. Charlie Smith, Sr. sat on the right side of the table closest to Nicole, Tommy was in the middle, and Libby Smith was at the far left. Tommy had decided he did not wish to have a paralegal or associate sit with him, as he wanted the jurors to assume the plaintiffs could afford a larger legal team than the defendants.

Promptly at 9:00, Judge Graham took his seat behind the mahogany barrier that separated the advocates from the referee, and called the court to order. This was the judge's second civil trial since he'd left the U.S. Attorney's Office and he enjoyed the power of being in charge of the courtroom, compared to his previous role, a lawyer representing the people.

After 24 potential jurors were seated in the jury box in four rows of six and the judge gave his initial instructions, the voir dire process—the selection of the jury—began.

Anderson rose, positioned himself behind the podium in front of the jurors, and spoke. "This will be the only time during the trial, ladies and gentlemen, when I will be able to speak directly with you. The purpose of voir dire, which is a French saying for 'to tell the truth,' is for the lawyers to learn about everybody's backgrounds so seven fair jurors can be chosen to hear the case."

Of course, Anderson, like all trial lawyers, wasn't looking for neutral jurors. He wanted to end up with seven people who would lean toward his side of the lawsuit and be more likely to believe what his clients said had happened.

Anderson's first question was whether any of the 24 had ever lost a child. When potential juror number 17 mentioned her 11-year-old son had drowned, Anderson felt sorrow on a personal level but knew that her words would have great effect in the courtroom and on the other prospective jurors. He had the mother describe in painstaking detail her grief since the death.

Next, Anderson covered the issue of alcohol. By cleverly wording his questions he had everyone agree that adults should not promote or allow the consumption of liquor by children less than 21 years of age.

Anderson had decided to conclude his voir dire questions by returning to the strength of his case—sympathy. Potential juror number six had earlier revealed she was a pediatric nurse, so Anderson directed his final area of inquiry to her.

"Are you familiar with the term 'descending aortic tear'?" he asked.

Proud of her medical training, the nurse acknowledged she did know of the medical condition and proceeded to give a detailed description of how the tear bleeds into a person's chest cavity, causing the victim to die from loss of blood pressure.

As Anderson closed his file and prepared to return to plaintiff's counsel table, he asked one last question. "Ms. Richardson," he began, slowly and quietly, "is death as a result of a descending aortic tear a painful experience?"

"Almost always," the nurse said firmly. "It's a terrible way to die. The person likely feels the accumulation of blood in their mid-body and has to fight for their last gasps of air."

Anderson was inwardly pleased as he sat down. He looked over at Charlie Smith, Sr. with a disapproving glance. Nicole leaned over to him and whispered, "You're awesome!"

He gave a hint of a smile, but he found himself wondering when his wife had last said anything like that to him. He couldn't remember.

Tommy was dressed conservatively with a white shirt and a gray tie, which complemented his dark-blue suit. After he ingratiated himself with the group, he redirected their attention away from medicine and sympathy.

"I would like to talk about seatbelts," Tommy announced. "Does anyone have training as to the mechanics of car restraint devices?"

Potential juror number 15 raised his hand to say he was a mechanic for a local Ford dealership. Tommy milked the young man's knowledge for all it was worth. He concluded his questioning on the issue by asking if it was possible for a driver to go through the windshield upon impact if a shoulder harness was being used.

"Absolutely not. Ford engineers design seatbelts so this will never happen. And of course it's the law that operators of cars must wear their restraint devices."

Tommy wanted to build upon his reference to the law. "Would everybody agree," he asked the potential jurors, "that drivers, whether they are 17 years old or 60 years old, should follow the law?"

"Yes," the 24 responded in unison.

"And if a driver doesn't follow the mandate of our legislature and as a result is ejected from a vehicle, strikes a pole, and then dies from those self-inflicted injuries, should a third party be held responsible for damages?"

Although the group did not understand the intent of the question most of them shook their heads.

Tommy was on a roll so he continued. "And while we are on the subject of the law, does everybody agree that a person should not operate a motor vehicle if they are under the influence of alcohol?"

Potential juror number nine, a black man in his 60s, was the first to respond with the words "I agree." Tommy asked him why he felt that way.

"I was rear ended by a drunken young troublemaker and my F150 was totaled."

"That's terrible," Tommy said, shaking his head indignantly, and the other potential jurors murmured agreement.

It was time for Tommy to move on to the last area he wanted to cover in his juror questioning. He walked to the front of the podium so he could be closer to the jury and stated, "You are all intelligent people and have figured out Mr. Parker is trying to take money from Charlie and Libby so he can enjoy a windfall with his clients—"

"Objection!" Anderson said as he quickly rose to his feet. "Defense counsel is not asking questions. He is making unsupported and fabricated statements."

"Enough talking from both of you," said Judge Graham. "Objection sustained. Sir, ask questions."

Tommy continued. "Yes, Your Honor. As I was about to say, have you noted Mr. Parker spends almost all his time trying to evoke sympathy? Judge Graham will instruct you after the lawyers' closing arguments that sympathy should play no role in your decision. Can each and every one of you decide this case on the law and the evidence solely without letting your good judgment be altered by feelings of sympathy?"

After all 24 assured Tommy they would be able to do that, he told the judge he was through with his voir dire questions.

It took about 50 minutes for the lawyers to finally decide on seven jurors, six to decide the case and one alternate should a juror become ill or be dismissed. Following a late lunch break, and exactly in keeping with Anderson's time plan, the trial resumed with plaintiff's opening statement.

Anderson had made a strategic decision to give a brief opening that did not detail the evidence he was going to present. He addressed the jury without any notes.

"Ladies and gentlemen of the jury," he began, "this is the stage of the trial when the lawyers tell you what the evidence will be. Let me start by describing what you will hear about how Jana's horrible death has affected her living parents. This is an undisputed issue."

For about 20 minutes Anderson described the loving family and how everything changed on the night of Charlie, Jr.'s birthday celebration.

He then moved to the liability aspect of the case. "Unlike the facts surrounding the Bensons' pain, there is no agreement as to what happened at the house that night. I am not going to tell you what the evidence will be as to the drinking because that is for you to decide. My job as a lawyer is to bring the witnesses to this courtroom who can tell you what they saw and heard. Mr. and Mrs. Smith will be called to the stand and they will tell you what they did and didn't do. You can then make an educated decision based upon the facts presented to you during the trial. "

Anderson was trying to give Mr. Smith the impression that he and his wife would be the only witnesses regarding the party. He always believed in telling the truth and took his oath as a lawyer seriously. Anderson would do all he could to advocate effectively on behalf of those who were injured physically, mentally, or in both ways, but he would not cross the line and lie or cheat to fulfill his mission. Anderson was not lying when he said he would place the

Smiths on the stand. He would. But there would be two additional witnesses who would discuss the drinking, and he chose not to mention this little fact. He ended his opening statement by asking the jurors to listen carefully to all the evidence and then decide the case based upon the truth.

Tommy brought a legal pad to the podium, which contained a detailed outline of the defendants' opening statement. After his introduction and a little bit of small talk made in an attempt to bond with the jurors, Tommy told them he was going to cover four areas of evidence in his argument. He spoke in a manner indicating he knew the facts of the case clearly and was confident the evidence would indicate his clients were not responsible for the death.

The first point he made was that since Jana had a history of stealing alcohol from her parents' house, Mrs. Benson should have taken precautions to prevent access. Tommy suggested that because her mother had not done this, there was justification for the assignment of negligence to Mrs. Benson for the accident that evening.

The second issue he highlighted to the jurors was that it was Jana who brought the rum to the Smith's house. Tommy suggested this act was evidence of Jana's negligence. Then Tommy brought up the fact that after Jana drank she drove a vehicle even though she had to know her ability to drive and react was affected by the alcohol she had consumed. Additional negligence, he told the jury.

Finally, Tommy outlined how Jana's failure to wear a seatbelt caused her to go through the windshield, strike the pole, and suffer an injury that resulted in her death. His last comment was that the accident and lawsuit could have been avoided if Jana had not taken and consumed the alcohol, or if she had not driven while intoxicated, or if the seatbelt had been used.

Anderson was impressed with Tommy's opening statement. It set up numerous hurdles he would have to overcome if a verdict was to be returned in his clients' favor. As he smiled inwardly, Anderson thought Tommy's biggest problem was that he didn't know alcohol was provided by Mr. Smith. It appeared that Charlie Smith, Sr. had withheld valuable and critically important information from his lawyer, or worse, had lied to him.

Judge Graham declared a mid-afternoon recess and then Michelle Benson was called as plaintiff's first witness. Anderson kept his eye on the clock. He wanted to make sure her direct examination consumed the remaining portion of the day.

Once on the stand, Michelle testified that it took two years for her to become pregnant with her only child and it was only possible after an extensive regimen of fertility drugs. She took the jury through their early years as a family emphasizing how the three of them spent so much time together. She described the numerous family fishing trips they took, and she displayed a picture of Jana and Joe hugging each other after they completed their first deep-water dive together. Michelle talked about Jana's future goals—how she had planned on attending St. Louis University's premed program to become a pediatrician.

After Anderson completed painting the portrait of a loving family, he moved on to life after Jana's death. This is when tears started to flow from the jurors' eyes.

Stoically, Michelle described how, after Jana's death, Joe would come from work and after he'd changed his clothes he would go sit on his late daughter's bed. Joe was adamant that Jana's room remain in the same condition it was in on the day of her death. She further discussed how Joe suffered from extended crying spells and was visiting with a psychiatrist two times per week.

With perfect time management, Anderson then moved to the night of the accident. No questions were asked regarding how Jana obtained the rum from their house. Instead, Anderson started with the phone call from Angela to Michelle and went forward slowly making sure that no sympathetic details were left out.

Michelle testified that she had to hold her daughter's face together while blood accumulated in her mouth; all the jurors were in tears. Michelle then demonstrated to the jurors how her only child died in her arms.

For the remaining portion of the day Anderson asked questions regarding her pain and suffering from the loss. Michelle's last answer described in horrifying detail her nightmares in which she would see her daughter's face as she tried to tell her mother goodbye or I love you, but no sound came out of Jana's blood-filled mouth.

Anderson concluded his direct questioning at precisely 4:58 p.m. and then tendered the witness to defense counsel, knowing that Judge Graham would call it a day. The judge advised the somber jury that testimony would resume the following morning at 9:00.

Anderson found himself glancing toward Nicole. He realized he wanted her approval. The look in her eyes told him he got it.

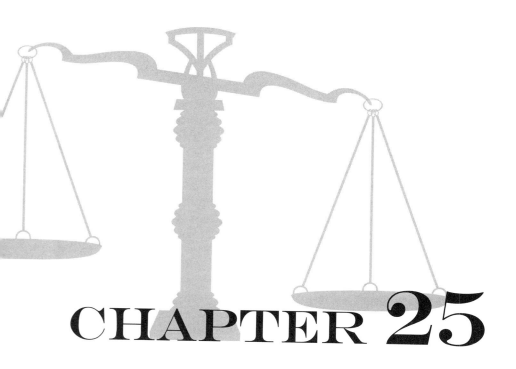

CHAPTER 25

That evening over Chinese takeout, Anderson, Nicole, Joe, and Michelle met in the main conference room of the law firm to discuss the first day of the trial and their strategy. Anderson sat at the head of the table and addressed the group.

"I like this jury," he began. "They were obviously moved by Michelle's testimony. Based upon Tommy's opening statement and Mr. Smith's demeanor, it appears to me that nobody on the defense team anticipates Caroline and Angela will be called as witnesses. I think we've kept the little secret to ourselves. Good job, everyone.

"Our first witness tomorrow after Michelle's cross-examination will be Libby Smith, and I'll establish that she did see the rum in the pool house. Then I'll call Charlie Smith, Sr. and I anticipate he will deny any knowledge of the drinking. Hopefully, he will be adamant and self-righteous about it. Then Angela and Caroline's testimony will be especially devastating to his credibility. Now, where do we stand with the coordination of our out-of-town guests?"

Nicole cleared her throat. "Our investigator is meeting their flights in the morning," she began, her tone most professional, "and he should have them to the courthouse by 10:00. I've instructed Larry to keep both Caroline and Angela in the witness room on the floor below ours so the Smiths won't see them. He will bring them up for their testimony when I call him on his cell phone."

"Good planning," Anderson said approvingly. "Michelle, Nicole is going to prepare you for your cross-examination by Tommy. I need to work on my questions for the defendants' seatbelt expert who will probably be called to the stand tomorrow afternoon. Enjoy dinner, and if you have any questions, I'll be down the hall." Anderson went to his office while Joe, Michelle, and Nicole remained in the conference room.

Nicole spread out her notes on Michelle's cross-examination and addressed her client. "Tommy wants to question you regarding Jana's drinking history, and specifically, how she had taken bottles from your liquor cabinet. Remember, he's trying to establish a factual basis for the jury to assign negligence to you. Although you must tell the truth, you should convey to the jurors that you had taken reasonable measures to stop Jana from taking your liquor and you had absolutely no indication she was looking for alcohol on the night of her death."

"I understand," Michelle responded.

"Anderson and I want you to be forthcoming in acknowledging Jana had used alcohol before because in closing argument Anderson is going to compare and contrast your preventative measures with Charlie, Sr.'s actions. One additional piece of instruction. We don't want the jury to forget about the sympathy aspect of this case. So when Tommy asks you whether you knew Jana had taken the bottle of rum, I want you to think back to when you held her as she died."

"That seems a bit cruel," Joe said.

"I'm just doing my job," Nicole said patiently, "which means we will do everything possible within the ethical guidelines of the law to make sure your family secures the monetary award you are entitled to as a result of the untimely and unnecessary passing of your daughter."

As Nicole spoke, she flashed for a moment on the odd fact that she had come to the firm to destroy Anderson, but her mission now included winning this case with him. Funny how things change, she thought. Well, I can do one and then the other. And I will.

"Michelle," she said, "please remember that Tommy's question, which I know he will ask regarding your knowledge of the rum being taken, will trigger the horrible memory."

Eyes downcast, Michelle said quietly, "I know."

"Okay, everyone," Nicole said, wrapping up. "Tomorrow's going to be a long day. Try to get a good night's sleep and I'll see you in the morning."

The clients thanked Nicole and took their leave. Nicole thought about going to Anderson. He might be vulnerable right now, she told herself. I could get him to a hotel or my place where I could take pictures.

And then she decided, no, not until after the trial. She wanted to fulfill her responsibility to Justin—and get paid—but she also wanted to fulfill her new responsibilities to Joe and Michelle. And to Anderson.

CHAPTER 26

When court resumed Tuesday morning, Judge Graham asked Michelle to return to the witness stand.

Tommy greeted her in a friendly voice. "Good morning, ma'am. I'd like to ask you some questions about Jana and her lifestyle before the night of her accident, if that's all right with you."

Michelle nodded warily.

"Despite her age, did your daughter consume alcoholic beverages?"

Michelle glanced uneasily at Anderson, looking for direction. He gave a small nod, meaning she should answer the question. "Yes, she did."

"Was there ever an occasion when you realized Jana had taken bottles from the liquor cabinet in your house?"

"Yes. Actually on more than one occasion."

Anderson was pleased with Michelle's demeanor as she testified. It was apparent to all in the courtroom she was telling the truth and was not trying to conceal information.

Tommy continued. "Why didn't you take reasonable measures to stop your daughter from underage drinking?"

"I did. In fact, I installed a lock on the cabinet, but apparently she found a way to get around it."

"Do you know if Jana took rum from your supply before she went to the Smiths' house?"

Michelle now stared at defense counsel and did not answer the question. It was obvious to Nicole her plan was working. She could tell from the look on Michelle's face that the vision of her daughter's last moments was vividly real.

Tommy followed up. "Did you understand my last question?"

Michelle's lips began to quiver and her eyes filled with tears. "I'm sorry. I was thinking about my daughter. How she died. How she tried to tell me she loved me. She couldn't do it. Her mouth was full of blood. My daughter's blood was all over my shirt."

Tommy realized he was losing the effectiveness of his cross-examination. The jury's focus had gone from what Michelle had not done to sympathy for the loss of her daughter. He needed to get her off the witness stand.

"No more questions," Tommy announced as he sat down.

Nicole, biting her lip, glanced approvingly at Anderson, who gave a small nod.

Anderson called Libby Smith as his next witness. His plan was to keep his questioning very brief. "On the night Jana died," he began, "did you see the kids drinking alcohol in your house or any evidence they might have been drinking?"

"I did see a bottle of rum, but I couldn't stop them from drinking because the container was already empty," she said.

"But you could have broken up the party and made sure no one drove. Did you take the car keys away from the kids who drank alcohol illegally in your house?"

"No, I didn't take their keys. Maybe Jana shouldn't have snuck rum into my house. There shouldn't have been any drinking!" Libby added angrily.

Anderson loved her answer. He wrote it down on his legal pad with a note to use her statement in his closing argument.

"No further questions, Your Honor."

Charlie Smith, Sr. was next in the witness box.

Anderson looked down at his pad. "Sir, I'm sorry. I didn't notice. Have you already been sworn in by the Clerk of Court to tell the truth?"

"Yes, I have been," he said.

Anderson was well aware the witness had taken an oath to tell the truth, but he wanted to emphasize the fact to the jury.

"On the night of Jana's death, did you know minors were drinking alcohol at your house?" Anderson continued.

Charlie paused for a moment and then turned towards the jury. "No, I did not."

Anderson had established the predicate for the two girls' testimony, but he wanted the defendant to commit himself a little further.

"If you had known the kids were drinking rum, would you have taken action to stop the partying?"

Charlie answered quickly. "Absolutely. Not only is it against the law, but it's dangerous."

Another quote to read back to the jury in closing argument, Anderson thought as he concluded his questions. The judge ordered an early lunch break at 11:45. Instead of eating, Anderson used the time to meet with Caroline and Angela downstairs.

When the trial reconvened at one, Nicole called Larry and told him to bring Caroline to the courtroom immediately. She signaled to Anderson to let him know she was on her way. Anderson announced Caroline would be the plaintiff's next witness.

Charlie Smith, Sr. looked uncomfortable and repositioned himself in his seat. Tommy seemed confused because Caroline's statement to the investigating authorities was consistent with the testimony at trial. He wondered why the plaintiff was bothering to call this witness who was going to give similar testimony.

Anderson did not want to appear to be leading or coaching Caroline, so he simply asked her to describe what took place at the house that night. Her testimony was consistent with the Smiths' sworn statements until she reached the part where she described how Mr. Smith came out and saw the empty rum bottle. Caroline told how he brought out a larger full rum bottle, poured drinks for the entire group, and then proposed a toast for his son. This revelation triggered looks of stunned disbelief on the faces of the jurors. This was clearly a totally different set of facts than what they had heard so far.

On cross-examination, Tommy turned to Caroline. "If you're now telling the truth about what Mr. Smith did that night, I assume you also told the investigating officer the truth?"

"I should have, but I didn't." She looked down at her hands.

Tommy, thinking that he had accomplished his job of discrediting her, turned to the judge, "No additional questions, Your Honor." He began to walk back to the counsel table when Caroline's voice stopped him in his tracks.

"Charlie begged me not to say anything—he said he and his dad would go to jail if we told what had happened."

The jurors' faces reflected their shock and anger at this new incriminating evidence.

Angela's testimony parroted Caroline's version of the night. Again, Anderson asked an open-ended question regarding what happened so he didn't appear to be coaching the witness.

"Why didn't you tell the police about what Mr. Smith did that night?" Anderson asked, knowing the question would be forthcoming from Tommy.

"I'm not proud of that. I shouldn't have listened to Charlie, but he was very persuasive. He told us we couldn't bring Jana back so why jeopardize his college acceptance and his father's reputation."

Angela looked toward the Benson family and said quietly, "I'm so sorry. Jana was a good friend."

Tommy had no ideas for a productive cross-exam. He was at a total loss for anything he could say or do to attack this line of questioning. The defendants' case was brief and focused on the seatbelt issue. Tommy only called one witness.

The hired gun, Mr. Albert, first explained to the jurors how a seatbelt functioned so a driver could not possibly go through a windshield. Then he demonstrated with the use of visual aids how Jana was thrown from the car and struck the pole. He ended by stating that if Jana had obeyed Florida law and worn her seatbelt, she would still be alive.

Anderson knew he couldn't attack the expert on his physics or his conclusion that a seatbelt would have stopped Jana from being thrown from the vehicle. He turned the focus back to the issue of alcohol.

"Isn't it true that if Mr. Smith had not provided rum to the minors, Jana wouldn't have driven into the pole and she would still be with her mother and father today?"

"That is possible," admitted Mr. Albert.

With that, testimony concluded, and it was now time for closing arguments. As plaintiff's counsel, Anderson spoke first. His argument first concentrated on the open house party statute. "The law of Florida," he told the jurors, "dictates parents are responsible for underage drinking at their house if they have knowledge of the activity and do not take affirmative action to stop it."

He then moved on to the critical testimony of the two friends. "Caroline and Angela had no reason to fabricate their testimony about Mr. Smith bringing out the bottle of rum. And as you heard for yourselves, their testimonies were entirely consistent with each other. There can be no doubt in your mind that they are telling you the truth."

Anderson returned to the plaintiff's counsel table to retrieve a legal pad. "I want to remind you of two statements made by the defendants during this trial. Ms. Smith testified there should not have been any drinking. Mr. Smith stated not only is underage drinking against the law, it is dangerous."

Anderson looked up from his notes and directly into the jurors' eyes. "The law was broken. Mrs. Smith did not try to stop Jana from driving even though she had seen the empty rum bottle and then

Mr. Smith even provided more alcohol. At least Michelle Benson tried to stop the drinking by installing a lock on her liquor cabinet!"

Anderson went over to the clerk's table, picked up his water glass and drank a sip for effect. He then continued in a less forceful voice. "The result of the alcohol consumption was tragic. Joe and Michelle lost their only child. Think back to how Jana tried to tell her mother she loved her as she died in her arms. Michelle was able to wash away the blood but the memory will never be erased. The family trusts you to be fair in your damages evaluation.

"Your justice must be equitable to both the Bensons and the Smiths. Some accidents are clearly caused by the negligence of only one party. But many unfortunate events take place because of the actions and inactions of more than one person. In fairness, the plaintiff admits some negligence should be assigned to Jana for her failure to wear her seatbelt, but the vast majority of the fault should be given to the Smiths. They are adults, not children. They allowed alcohol to be consumed in their home, and in fact, promoted underage drinking. Thank you for your time and justice."

This time, as Anderson took his seat, Nicole gave his hand a small squeeze below the table. No one in the courtroom appeared to notice. Tommy spoke next. He thanked the jurors for their service. Then he spoke in detail about the seatbelt and Mr. Albert's testimony regarding how Jana's injuries would have never occurred if the restraint were in place. Tommy also argued Jana should be held accountable for bringing rum to the Smiths' house just as her mother should be assigned negligence for her failure to secure the family's liquor cabinet.

The defendants' closing argument ended in a similar fashion to the plaintiff's. An admission was made that there was probably more than one party to be blamed for the loss. But Tommy's final comment to the jury differed from Anderson's.

"If justice is to be served based upon what Jana herself did that night, then less than 25% of the fault should be allocated to the Smiths."

After the jury retired for its deliberations, the Bensons hugged both Nicole and Anderson and thanked them for their hard work. A long two hours later, the foreman told the bailiff they were finished and had reached a decision. The jury reentered the courtroom, now tense and filled with family members, friends, reporters, and other onlookers. The bailiff published the verdict.

"Was there negligence on behalf of Mr. and Mrs. Smith?"

"Yes, 60%."

"Was there negligence on behalf of Jana Benson?"

"Yes, 30%."

"Was there negligence on behalf of Michelle Benson?"

"Yes, 10%."

"What are the total damages of Mr. and Mrs. Benson as a result of the loss of their daughter?"

"Two point two million dollars."

The size of the verdict caused gasps in the courtroom. Joe and Michelle embraced, sobbing. Anderson and Nicole smiled at each other—mission accomplished.

Tommy waited for Anderson on the front steps of the courthouse. As Anderson approached, Tommy extended his right hand. "Congratulations, Anderson. You presented a good case. I look forward to our next one together."

"Thank you for your professionalism," Anderson said as he patted Tommy on his shoulder. Normally, Anderson would call Ruth with news of a verdict, especially such a large one. But today, with Nicole right there, he didn't feel the need.

CHAPTER 27

When Anderson and Nicole arrived back at the office, the rest of the firm was waiting to celebrate. Everyone was pumped about this newest win. They all knew what a tough case this one had been and were excited to share in the thrill of the victory.

While the staff congratulated Anderson, Nicole went back to her desk and made some quick calculations. "Sixty percent of $2.2 million equates to a judgment of $1.2 million! My God...the 40% fee on 1.2 will be $528,000!"

"Wow," Nicole said as Anderson appeared behind her.

"I see we're doing a little bit of arithmetic," Anderson said, "Nicole, I want you to know these numbers were made possible by your hard work and I think there'll be enough to give you a nice year-end bonus."

"Well, counselor, as you once said, we are good together," Nicole said with a big grin.

"Yes, we are."

"Anderson, could I ask for a big favor?"

Anderson looked surprised.

"Would you be willing to meet me at the Marriott Waterside at 6:00 so we can celebrate with a drink?"

"With pleasure," Anderson said with a smile and headed back to his office.

Nicole watched his long, lean body move down the hall. Getting laid and getting paid, she thought. Doesn't get much better than that.

She got a text message on her cell from an anonymous source. It read: "UR NOT GETTING PAID TO WIN CASES FOR HIM."

She texted back. "JUST U WAIT."

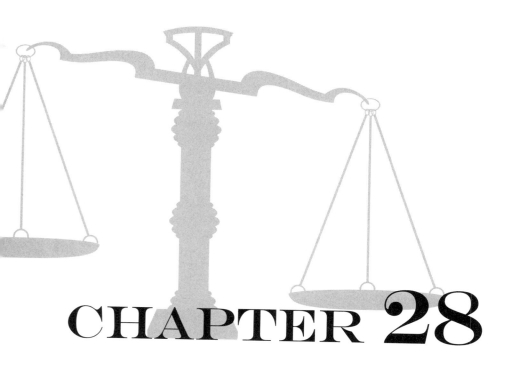

CHAPTER 28

Anderson entered through the revolving doors of the hotel lobby and saw Nicole seated at a small round table for two, sipping a glass of white wine. She was wearing a body-clinging red dress that left little to the imagination. Nicole looked up and saw Anderson staring at her.

"You—you look very nice in that dress," Anderson stammered.

"Thank you. You don't look bad yourself...for a tired, old trial lawyer."

Anderson grinned. As he sat down, the waitress approached. Anderson ordered a beer and Nicole asked for another Chardonnay. Nicole immediately broke the tension by bringing up the trial and the verdict. She was fascinated by the entire legal process and especially how Anderson's mind worked when it came to thinking through a trial and deciding how to handle each part of it. She kept asking him questions and getting him to talk about himself and the law. Anderson loved to talk about his work with anyone who appreciated the intricacies and minor details. He was in heaven. A beautiful, intelligent girl hanging on his every word.

Anderson had worked through the lunch hour, so he was starting to feel his drink. He began to loosen up a little bit and confided to Nicole, "You know, I was really impressed with how courteous and professional Tommy was after the verdict. It takes an honorable man to do that. "

"Well, I was very impressed by you today. Especially with how well you connected with the jury," Nicole said.

After more small talk and another round of drinks, Anderson said, "Nicole, I want you to be the paralegal who works on all my new cases in the future. Whenever I accept a plaintiff's case, it will immediately be forwarded to you for the initial workup, and if I'm not available when a client calls about a new matter, I want you to handle the intake," Anderson told her with a smile.

"That's quite an honor, Anderson. I really don't know how to thank you. But I did have an idea so I'm going to try in my own special way. If you don't mind waiting about ten minutes, I can have my surprise ready for you. Could you come to room 234 so I can give it to you?" And with that, Nicole slipped from the table and headed toward the elevator.

The waitress brought the bill for the drinks and Anderson, alarmed, thanked her and tossed his Visa card on the table. Sobering quickly, he ran after Nicole and caught her just as she was about to step into an elevator.

"You're a fast worker!" Nicole said approvingly.

"Maybe not as fast as I...as I wish I was," Anderson said awkwardly. "Listen, Nicole, about going upstairs..."

She came close to him, wrapping her arms around his neck. "We are good together, Anderson. I want us to be even closer." As her lips approached his, he reached behind him for her wrists and pulled her arms from around his neck.

"Nicole!" he exclaimed, shocked, and afraid that someone might have seen them together. Tampa, after all, was in many ways a small town, and this lobby was the Town Square.

"I'm sorry if I somehow gave you the wrong impression. We do work well together, but our relationship is strictly business. My wife and I are very happy together. I wouldn't want to lead you on by letting you think otherwise. This wouldn't be best for either of us."

Nicole felt as if someone had knocked the wind out of her. She struggled to speak. She somehow managed to keep her composure.

"I'm sorry, Anderson," she said stiffly. "I misunderstood. I thought you might be interested in...knowing me better." She paused and took a deep breath, dropping her hands to her sides. "I understand we only have a professional relationship. I hope you will forget this ever happened and I promise to never let it happen again."

Anderson didn't know what else to say so he turned quickly and left her standing at the elevator. He went back to the lobby, retrieved his credit card and signed the bill, and headed out of the hotel without another word or even a glance in her direction.

Nicole shook with anger. Anderson was no better than her father or Rick. I offer myself to him and he rejects me—just like they did. He thinks he's too good for me. All this time, he's been leading me on, getting me to do his work, making me think he cared about me, when all he wanted was the work. It's always the work and the money. I'll make sure he pays. That ungrateful, condescending bastard. Justin was right all along. She fumbled through her purse, looking for her phone. She punched in Justin's number.

CHAPTER 29

Even though it was evening, Justin was still working. In fact he was busy yelling at an associate for his most recent screw-up involving a recommendation the green lawyer had made to settle a case.

"Justin Cartwright," he barked into the phone.

"This is Nicole. We need to talk."

Justin abruptly dismissed the trembling young lawyer from the room and shut the door behind him.

With his privacy assured, Justin asked, "How's it going with our mutual friend?"

"You were right. He's arrogant, self-centered, and thinks he's Mr. Wonderful. I want you to know I will have your pictures for you soon."

"Excellent," Justin said, with a tight grin on his face.

"One last thing," Nicole continued. "You never did tell me what you were going to do with the pictures. When the time comes, I want to know every single painful detail. I'd like to think of him suffering. That would be my pleasure."

"I promise. Now get to work on obtaining my evidence. Remember, there's a big payday for you!"

As he hung up the phone, Justin knew he had definitely picked the right woman for the job. She was on a rampage.

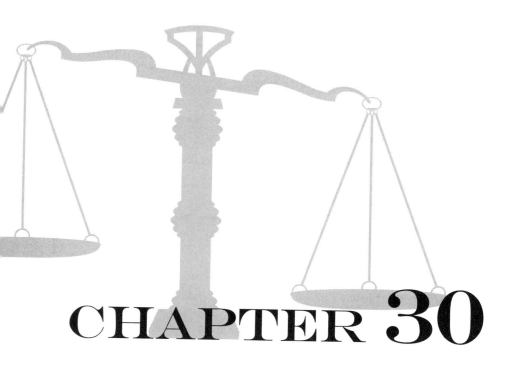

CHAPTER 30

The next morning, both Anderson and Nicole acted as if nothing had ever happened. When Anderson walked past her in the hallway, she greeted him cheerfully just as she did every other day. She hoped she had done no permanent damage the night before. Maybe he was too embarrassed to say anything. Whatever. That would certainly work in her favor. She needed to keep her job so she could accomplish her long-range plan.

During her lunch break Nicole politely declined an offer to go to Bennigan's with the rest of the office staff. She needed to get away and do some research on a computer where the search trail could not be traced back to her. She went to the same Internet café where she had gone before she came to work at Anderson's firm and pulled up all the information she could find about date rape drugs.

The most common drugs mentioned were Gamma-Hydroxybutyrate (GHB), Rohypnol (roofies), and ketamine. After reading about all of the effects of the drugs, she decided roofies would be her best bet. The pills could easily be slipped into a person's drink without being detected, the drug's effects began within 30 minutes, rendering a person defenseless against sexual assault, and the best news of all, the person usually suffered from temporary amnesia. Perfect.

Next, Nicole called the pharmacy at Bayside Drugs, a few blocks from the office. At the Athletic Club, where she worked out, she had gotten to know some of the bodybuilders, who got their illicit drugs from a clerk at that store. Nicole and the pharmacist, Howard, had gone out a few times, but nothing had ever happened between them, much to Howard's dismay.

"Bayside Drugs, Howard here. May I help you?"

"Hey, it's Nicole. I need a big favor and this request must stay between the two of us."

"Anything for you, doll."

Nicole hesitated before she spoke. "I need to get a hold of enough roofies to knock out a 200-pound man for an evening."

"Nicole, you devil! What sexual deviancy do you have planned? You do know Rohypnol is a very dangerous date rape drug, don't you?"

"I know."

"Darling, with your looks you shouldn't have any trouble finding sex." Howard lowered his voice to a whisper. "What in the world do you need roofies for?"

"Look, that's my business. How much would I need and can you get it for me?"

"You're going to owe me big. I don't exactly carry roofies behind the counter, but I can probably get some for you. To do what you're talking about, you'll need a two-milligram tablet. Crush it and put it in your man's drink. It's tasteless so he won't even know it's there.

"Now, remember, he'll be incapacitated for up to eight hours so you better be near wherever it is you want him to end up once he's unconscious or you'll be trying to lug him out of the bar. And somehow I don't see that happening."

"Okay, Howard. I get the picture. Now, can you help me or not?"

"Hold on, hold on. I told you I thought I could. Tonight when I'm at the gym I'll leave a small box for you up front with three two-milligram tablets in it. Nicole, have fun, but please be careful. And of course, this conversation never happened. Maybe I can take you to a movie sometime?"

"Maybe," she said noncommittally, and she hung up the phone.

CHAPTER 31

Work at Anderson's firm was relatively quiet until Nicole received a phone call the following Wednesday. Anderson was out of town covering depositions in a chemical poisoning case when the receptionist forwarded the call from a Mrs. Radis.

"Nicole Babson, paralegal to Anderson Parker. May I help you?"

"I need Mr. Parker. My son has been badly injured and my friend and neighbor Dr. Terry Harmon told me I should call Anderson Parker immediately."

"Unfortunately, Mr. Parker is out of town for the day, but I am in charge of intake for his new cases and I would be glad to help you."

"My son's been in an accident and I must speak to someone right away. May I come to your office and meet with you now?"

Mrs. Radis, an attractive woman in her early 40s, was clearly distressed. Nicole took her back into Anderson's office and brought her a glass of water.

"Mrs. Radis, take a deep breath and see if you can tell me what happened. Take as much time as you need. It's okay."

"Thanks. I'm a wreck, but I've got to do something. It's just too horrible. I don't even know where to start."

"That's okay, Mrs. Radis. Why don't you tell me about your son? What's his name?"

"Well, Danny—that's my husband—Danny and I have two sons. Our oldest is Andy. He's a world-class tennis player. He played one year at Stanford and then turned pro. Recently, he's won matches at some of the major tournaments so his world ranking has climbed to 37. Finally, after all the years of scraping to make ends meet, he now makes a good living from the tournament prize money and through his contracts with clothing companies, racquet makers, and other corporations when he endorses their products."

She took a sip of water.

"Andy lives and trains at Saddlebrook Resort here in Tampa. Although he's busy with his tennis and traveling, he does have a girlfriend. Andy just finished a long roadtrip last week so he took Dorothy to Key West for a three-day vacation.

"Dorothy called last night and told me Andy'd been attacked by a barracuda. He's in intensive care at the Key West Hospital. From what the doctor told her, the barracuda's teeth sliced Andy's leg right below his knee and now he has what she called a, um, a severe peroneal nerve injury. At least, I think that's what she called it. I'm so upset, I can't remember much of what she said. But I do remember she said he almost bled to death because it took so long to get him to the hospital. The doctors told Dorothy that most likely Andy will have a significant disability in his right leg and there's the chance they'll have to amputate his lower leg. How can this be happening to my boy? Everything Andy's worked so hard for is going to be lost. And I can't even go be with him because my mom's got Alzheimer's and I can't leave her alone."

As Ms. Radis sobbed and held her head in her hands, Nicole's mind worked rapidly, thinking of all the questions the accident brought up. She wrote her notes and questions on a legal pad while keeping an eye on Mrs. Radis, ready to offer a tissue, if needed. Another thought entered Nicole's mind as she ran through the issues. The investigation of this case could be her chance to get Anderson.

With Mrs. Radis's permission, Nicole called Dorothy and put her on speakerphone. Dorothy could only be with Andy for brief periods because he was still in intensive care. Apparently, the doctors were trying to decide whether the right lower extremity could be saved. The blood loss had been so severe that the circulation to Andy's foot had been almost nonexistent for an extended period of time. Even if the leg could be salvaged, the doctors felt there would be peroneal nerve palsy although it was too early to determine the extent of functional impairment.

Dorothy described the accident in detail. Andy and Dorothy were snorkeling together, holding hands in about six feet of water, when a large barracuda—she guessed it was about five feet long—shot in like a bolt of lightning and sliced Andy's leg just below his knee. Dorothy said there was blood everywhere. The first mate jumped in the water and carried Andy up the ladder. The other snorklers were screaming. She described the wound—how his blood was spurting out all over the floor of the boat and his leg looked as if it might fall off, the gash was so deep. The captain tied a tourniquet above his knee and then the boat sped to a dock where Andy was rushed to the hospital.

Nicole obtained additional background information from Dorothy and told her she would call back in a few hours to let her know what time tomorrow the representatives of the law firm would meet with her in Key West. She assured Mrs. Radis she would call her later in the afternoon to let her know about her research and any actions the firm planned to take on Andy's behalf.

The case appeared to be a moneymaker, so Nicole wanted to make sure she covered all the bases in the early stages. One thing was clear—there were large damages. A young man was probably going to lose a productive professional tennis career and maybe a portion of his lower leg. That equated to big dollars.

Dorothy had told Nicole that she and Andy had found out about the snorkeling trip from a search on the Internet, so Nicole began her research by going to their website. It was definitely impressive. A video clip showed the boat taking tourists out to the reef on a beautiful sunny day. Shots of underwater sea life interspersed with the happy smiles of snorkelers swimming in the crystal-clear waters enticed future clients with promises of a top of the line trip on a custom 35-foot boat and complimentary champagne for the sunset cruise back to Key West Harbour. The operation smelled of money and Nicole was confident there was a big fat liability insurance policy at the end of the rainbow.

Nicole had to convince Anderson it was essential the two of them go to Key West and take a trip on the boat. The best way to develop their strategy for the case would be to see the snorkeling setup first-hand so they could develop their theories of liability. She knew she'd be able to sway him.

And although Nicole was in charge of the intake for Anderson's new plaintiffs' cases, she still had to clear any major plans with him first.

Anderson glanced at his BlackBerry between questions at the deposition and saw Nicole's message. He asked for a short recess and left the room. After Anderson heard the background of the case, he agreed with Nicole's suggestion and told her to go forward with the travel plans. He sent an email to his secretary, telling her to clear his calendar for the next two days. Good work. You handled this well. Could be a big case, he emailed to Nicole as he walked down the hall back to the deposition.

Nicole dialed the toll- free number.

"First-Class Reef Experience. May we help you?"

"Yes, I'd like to book a trip on your boat for tomorrow. Do you have an opening for two?" Nicole asked.

"Today's your lucky day. Our afternoon sunset snorkeling trip has two openings."

"Great. We'll take it." She booked airplane tickets for a Thursday morning departure with a Friday mid-morning return and then made reservations for two rooms at the Pier House. The hotel advertised itself as a romantic getaway overlooking the water, and she was counting on the magic allure of Key West to do its work.

When Anderson returned to the office at 4:30, he called Nicole to request a meeting in the conference room. The results of her investigation covered the conference table. She had gathered information on the First-Class Reef Experience including their official business records from the state of Florida, medical research on peroneal nerve injuries, newspaper articles on Andy's tennis career, and travel information for the Key West trip. Anderson liked the damages element of the case. The negligence aspect of the case could be established once they'd done further research in Key West.

"People aren't supposed to have their legs eaten off by barracudas when they pay to go on a snorkeling trip," Anderson said.

Nicole called Dorothy and confirmed a 10:00 meeting at the hospital the next morning. She had prepared a file for Anderson to take home with a copy of all her research and his itinerary for the flight the next morning. He gathered up all his files and headed toward the elevator.

"You've done a great job on this, Nicole."

"Why, thank you, kind sir. Just make sure you do your homework tonight. And don't forget to pack a bathing suit."

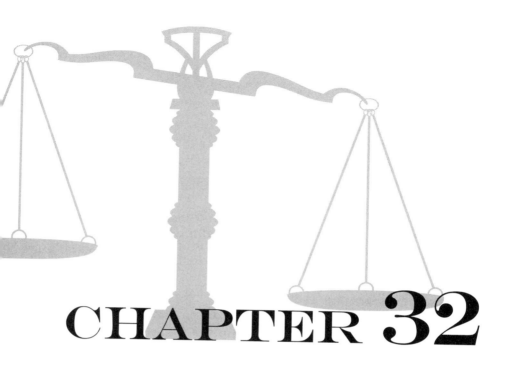

CHAPTER 32

A nderson and Nicole met at the airport gate early the next morning and boarded the puddle jumper to Key West. After renting a car, they drove straight to the hospital and met Dorothy in the lobby. Andy was still in intensive care so they could only visit with him for ten minutes. His appearance was shocking—his leg was raised and heavily bandaged. Tubes protruded from his knee and monitoring equipment beeped and hummed all around the bed. His face was pasty and gray.

Dorothy rested her hand softly on Andy's arm to see if he was awake enough to talk to them. He slowly opened his eyes and groaned, "Hey baby, what's up?" with a crooked smile. Dorothy introduced Anderson and Nicole and did her best to explain what was going on, but it was clear Andy had no idea who they were or why they were there.

"Andy, these people want to help you. Can you tell them how you were hurt?"

"I'm not sure I know, but my leg sure hurts like hell. I can't wait to get out of this damn bed and get back on the tennis court."

It was obvious that Andy wasn't going to be much help in establishing background facts. Everything had happened so quickly and he was still too drugged to even try to remember. Anderson, Nicole, and Dorothy went to the hospital cafeteria where they talked while sipping coffee. Dorothy stirred her coffee, staring down into the black whirlpool she created with her spoon.

Nicole rested her hand gently on Dorothy's arm. "I know you've had to tell your story too many times already, but it would really help us if you could do it again. We need every single detail that you can remember, even those that don't seem important to you. Could you do that?"

Dorothy continued to look down into her coffee, almost as if she could pretend she wasn't there by not facing them as she spoke. She gave a slight nod.

"The snorkeling trip appeared to be top-of-the-line. When we arrived at the dock, the first mate introduced himself and helped us aboard. His name was Matt. I particularly remember him because he was so good-looking—great smile, curly blond hair, nice body. There were three other couples going on the trip and we chatted with each other during the 30-minute ride out to the reef line. The boat was very comfortable. I believe the captain told me it was a Cabo 35.

"After the crew anchored the boat, they offered us cold drinks and chips while they showed us how to use the gear and told us the rules about snorkeling. The captain reminded us we had to wear our vests when we were in the water and that we needed to stay within 50 yards of the boat.

"As we were putting on our life vests, the first mate told me to stay close to him. He said he'd release food that would bring the prettiest fish right up close to him. Actually, I think Matt was hitting on me even though I was clearly with Andy.

"We swam around for a long time. Fish of all sizes and colors were everywhere. I did notice a couple of big barracuda following us, but when I asked Matt if they were dangerous, he told me if I didn't harass them they wouldn't bother me.

"We were floating next to the swim platform at the back of the boat waiting to reboard when Matt emptied the last bit of food into the water. All of a sudden, all these little fish appeared. I was kinda scared when the fish started touching me, so we turned to swim away. That's when this huge barracuda darted in front of me and attacked Andy.

"The water turned bright red, and I was terrified because I'd seen on the Discovery Channel that blood attracts sharks. I tried to pull Andy to the boat, but he was too heavy. Matt jumped in and helped Andy up onto the platform. The captain came down from the flybridge and immediately placed a tourniquet above Andy's knee to try to slow down the bleeding.

"It was awful—Andy was screaming in pain, everyone else was

freaking out too because they weren't sure what was going on. There was blood all over the boat and all over Matt and me. I held on to Andy and managed to calm him down a bit as the captain tried to get the boat back to the dock as quickly as he could. I was so worried because it seemed like Andy was going into shock from loss of blood. Finally, we arrived at a dock where, thankfully, there was an ambulance waiting and they rushed us off to the hospital."

"I know it's painful to recall the details, but every bit helps us in our investigation," Anderson said. "Nicole and I have booked a trip with the same group for this afternoon to check things out. We'll let you know what we find."

Anderson and Nicole drove from the hospital to the Pier House, passing through historic Key West. Even though Anderson was focused on the case, he couldn't help but notice the beautiful old homes and the abundant tropical foliage. The island was a lover's paradise. Ruth would love this place, he thought. He made a mental note to plan a surprise anniversary trip and bring her here.

They checked into the hotel with just enough time to change quickly and get to the dock for the snorkeling trip. As Anderson put on his bathing suit, he caught a glimpse of himself in the mirror. He'd definitely been working too hard. Where did that belly come from? Time to start running again. Oh well, he'd worry about that later. He grabbed a towel and threw it over his shoulder.

Nicole and Anderson walked down the finger dock to the Cabo 35 where a young man greeted them.

"Welcome to the First-Class Reef Experience. I'm Matt, the first mate."

Just as Dorothy had described, Matt had curly blond hair and a big smile, and he was very attractive. Nicole asked Matt to take a picture of the two of them in front of the boat before they pulled away from the dock.

"I would be honored."

"We want to have a perfect picture for memories' sake so let's use my tripod. That way it won't be blurry," Nicole said as she set up the picture. Nicole made sure the company logo on the side of the boat was included in the picture. Matt might think she wanted a picture to show her friends back home, but this was business—for the potential lawsuit and any information it might provide.

On the way out to the reef, Anderson joined the captain on the fly bridge.

"I don't get out on the water much. Is it safe out there?" Anderson asked in an attempt to break the ice.

"Nothing to worry about. It's a beautiful calm day. Don't swim too far from the boat and you'll be fine."

"Any sharks or anything that could bother us?"

A slight pause.

"Doubtful."

Once the boat reached its destination over the coral, everybody prepared for the water. As Anderson reached into the bucket to grab a snorkel, he looked up and saw Nicole standing right next to him. She'd pulled her dress off and was adjusting her blue bikini. He couldn't help noticing how good she looked. Nicole turned and saw him staring. She grinned and gave him a little wink. Anderson blushed and quickly focused on adjusting the buckles on his life preserver, acting like nothing had happened.

"Have you noticed anything?" Nicole said in a soft voice.

Plenty, Anderson thought. Still uncomfortably aware of her body, Anderson kept his head down. "Um, hold on. I'm having trouble with this old zipper."

"Exactly! These aren't the same jackets that the website pictures showed. I wonder what's up with that? Why would they use these old ratty things if they've spent money on new ones?"

"You're right. We better follow up on that somehow," Anderson said. He'd better get his mind back on the job, he thought.

They jumped in and the silence of the cool blue water surrounded them. The underwater world fascinated Anderson. Yellowtail snapper, angelfish, grouper, and amberjack darted in and around the rocks below. Tiny, bright tropical fish nibbled on the coral. He could see lobster hiding in the crevices. The surreal underwater landscape was peaceful and serene. He couldn't imagine Andy's devastating and bloody accident amidst such beauty. And yes, the dreaded barracuda swam lazily around the reef, but they didn't bother anyone that day.

The group celebrated their successful marine adventure and the picture-perfect sunset with glasses of champagne. The boat powered up and headed back toward the dock, passing the raucous crowd partying in Mallory Square among the many entertainers working hard for tips. The Cat Man was mid-performance, chasing and yelling at his uncooperative feline performers. The Silver Man was perched amidst throngs of children who were trying to attract his attention and spoil his cool demeanor. Another couple performed acrobatic feats through hoops of fire. All in all, it was a typical Key West evening, but for Anderson and the rest of the visitors to the island, it was a spectacle to behold.

Nicole walked around the boat and stood next to Matt.

"Seems like a great job you got here. Spend all day out on the water and get back in time for a night on the town. That's the life. You been doing this long?"

"Nah, only about two weeks. I replaced Keith when he left to work for the *Key West Queen*. But I do like it so far. It's pretty easy work and I get to meet a lot of nice people." He cut his eyes over toward her, a little grin on his face.

"Well, you sure are good in the water. Do you ever run into trouble on the boat? You know, with drunk, obnoxious tourists or cute girls who flirt with you too much?" Nicole stood closer so that her arm brushed against his.

"Yes, to the obnoxious tourists, that's for sure. And a definite no to the second. A guy can never have too many girls flirting with him. That's the best part of the job!"

"What about in the water? That could get pretty scary if someone got stung by a stingray or a shark attacked or something like that."

"Uh, no, not really. Um, I gotta go now and get ready for docking." Matt backed away. He got busy moving ropes, putting away supplies, until the boat nudged the dock and he helped everyone off.

Nicole made one last attempt as she was leaving. "We're probably heading down to Duval Street tonight. You going to be around? I'd love to meet up with you later. You could show me the fun spots around here."

"I'm not really into the night life so I probably wouldn't be much fun."

Nicole turned to Anderson as they walked down the dock back to the hotel. "Something's up. No way he'd turn me down."

Nicole walked quickly down the dock. "I have an idea. Just follow my lead." Anderson, surprised, did as told. Her instincts were good, he decided. He would follow her just about anywhere.

An older man with the look of a local was cleaning fish by the side of the dock.

"Could you tell me where the *Key West Queen* is berthed?" Nicole asked him

He pointed behind him. "Three docks over. She's the big catamaran."

"What's up, Nicole?" Anderson almost had to run to keep up with her.

"Come on. I'll show you," she said. As they approached the boat, a young man came down the ramp carrying a cooler.

"Is Keith around?"

The man pointed to a kid with a dark tan, mopping the deck.

Nicole pulled Anderson over to the information booth at the end of the dock. "Matt happened to mention that Keith used to work for

First-Class. He just recently quit. I'm thinking we might be able to find out something from him so let's just wait for him to finish up."

When Keith completed his chores, he slung a backpack over his shoulder and headed down the pier. Nicole ran after him.

"Hey, are you Keith?"

"Yep, that's me," he said with a smile.

"I was told you're from around here and could tell us what's fun to do. My friend and I are visiting, and we don't know where to go to have a good time. Would you have a few minutes to let us buy you a drink and pick your brain?"

"Anything for a pretty lady," Keith said, winking.

The three of them walked the short distance to the Schooner Wharf Bar and ordered a round of Coronas. Nicole chatted with Keith about what it was like to grow up in Key West. Eventually, the subject switched to the local scene. Anderson let Nicole do the talking, but he made sure to keep the Coronas coming.

"You know, we'd really like to go on a snorkeling or dive trip. Can you recommend a boat? There seem to be so many, it's a little overwhelming. I don't want to go on a third-rate boat and waste our time."

"Well, I work on the *Key West Queen* and she'd be a good choice," Keith replied.

"Yeah, we saw that one, but she seems too big. A friend back home mentioned a smaller cabin cruiser of some type. I think the group was called Reef Experience or something like that. Do you know if that company is still around? Would they be worth checking out?"

"I think she must've been talking about the First-Class Reef Experience. I used to work for them. But I wouldn't recommend them."

"Why not?"

"Well, it's run by a captain new to this area who thinks he knows everything. The crew does things differently on that boat, and I don't think they're too worried about safety concerns."

"Oh, really? That's interesting. My friend spoke highly of her trip and how nice the boat was. What do you mean about safety problems? Has anything happened?"

Keith looked around the bar.

"Well, I shouldn't be talking out of turn, but you two seem like nice people and I wouldn't want you to get hurt. You've treated me to drinks so I'll give you a little bit of advice." He tilted his Corona upside down and the lime floated to the bottom of the bottle. "But I'll deny it if you say you heard it from me." Nicole nodded, leaning closer to Keith. Anderson watched his paralegal work her magic.

"You have to remember the fish on the reefs are wild animals. They don't particularly like humans, but they'll tolerate the interaction. Some divers release food particles or pellets into the water to attract fish for the tourists. That just isn't a good idea, even though the tourists love it. I've never heard of a person being attacked by a shark or barracuda from the food pellets, but it's still a bad idea. The bigger fish come in when the little fish gather for the food. It's just the law of the sea. But here's my main problem with First-Class. The owners had these fancy vests made to coordinate with the boat's colors and company name. Each vest had a silver logo attached to the end of the zipper. They look great, but they scared me. When the tourists snorkel on the surface of the water, the logo dangles down in the water." Keith paused to take a large gulp of his beer.

"So? What's the big deal?" asked Nicole.

"Well, there's nothing a barracuda likes more than shiny silver. Those logos glitter and sparkle in the water when they catch the sunlight. Everyone who knows anything about fishing and the water around here knows that. But not these idiots. Fishermen troll with silver spoons to catch barracuda and that's just what those shiny tags looked like. Barracuda bait! So I figured we might have a problem—shiny items plus schools of feeding fish do not make a good mix, especially with humans swimming in the middle of it all.

'So I mentioned it to the captain, thinking he'd be concerned, too. But nah. He laughed. Said he knew what he was doing and maybe I'd be happier on another boat. Obviously, he didn't like anyone questioning him. Whatever. I moved on."

Anderson kicked Nicole under the table he was so excited about this information. She ignored him and continued. "Wow, that's scary. Do you know if anybody's been hurt?"

"Well, that's why I want this conversation to stay between us. There was an accident on their boat just recently. A young guy was bitten by a barracuda, and they brought him in to the hospital. Blood was all over that boat! Everyone's been talking about it. I don't know any details because I'm trying to mind my own business. I don't want to get mixed up in that shit. And I don't know how or why it happened but I sure hope the captain doesn't use those vests anymore."

Keith stood up and stretched. "Time to get ready for a night on the town. I'd suggest you head over to Irish Kevin's. That bar's always a big hit with the new folks in town. You'll like it. See you 'round, and thanks again for the beer."

CHAPTER 33

Y ou're amazing, Nicole," Anderson said admiringly as they
walked down Front Street back to the Pier House. "He never
would've talked to me."

Nicole gave a proud half-smile, but didn't speak.

"Now we definitely have something to work with," Anderson continued. "Sounds to me there's a pretty good chance the barracuda
struck Andy because of those dangling logos combined with the fish
food in the water. That's negligence, for sure. As soon as we get back
to Tampa, let's get the lawsuit drafted and filed down here immediately. That way we can schedule Keith's deposition before he relocates
or disappears." He opened the door to the hotel lobby and held it for
her. "I guess you were lucky today you weren't barracuda bait in your
blue bikini." Nicole laughed and elbowed Anderson in the ribs as she
walked past.

"I know it's been a long day, but we've got to go out and celebrate on Duval Street. No way we can come all the way to Key West
and not check out the night life. You up for it, old man?"

"Absolutely! I'll meet you downstairs in an hour. Sound good to you?"

Instead of going straight back to her room to shower and dress,
Nicole stuck her head in the restaurant door. After a brief discussion with
the headwaiter, she headed up to her room. She only had a few minutes
to get ready. She dressed in a low cut sundress, no bra and a thong.

✧ ✧ ✧

"You look absolutely stunning." Anderson tried to keep from staring. At that moment, his cell phone buzzed. It was his wife. He pressed Ignore and put his phone back in his pocket.

"Why, thank you." Nicole spun around and curtsied. "Let's go have a toast on behalf of the insurance company for the First-Class Reef Experience."

First stop was world-famous Sloppy Joe's Bar. Dinner was a shared appetizer of crab cakes and delicious salty margaritas, quickly followed by two chilled Coronas. The day of traveling, swimming, and drinking was beginning to add up. Anderson was starting to slur his words a bit, but he wasn't about to admit defeat. He could keep up with Nicole. No way he'd be an old man and go home to bed, even though that's what he really wanted to do.

"Let's go next door to Irish Kevin's," he said.

When they entered the bar the music stopped and the entertainer shouted into his microphone, "My, my! Look what just walked in. Hey, babe," he shouted at Nicole. "Whatcha doing with that old guy? You oughta be with me. I sure hope he has a lotta money, honey!"

The patrons all laughed and Anderson and Nicole pulled up their stools to a small table. Anderson didn't mind the joke; no doubt it was part of the routine. Still, he had to admit Nicole certainly drew attention wherever she went. She was definitely hot, especially the way she was dressed right now.

Nicole's head was starting to get a bit fuzzy, but she told herself to stay focused because she had a very important task to accomplish that night. She ordered two more margaritas.

"A toast to a good team." Nicole held up her drink and leaned over to touch her glass to Anderson's. When Anderson turned his head to listen to the joking at the microphone, she poured half her drink into the potted plant next to her. Anderson drank on, trying to keep up with her.

Nicole looked at her cell phone. It was 10:00. Time to start her plan. She couldn't put it off much longer or Anderson would be too out of it for her scheme to work.

Nicole leaned close to Anderson's ear and yelled over the music, "I'm tired, Anderson. Do you care if we call it a day? A very successful and fun day, for sure, but definitely a long one. This party girl needs her sleep."

"Sure," Anderson said. He was feeling guilty about not having taken his wife's call and wanted to get to the hotel and call her back. The two made their way back to the Pier House. When the elevator door shut, Nicole turned toward Anderson and put her hand on his forearm.

"Come by my room for one last drink. I ordered a bottle of champagne so we could celebrate our discovery today. We can look at the water and talk a minute."

"I'm not sure that's a good idea." Anderson burped and covered his mouth with his hand. "That was the liquor talking. I'm usually not that rude in the presence of a lady." He grinned and sat back against the elevator handrail.

"C'mon," Nicole teased. "Just one small drink then you can get to bed. We have to be out of here early in the morning anyway to catch our flight."

"Well, I guess that'd be okay," Anderson finally said. He didn't want to hurt her feelings. She'd been too valuable that day to risk losing her over some minor thing.

Nicole walked with Anderson out onto her porch overlooking the main channel leading into Key West Harbor. A sliver of moon glimmered in the dark sky and the stars spread like a canopy over the water.

Anderson dropped into the chair and propped his legs up on the railing. Nicole went back inside and opened the chilled champagne she'd had delivered while they were out. She filled two flutes about halfway. Glancing over her shoulder, she popped a two-milligram roofie out of its pre-sealed bubble pack, crushed it on a piece of paper on the table, and poured it in the second flute. The powder dissolved quickly. Supposedly, the additive would be tasteless in the bubbly liquid, but she knew Anderson wouldn't even notice in his present condition. Nicole handed the glass to Anderson and sat down in the chair next to him.

"To the legal system. Cheers!" Nicole tipped her glass and drank. Anderson touched his glass to hers and smiled.

"We did great today. You're the best, Nicole. Never coulda done it without you." He finished his drink in two quick swallows. It would be about 30 minutes before the drug would begin to take effect—so she kept talking. She knew she could play on Anderson's sympathy if she talked about herself. He would never walk out if she started telling him her life story. Anderson was always polite, even at his own expense. So Nicole talked on, but her mind wasn't on her words. She was thinking of her father and Rick, letting her anger at their rejection build. Men were such assholes, no matter how nice they might pretend to be. It was all an act.

"Nicole?" Anderson said uncertainly. He leaned forward in his chair and rested his elbows on his knees with his face in his hands. "I'm feeling a little dizzy. Maybe a bit too much alcohol for one day,"

"Yeah, you don't look so great. Here, let me help you. You can rest a bit before you go back to your room. I'll get a cold washcloth for your head. That'll make you feel better."

She put her arm around his waist to help him stand. He stumbled to the bed and fell across it clumsily. She rolled him onto his back and he began to snore quietly. Just to be safe she waited a half hour before she began to set up her camera gear.

"Anderson, can you hear me?" No response. She worked quickly, taking off his shoes, then his shirt. He still didn't appear to be aware of anything so she pulled off the rest of his clothing. She set the camera on its tripod, making sure it had the perfect view. Then Nicole took off her clothes and arranged herself as required for the job. The camera clicked away on its time-delayed function. For over an hour, she posed and repositioned herself so she would be sure to have plenty of shots from which to choose.

She went into the bathroom and poured the remaining champagne down the sink and rinsed the glasses thoroughly. She flushed the two unused roofies down the toilet. Returning to the room, she stored the camera and its tripod in her suitcase and climbed back into the bed with Anderson. She leaned over his inert body and patted him on the head.

"Thank you for the money, Mr. Hotshot. Think you're still too good for me now?"

The wake-up phone call rang three times before Nicole opened her eyes. When she looked over, Anderson's eyes were open. He looked confused.

"Good morning, sunshine!" she chirped. "Thanks for a great night! You were fantastic!" Anderson sat up.

"Oh my God," he said, his head feeling as if it would split at any moment. He put his hand to his forehead. "What have I done?" he asked.

Nicole watched as he rolled out of bed and tried to put his clothes on as quickly as he could. He barely had his pants on and his shirt was still unbuttoned as he ran to the bathroom and threw up violently in the toilet. Nicole could hear water splashing in the sink.

"Hey, tiger, we need to leave in a few minutes so I'll get the rental car and meet you out front. You don't look like you're in any condition to be driving. But you sure were fun last night!"

Anderson stared at her blankly then stumbled out of the room.

Neither spoke on the flight back to Tampa. Anderson rested his head on the cool glass of the window, head throbbing, trying to remember what had happened.

CHAPTER 34

Anderson couldn't recall ever having such a bad hangover. As he watched the luggage travel in a circle on the belt, he wanted to ask Nicole for details about the night before but was afraid of what she might tell him. Maybe it would be better to just keep quiet. Nicole enjoyed watching Anderson suffer.

"See you back at the office." Nicole rolled her bag toward her car.

"I think I'm going to take the afternoon off. My head is still killing me. Please tell Gwen I won't be in until Monday."

"Okay." She drew out the word. "It's hard to hoot with the owls and then soar with the eagles, isn't it?" Nicole waved as she pulled out of the parking lot.

Anderson drove home slowly, thinking about his predicament. He had never lied to Ruth before. So how could he walk in the house and act as if nothing had happened? Had anything even happened last night? Maybe he'd just fallen asleep. He couldn't tell Ruth when he didn't even know himself. How could he put that burden on Ruth? It wouldn't be fair. He'd have to figure it out on his own. But man, did he feel like a piece of shit.

Anderson entered the house through the garage door, dropped his bag on the hallway floor, and headed for the bedroom. Ruth was in the kitchen and stuck her head around the corner when she heard him come in.

"Anderson! You're home. I didn't expect to see you until dinner. How was your trip?" She walked over and gave him a hug. She took a step back and looked up at him. "You look terrible. What happened?"

"I think maybe I got food poisoning. The investigation went well so we celebrated with dinner. The grilled grouper apparently didn't agree with me."

Ruth raised an eyebrow. "And who is we?"

"Oh, yeah. I forgot to mention the firm's new paralegal, Ms. Babson, went down there with me because there was so much work to be done. I've told you about her. She assisted me on the trial involving the drunken teenagers."

Ruth looked apprehensively at her husband. "I've told you before I don't think it's a good idea for you to stay out of town with female staff. But let's get you to bed now. You look like you're about to pass out."

Anderson's guilt rose another thousand degrees as he let Ruth gently lead him to their bed and tuck him into the cool sheets. "I'm going to bring you a Coke with crushed ice. See if that helps your stomach. I'll be right back."

Anderson watched through half-closed eyes as Ruth turned out the lights, pulled the curtains, and tiptoed from the room. He rolled over and groaned softly.

✧ ✧ ✧

Nicole balanced her cell phone against her ear as she drove down the interstate. "Justin, it's Nicole Babson. We need to talk."

Silence on the other end. And then, "Yes, Your Honor, I understand you need to speak with me and opposing counsel. I'll conclude my meeting and call you back in five minutes."

"Very cute," Nicole said when he called back a few minutes later. "I have your pictures and I want my money. When I have the money, the pictures are yours."

"Excellent!" Justin exclaimed, thrilled. "That's very good news! So, how'd you accomplish it?"

"The deal was for pictures, not details, so let's keep this to business. My cousin and her boyfriend are out of town so come to my place on Harbour Island at 8:00 with the money. I'll make six copies each of the four best pictures and have them ready for you tonight."

"I can't come. I'll send a courier to meet you in front of the ticket booth at the Channelside Movie Theater for the exchange. And good job, Nicole. I knew you'd get it done."

Nicole next went to a large office supply store over in Brandon, far enough from south Tampa that she wouldn't see anyone she knew. There, she paid cash for a top-of-the-line photo printer. Returning to her apartment, she hooked it up to her computer and printed out the photographs. Admiring her handiwork, she thought of the big payday that would be coming her way very soon. She smiled to herself as she tucked the photos into a drawer and changed to go out for a run.

That evening, a courier wearing dark glasses, jeans, a Tampa Bay Buccaneers jersey, and a Tampa Bay Devil Rays baseball cap, carrying a beat-up old briefcase, showed up at the movie theater a few blocks from Nicole's home. He looked a little old to be a courier. When he took the glasses off, Nicole was not surprised to see it was Justin.

"I couldn't trust anyone else with the cash," he explained in a quiet voice as they found seats in the back row of the new James Bond movie.

"Why am I not surprised?" Nicole said, rolling her eyes.

Justin laughed softly as he looked through the pictures she displayed but did not hand over. She wanted the money first.

"Looks like you had a good time," he said happily, "but I think you wore Anderson out, the sucker."

"Well, the jerk wasn't exactly a willing participant. I had to give him a little assistance to get him in the mood, if you know what I mean."

"No, I don't know what you mean. What did you do to the guy?" Justin's eyes opened wide in shock.

"Oh, it's not a big deal. I just gave him a little something in his drink so he wouldn't be so uncooperative. And it worked. So don't complain, okay?"

Nicole jerked the briefcase from Justin's hands and began to count the money.

"You are some daring broad. I'll give you that." Justin said, "So, what'll you do now?"

"I'm going back to the West Coast as soon as I can catch the next plane. I'm starting a new life with this money, and I'm gonna make Rick wish he'd never left me. He's going to realize that he made the biggest mistake of his life when he walked out my door." Nicole ran her fingers through the stacks of bills. "I plan to give my notice to the firm and let them know I'm leaving on Wednesday. I'll just tell everyone I miss California too much and I'm heading back home."

Nicole began to hand the photos to Justin, but he shook his head. "I don't want to touch those things. No fingerprints. They're dynamite. Just put them back in that envelope. I don't want anything to be traceable back to me."

"Justin," Nicole turned from the briefcase "I'm not sure what plans you have up your sleeve but I know whatever you do, Anderson isn't going to like it and he's going to be hurt. I want to hear every detail once you spring your trap. Will you call me and tell me everything? I don't want to miss out on a single juicy morsel."

"I would be honored to let the star of the show know how her performance is received."

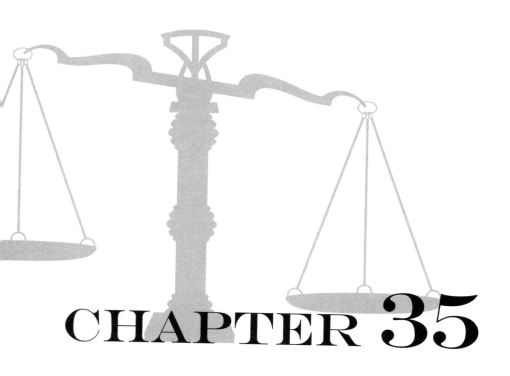

CHAPTER 35

Sunday night, Anderson tossed and turned in his bed. He wished he'd never gone to Key West. So what if it'd helped his case? Nothing was worth this. No matter how hard he tried to concentrate, the last thing he could remember about the night was sitting on Nicole's balcony looking at the stars. Everything after that was a total blank. And the questions wouldn't stop. Did he really sleep with her? He'd woken up in her bed without his clothes. That much was a fact.

His biggest question of all was whether to tell Ruth. She'd be affected too if he'd slept with Nicole. STDs, pregnancy ... Oh, man, there were too many things that could come of this, and he didn't even know where to start—or stop. But he didn't want to hurt Ruth and he sure didn't want to disappoint her. She always had such faith in him. How could he admit his failure to her? She'd never trust him again—and with reason. If he had contracted an STD, what would that do to their marriage? That question alone overwhelmed him. Anderson never made a decision in haste, but he also knew he couldn't procrastinate forever. He decided he would set himself a Thursday-night deadline. By that time, he'd have to determine one way or the other how he was going to handle this situation.

Sunday had been a beautiful day. Nicole had counted her money four times, fantasizing about her triumphant return home. She could hardly wait to see Rick's face when she drove up in her new car with her new wardrobe. He was definitely going to wish she was still his. She was going to show him.

Monday morning came, and as usual, Nicole was the first to arrive at the office. She planned to act as if nothing had happened. She'd treat Anderson just the way she always had, friendly yet professional. But she did plan to head straight to Gwen's office and give her resignation that afternoon. She knew it was short notice, but she couldn't wait any longer. Her newfound wealth was making her impatient to move on. She'd be on a plane by Friday, flying back to the West Coast. She was ready to get back home, and she sure as hell didn't want to be around when Justin dropped his bomb.

Normally, Anderson would check in with Nicole first thing every morning, but when 10:00 rolled around and still no word from Anderson, Nicole decided to break the ice.

"Good morning, Anderson. I put the Key West file materials on your desk Friday afternoon so you'd be prepared to draft the complaint. Do you need anything else?"

"No. That will be sufficient, Ms. Babson." Anderson kept his head buried in his paperwork.

Oh, so now it's Ms. Babson, is it? She wondered what he'd call her after he saw the pictures.

Anderson tried to concentrate on the work in front of him but everything was blurry and his mind kept returning to that moment when he woke up in Nicole's bed. The phone rang, startling him from his descent into despair. Gwen's baritone voice came through the receiver.

"Anderson, Nicole Babson just came to my office and gave notice. She's leaving the firm on Wednesday."

"That's too bad," Anderson replied, suddenly perking up. "She is such a good worker."

"I can't imagine why she'd want to leave so suddenly. It's very unusual. Nicole said she missed home, but I'm concerned about her. I know she's had some trouble back in California and I think

Tampa's been good for her. I tried to convince her to stay, but she was adamant. We're going to miss her. She did great work and I really like her—everyone did. I'd like to have a going-away party for her on Wednesday afternoon, if that's okay with you?"

"Yeah, that's a good idea. Unfortunately, um, I have a meeting out of the office at that time so I can't be there—but go ahead without me. And, Gwen, even though she didn't give us the usual two weeks' notice, prepare a severance check for ten days' salary. Nicole did a good job for our clients."

Wednesday came and went and Anderson was relieved. His potential problem was gone and he was not sorry at all. He'd made a big mistake in Key West, but he would never again be that careless. His main concern was what to do about Ruth. Although he didn't like keeping things from her, he knew he had to make an exception this time. Final decision—Nicole was gone and he would no longer worry about what had happened in Key West. He would act as if nothing happened. He wouldn't share this dirty secret with Ruth. That was the best decision for his marriage.

CHAPTER 36

Even though Nicole had been gone for two weeks, Anderson thought of their Key West trip daily and the guilt was eating him up. Her departure had also left a void at the firm. Nicole had done an excellent job on Anderson's files and now many tasks were being left undone. To make matters worse, a large complicated trial was starting next week and Anderson had to put Teresa, a new paralegal, on the file.

One night at dinner, Ruth noticed Anderson seemed to be a million miles away. She watched as Beatrice, their oldest daughter, chattered on and on about her field trip to Lowry Park Zoo. She described the panda bears and the monkeys, her favorite animals of the day, in great detail. "Which animals are your favorite, Dad?" she asked as she wiped the spaghetti from her mouth with a napkin.

Anderson looked up from his dinner. "Favorite what? I'm sorry, Beatrice. I drifted off there for a minute and missed your question."

"Dad! I was telling you about the zoo today. Were you even listening?!"

"Yeah, Dad," mimicked Emily, her little sister, "I don't think you were listening."

"Girls, your dad's had a long day," Ruth interrupted. "Go on upstairs for your baths and we'll let Dad have some quiet time. I'll take care of the dishes tonight. Okay?"

The girls ran giggling up the steps, happy to be freed from their chores. Ruth began clearing the plates, waiting for Anderson to say something. When he was still silent, she stopped and sat down at the table next to him.

"Anderson, what's wrong? You haven't been yourself lately."

Anderson wanted to tell her everything. He could feel the words on his lips. But he couldn't. He just couldn't do that to her. Instead, he blamed his stress on the approaching trial.

"Oh, honey. You know how it is when I'm preparing for a trial. I get so focused I zone out. I'll be fine. I just have a lot on my mind. I need to go work on my opening statement."

"Okay, I have an idea. You go on into your office and start working. I'll finish the dishes and then join you. You can tell me all about your case and maybe that will help you pull your thoughts together. Remember, we always manage to figure things out when we work together." Ruth touched his shoulder gently as she stood to go back into the kitchen.

Slowly, he lifted himself from his chair and headed to the office. When Ruth joined him a few minutes later, he'd barely looked at his files. He was staring out the window as she entered the room.

"Baby, it's gonna be okay. Let's see what we can do. Okay? Tell me what it's all about," Ruth said softly while she rubbed his neck.

Anderson spread out his materials and looked down at the paperwork to refresh his memory. "Well, let's see. The name of the case is Beverly Harrell as guardian of Arlee Harrell versus Sunfun Rentals and Turbojet, Inc. Two summers ago, the Coflit family came down from Indiana for their vacation on St. Petersburg Beach. Their sixteen-year-old son, Paul, wanted to rent a jet ski. So his father walked over with him to the Sunfun Rentals, which was right on the beach next to the hotel, and paid $60 for a one-hour rental. The father left the beach and went back to his room after paying the rental fee. According to Paul, the operator asked him if he knew how to operate a jet ski. Paul told him he'd never driven one before and didn't really know what he was supposed to do. The owner said it was very simple. Just follow four rules: Squeeze the switch on the right handle bar to make the jet ski go. Stay within the area marked by the yellow buoys. Wear a safety vest. And, most of all, have fun.

"In his deposition, Paul said he asked the owner if the two of them could go on a short checkout run, but the man told him he was too busy to leave the beach and couldn't do it right then. He told Paul to get on the jet ski and helped him buckle up his vest. He showed Paul how to operate the gas on the handle and told him he'd be fine.

As Paul headed out into the water, he went slowly at first as he got a feel for the way it operated. As his confidence grew, he began to drive faster and take it toward the edges of the marked boundaries.

"That same day, the Harrell family from Tampa was spending the afternoon at the beach as well. Twelve-year-old Arlee was an excellent swimmer just like most girls who grow up in Florida. Arlee's mom, Beverly, had staked out an area on the beach with her umbrella and blanket. She'd opened her picnic basket and spread out their lunch. Her husband, Rob, walked down the beach with their son, Brett. Arlee couldn't wait to get into the water, and after asking her mom's permission, went dashing off to play in the waves. Arlee probably noticed the jet skis speeding around in circles in the area nearby, so she swam over next to the marker so she could watch the kids having fun.

"Paul only had about ten minutes left before he had to return the jet ski to the beach so he was trying to use his last bit of time to learn some of the fancy tricks he'd seen the other kids doing. The Turbojet 400 was speeding at about 30 miles per hour when Paul turned the handlebar quickly to the right to make a tight spin. Instead, it went out of control and went sliding across the water past the yellow marker and straight toward Arlee.

"Arlee had been splashing in the water and waving to her mom. She turned and saw the Turbojet heading directly toward her. The nose of the jet ski struck Arlee directly in her forehead as her mother watched helplessly from the beach. The impact fractured her skull. Subdural and Subarachnoid hemorrhaging began immediately. Loss of consciousness was instantaneous. Arlee's mother ran into the water and pulled Arlee to the beach. A purple knot formed on her forehead. Despite repeated questioning, Arlee did not respond."

Ruth interrupted. "How horrible. Poor little girl—and her mother! I can't imagine. And what happened to Paul?"

"Hold on. I'll tell you the entire story. Paul jumped off the jet ski as it skidded out of control, and he swam to the beach. He ran over to where Beverly had pulled Arlee onto the sand. He kept apologizing over and over to her, saying that the handlebar had slipped just before he lost control. The beach patrol loaded Arlee onto a stretcher and took her to the parking lot where an ambulance was waiting to take her to Bayfront Medical Center. She was in intensive care for four days until she came out of her coma.

"The brain damage was permanent. The injured area in the front of the cortex impairs her cognitive functioning and she will always act and think like a ten-year-old. The bleeding in the back of her brain has adversely affected her ambulation and motor coordination of her upper extremities. When her treating neurologist told Arlee's parents that their daughter's injuries would affect Arlee for the rest of her life, they came to me to find out if there was a basis for a lawsuit that could pay for future medical expenses and rehabilitation."

"I hope you're suing Paul for all of his insurance money," Ruth said.

"Well, that's one of the problems. Paul didn't have any insurance, so I filed a lawsuit against Sunfun Rentals and Turbojet, Inc. The complaint alleges the jet ski concession negligently entrusted the personal watercraft to Paul without properly training him on its operation. We also made a claim on behalf of Arlee against the manufacturer of the craft, Turbojet, Inc., pleading that the company negligently designed and manufactured the jet ski, and thus it was inherently dangerous."

"What was wrong with it?"

"Well, remember Paul kept saying right after the accident that the handlebar slipped. I had an engineer examine it and he found evidence that the bolt connecting the handlebar to the steering mechanism was slipping. My expert concluded the watercraft was designed and built where it could uncontrollably veer when the handlebar was turned at high speeds. Of course, the manufacturer denies there is anything wrong with its product and their lawyers have high-priced experts to support their innocence. I had hoped the two defendants would point fingers at each other, but they've decided to present a united front and argue that the unfortunate event was totally caused by Paul's actions."

Ruth sat on the arm of Anderson's chair. She kissed him on the forehead. "I see why this one could make for a tough trial. Just do your best. You always do. And don't let it get to you so much. You won't do them any good if you're too stressed. I know I've been upset with you lately, but it's just because I love you so much and I feel like I'm losing you to the office again. Remember, the girls and I love you very much, whether you win or lose. We're always there for you. "

CHAPTER 37

There was another lawyer who was monitoring the jet ski lawsuit closely. Justin had learned of Anderson's approaching jury trial through a circuit court bailiff. He saw the trial as the perfect time to mess with Anderson's head by unveiling his pictures. He knew Anderson would be totally focused on the trial, and by revealing the incriminating photos, Justin could throw Anderson out of sync and make his life completely miserable. But he had to make sure the case didn't settle, as sometimes happened. He wanted this revelation to occur during the midst of a big money trial.

When Justin researched the information regarding the case on the court's website, he was thrilled to learn that Peter Baldwin was one of the defense lawyers. Peter had served on a Florida Bar Trial Rules Committee with Justin the year before. Justin picked up the phone.

"Peter, this is Justin over in Tampa. How are the billable hours treating you? How's Orlando?"

"Well," Peter replied, laughing, "between us defense boys, I wish there were more hours in the day. But I guess it really doesn't make any difference because I bill like there are anyway. Let me tell you a little story. Last Sunday I'm walking down the street with my ten-year-old son when I see that the panel door on the phone company's electrical box on the street corner has been left open. I show Steve how dangerous it could be if someone touched the exposed electrical boards—his or her skin would fry and totally sizzle off their bones—which, of course, would lead to more work for Dad.

"So, get this. Steve looks up at me and asks if I want people to get hurt. I told him, 'Not too many,' and he laughs. Damn, I love my son. I think he's going to develop into a fine defense trial lawyer when he grows up." Peter laughed.

"Congratulations, Peter. Sounds like you're training him right. Wish I had one of those. Now, listen, don't worry. This call is billable. I want to talk to you about the Harrell case."

Peter interjected. "I wanted to talk to you about this case. Didn't Anderson used to be your associate?"

"He was. But then he got a little too big for his training pants. I wanted to give you a heads-up. Anderson doesn't perform well in product liability cases and he gets very nervous at trial. From what I heard from the bailiff on this one, it should be a defense verdict. I wanted to make sure you were hanging tough. Don't be a pussy and settle."

"No worry. I've told my client, First Casualty, not to put a single dime on the table."

"Pardon me. But technically, isn't your client Turbojet, not the insurance company?"

"Well, excuse me," Peter said sarcastically. "My paycheck comes from the home office of the big bad insurance company. So in my book, they're the client—not some upstart jet ski company. They don't have the money to pay my bills so I'll do just what First Casualty asks. Hey, but please don't tell the Florida Bar about my confusion."

"Now, Peter, you know I wouldn't say a word. I'm in the same boat with most of my cases, too."

"Okay, let's get back to this case, since I'm planning on billing First Casualty for our little phone call. I wouldn't want to be dishonest about billing my time, now would I? The only danger I can see in this case is if the jury feels sorry for the little girl. Personally, I think she was a dumb ass even before she kissed the front of the jet ski. Let me get up on my soapbox for a second. After I win this case, the little brain-damaged kid will suck off of social security disability. Or maybe the Democrats will create another program so somebody can get paid to wipe her ass. It'd save us all a lot of hard-earned tax dollars if someone just put her down like a racehorse with a broken leg."

"You're my kind of man," Justin said, grinning into the phone. "Since I'm not billing for this conversation, I have to move on to moneymaking ventures, but first I'd like to ask a small favor. Could you have a paralegal call me on my private line the day before closing arguments and let me know when they begin?"

"No problem. We start the trial on Monday, so most likely closing will take place on Friday. But just to be safe, Janice will call. I assume you want to watch me perform and then witness the jury throwing the little brat out on her ass."

"You bet. I'm looking forward to watching that happen. Talk to you soon." Justin leaned back in his leather chair, placing his expensive shoes on his desk. He folded his arms across his chest and smiled.

That night Justin worked on the Anderson project at home. Before he took the envelope out of his desk drawer, he checked his office door to make sure it was locked. He wasn't really too concerned about his privacy because he'd warned Catherine and the girls never to enter his sacred space unless he gave permission first. This room was his and his alone.

He opened a cardboard box and pulled out a pair of latex gloves, slipping them over his fingers and down onto his hands. Justin made sure he never touched the pictures, envelopes, mailing labels or stamps with his bare hands. He wanted to make damn sure nobody would ever be able to trace the photographs back to him.

The plain manila envelopes were spread out on the table in front of him. He checked the computer-generated mailing labels for accuracy: one hand delivery to Anderson, the remaining envelopes to be mailed to Ruth Parker, Gwen, Anderson's office manager Kelly, Anderson's secretary, two lawyers from Anderson's first law firm, two lawyers from his present firm, and four of his closest friends.

Justin placed two incriminating photos in each of the 12 envelopes. He stuck self-adhesive stamps on all the envelopes he planned to mail, making sure the postage was correct, and then slid everything back into his drawer, locking it firmly and pocketing the key. No photographs would remain in his possession once these were on their way to their designated recipients. Justin was like a child waiting for Christmas. His favorite vision was of Anderson's wife when she first recognized her husband in the pictures with the naked Nicole.

"Just one more week until Anderson pays for all he has done to me," Justin said out loud as he stood up from his desk chair.

CHAPTER 38

The first day of the trial had been tough for Anderson. He had planned to stack the jury with women who would sympathize with Arlee and her mother. But the two defense lawyers, Lee Cantrell, who represented Sunfun Rentals, and Peter Baldwin, the attorney for Turbojet, had successfully used their preemptory challenges on potential jurors so that five older, hardened gentlemen were remaining along with a 30-year-old female public school teacher. Anderson hoped the lone female would assert herself in the jury room.

The defense lawyers were also very effective in their opening statements. Their theme, which they repeated often and in various ways, was that the unfortunate accident was totally caused by Paul's reckless driving. They suggested Anderson was blaming parties that were not at fault solely because of a potential payday. Peter, in particular, spent a good portion of his opening statement discussing sympathy and reminding the jurors that the law dictated that their emotions could not influence the verdict.

Anderson started his case on Monday afternoon by calling Beverly Harrell to the stand. Anderson asked her to describe the accident as she had witnessed it. Then he moved on to questioning her about the current condition of her daughter. The female juror had tears running down her cheeks as Beverly described how her daughter would forget at times who her mother was and how Arlee would scream in horror when she'd have flashbacks of the day at the beach.

That night, Ruth and Anderson talked about the first day of the trial as he ate his reheated dinner. He tried to keep his mind focused on the conversation and not on his experience with Nicole.

"I'm very concerned about the five male jurors," Anderson said between bites of lasagna. "Not only do they not seem to be moved by Arlee's catastrophic injuries, but they look at me like I'm an ambulance chaser."

"You need to stop guessing what they're thinking. Concentrate on making your case."

"Good advice as usual, honey," Anderson said, nodding. "I know you're right. I plan on being very reasonable with this jury and admitting that Paul is partially at fault for the accident."

"I'm a little confused. Last week you told me Paul wasn't a defendant. So how does the jury determine whether or not he is responsible if he's not even involved in the case?"

"Excellent question. The defense lawyers petitioned the court for the right to have an allegedly at-fault non-party placed on the verdict form and, over my objection, the trial judge granted the motion. They're hoping to spread the blame. The jury will divide 100% of the fault between Paul, Sunfun Rentals, and Turbojet and that will keep their final cost lower. Remember, a judgment is entered against a defendant only as to that party's percent of fault in regard to the total damages award. I'm hoping that at least 70% of the fault will be split among the named defendants."

The two of them talked until midnight about the case, the firm, and their children as Anderson tried to wind down from the stresses of the day. The more Anderson opened up about what was going on at work, the more Ruth responded with encouragement. Anderson thoroughly enjoyed her attention, feeling almost like things between them were returning to the passion and like-mindedness of the old days. But he couldn't get past what had happened with Nicole. The guilt ate at him even though he tried to put it out of his mind. If he told Ruth, everything between them would be destroyed. She'd never trust him again. He couldn't lose her.

On the second day of the trial, Anderson called Paul to the stand. Paul consistently testified he received no real training on the operation of the jet ski. Paul held up well on cross-examination and Anderson's confidence level rose.

Tuesday afternoon was consumed by testimony from Anderson's experts. First, the plaintiff's engineer explained why the Turbojet 400 was defective, especially when turns were made at high speeds. Later, Anderson elicited opinions from his expert neurologist, his vocational rehabilitation consultant, and finally his economist. Some good points were made on cross-examination by the defense team, but overall, Anderson thought everything was going well for Arlee's case.

Anderson saved his best witness for Wednesday morning. The strength of Arlee was not so much in what she said, but in how she spoke. Her wandering thoughts and inability to focus on the questions clearly evidenced her cognitive disabilities. Anderson rested the plaintiff's case at noon on Wednesday. He was confident there would be a substantial damages verdict.

Since Sunfun was the first named defendant, Lee started his case next. The concession owner was called after lunch and his story differed in many aspects from Paul's version of the facts. With practiced sincerity, the owner told the jury about the extensive training he gave Paul on the tragic day. He claimed he offered Paul a test ride, but Paul declined the training, saying it wasn't necessary since he'd been riding jet skis for years.

Anderson was concerned the Sunfun Rentals owner had appeared truthful to the jury. He knew the results of the trial depended on the creditability of the witnesses for each side. Wednesday concluded with testimony from a neurologist retained by Lee to minimize Arlee's injuries and to suggest her medical conditions would improve in the future. After the jury was dismissed at 5:30 on Wednesday, Lee told the judge Sunfun Rentals would not be calling additional witnesses. Peter advised the court he would be placing three experts on the stand Thursday: two engineers who would testify about the design and manufacturing of the Turbojet 400, and an economist who would refute the plaintiff's projection of future damages.

Counsel all agreed the live testimony would be completed on Thursday and closing arguments could start on Friday morning. Anderson, packing his trial briefcases, glanced toward the rows of seats and thought he saw a woman who looked like Nicole. He couldn't get her out of his mind.

Later that night, Peter's assistant Janice called Justin as promised. Justin settled into his office to work on the best way to execute his plan the next day. He carefully placed the envelopes in his briefcase with his gloved hands. He couldn't remember the last time he'd been so excited about an approaching workday.

CHAPTER 39

On Thursday, Justin told Eleanor he would be leaving at 4:00 to play racquetball. She was surprised since Justin very rarely left the firm early, but she was glad to get him out of the office. At the club, Justin changed into sweat clothes and tennis shoes. He went back to his car, where he pulled Anderson's envelope out of his briefcase. The label read: Hand Delivery for Anderson Parker. Materials to be used in closing arguments in the Harrell case. To be opened only by Mr. Parker. He then drove to Anderson's office, put on the same "courier" outfit he had worn to the movie theater to meet Nicole, and walked up to the guard's desk on the first floor. Justin looked down at the ground, not making eye contact with the guard who was half asleep.

"Hand delivery for Mr. Anderson Parker. He has to get this immediately. Please take the envelope to him now," Justin mumbled.

"Will do," the guard replied as he stared at one of the surveillance screens.

On his way back to the athletic club, Justin stopped at the downtown post office and dropped the remaining eleven envelopes into the mailbox on the curb. Once on the court, Justin laughed as he smashed the racquetball against the front wall.

"You're on fire today, Justin. You must've had a good day at work," complained Harley, his longtime racquetball opponent.

"It was one of the best days of my career. Today, justice prevailed. My father would be proud," Justin replied as he unveiled yet another forehand smash. "And it's only going to get better."

CHAPTER 40

The engineers retained by Peter on behalf of Turbojet did an excellent job of suggesting to the jurors there was nothing wrong with the jet ski and the impact was solely caused by Paul's careless and reckless driving. Anderson was successful in eliciting testimony from one of the hired guns from MIT that other drivers had complained about slippage of the handlebar during tight turns causing the watercraft to lose control.

The last witness in the trial, Turbojet's retained economist, Dr. Roberts, began her testimony at 2:30. She told the jury that in her expert opinion there was a substantial amount of padding in plaintiff's projected economic damages regarding Arlee's future maintenance. Anderson was able to get Dr. Roberts to admit that even pursuant to her accounting methodology, the minimum future cost of medical and attendant care was $1.6 million.

The testimony concluded at 4:00 and the judge advised the jury the trial would end early that day so counsel could start closing arguments promptly at 8:30 the next morning. For planning purposes, the trial judge told the panel of jurors the matter would be given to them for a decision around lunchtime and food would be brought in so a verdict might be reached by mid-afternoon on Friday.

Anderson was tired as he packed up his trial supplies with Teresa and the Harrells. The week had not been any more stressful than his other trials, but despite his decision to put the Nicole situation behind him, the guilt lingered. Anderson's trusted secretary had developed a working plan for dealing with the multitude of emails, faxes, phone calls, and mail that came in during the days he was in trial. Kelly would review and screen everything, deciding what could wait until later and what needed his immediate attention.

"Ready to sit down and discuss where we are?" Anderson said as he stuck his head in Kelly's office.

"Why don't you get a cold drink and relax a minute? I'll be in with my folders in ten minutes."

Anderson was thankful Kelly understood the pressures of a jury trial. He sat down on his sofa and put his feet up on the coffee table.

"How's it going with the jury?" Kelly asked while walking into his office with a large stack of mail and messages.

Anderson sighed. "As usual, nobody knows except for our six chosen friends. I think we've proven the damages aspect of the case, but the liability determination of fault is anybody's guess. The Harrells and I are hoping the jury allocates at least 70% of the fault to Turbojet and Sunfun."

"Good luck. Not too much going on here at the salt mine that you need to worry about now. Defense counsel in the new Johnston case wants a ten-day extension on the filing of his answer. I assume that's acceptable."

Anderson nodded in approval.

"We received discovery responses in the Bryon case. And that's about it. Oh, yeah, except you just received a hand delivery, which referenced closing arguments in the Harrell case. I haven't even had a chance to open it. So here it is. Besides all of that, you're current unless you need anything else from me."

"Kelly, thanks as always for holding down the fort while I'm off fighting against the forces of evil," Anderson joked. "On your way out, would you shut the door and hold my phone calls? I have to write out plaintiff's closing argument speech."

As was his practice, Anderson started to formulate his speech in his mind and then create a written outline. Leaning his head back against the sofa, he reviewed the evidence when the envelope on the table caught his eye. He wasn't expecting any materials to be delivered in the Harrell case, but he opened the envelope just in case. His heart froze as he pulled the pictures from the envelope. Although his face was not clear in the picture, he recognized his own naked body. Nicole straddled him in apparent throes of ecstasy. Anderson immediately recognized the setting—her hotel room in Key West.

"Oh my God," Anderson murmured. His vision began to blur and black spots appeared before his eyes. Quickly, he put his head down between his legs. Concentrate, he told himself. Focus. You have to get your act together and figure out what to do! You cannot give in to this. Your whole life depends on what you do next.

Slowly, Anderson lifted his head and reached out with a shaky hand to pull the envelope closer. No return address and only a computer-generated mailing label. Who sent these? It had to be Nicole. She must want money. Obviously, she was the only other person there that night. Or was she? Who took the pictures? Nicole or someone else? He still couldn't remember anything about what happened after he sat with Nicole on her porch.

The room began to spin around him and a violent wave of nausea wracked his body. He grabbed the trash can just in time as his stomach heaved up almost everything he'd eaten that day. Anderson rested his head against the edge of his desk as he hovered over the can. I am so totally screwed. Nicole, or someone, is going to use these to blackmail me or expose me or both...my marriage, my family, my career...it's all over.

He pushed himself upright and walked to his sofa where he lay down with his arm over his eyes. He tried to think through his options rationally. But his brain was totally scrambled and there was no way he could even begin to think about what to do. No matter what, his life would never be the same.

After a few moments, Anderson sat up with determination. All he knew for sure was he still had the trial to get through. He would keep his mind focused on that for now. It was the only thing he knew to do. He did the best he could to prepare his presentation for the next day, but the pictures constantly crept into his thoughts. On the way home from work, he tore the photos into a hundred small pieces and tossed them into a Dumpster behind the Publix grocery store on Bayshore Boulevard.

✧ ✧ ✧

Ruth and the girls were sitting at the kitchen table when Anderson came home. A chorus of "Hey, Dad!" welcomed him.

"How is the trial going?" Ruth asked, putting her arm around her husband and kissing him.

"Okay, I guess," Anderson responded. His voice sounded dull and small to him, as if he were speaking from the bottom of a tunnel. When Ruth turned around and looked directly at her husband, she immediately noted the stress on his face.

Ruth put her hand on his forehead and asked, "Are you getting sick?"

"There is a lot going on with me right now," Anderson admitted.

"After I finish the trial tomorrow, I would like for us to sit down some-place and talk. Can we call a babysitter for the girls?"

Ruth smiled and responded, "A romantic victory dinner at my fa-vorite Italian restaurant would be in order. I'll make the arrangements."

"Actually," Anderson began, his voice hesitant, "I want to order pickup and eat in. Let's have the babysitter take the girls to a movie so we can talk."

"Is everything okay?" Ruth asked, concern in her voice.

"There are some issues from work, but I know we can work through them just as we have handled challenges in the past. But tonight I'm tired and need to practice my closing argument one more time. We will have time together tomorrow night."

That night, Anderson was in bed doing his best to concentrate on the Harrell trial, but the pictures remained front and center in his thoughts. Ruth came to bed around midnight. She thought Anderson was asleep so she quietly eased under the sheets. He lay staring into the darkness. He thought he might never sleep again.

CHAPTER 41

The next morning, Anderson looked at the stranger's face he saw reflected in his bathroom mirror. The bloodshot, hollow eyes drooped pathetically. Who have I become? Anderson thought as he opened the medicine cabinet, avoiding the stranger's questioning look. Running the hot water, Anderson was forced to stare in the mirror once more as he began to shave. He knew he had to pull his act together, no matter what it took. He had to pretend that nothing had happened so he could focus on the trial. The Harrells deserved that much from him. If he couldn't deal with his personal life, he could at least do his best professionally. It might be all he had left and he was going to fight for it.

Teresa met Anderson at the entrance to the courtroom. Immediately, she knew he'd had a rough night. "Are you going to be okay today, Anderson? You don't look so great." She handed him a steaming cup of coffee.

"I'll be fine, Teresa," Anderson said, and he grimaced as he took a sip. "Really. I'll be okay. And thanks for the coffee. Just what the doctor ordered."

Beverly stood up and gave Anderson a big hug as he slid into his chair at the counsel table. "Today's the big day, Anderson. We know you're going to do a great job. We trust you and are certain you're going to convince the jury to find in our favor."

Anderson could not remember ever feeling such pressure. It wasn't the closing argument that unnerved him. He could summarize to a jury without too much preparation. The challenge was to block the pictures from his thoughts so he could concentrate on the task at hand. Even the trial judge noticed Anderson was out of character. Anderson's usual passion wasn't present. Occasionally, he stopped mid-sentence, as if he couldn't remember where he was in his argument. Twice he used the wrong names when discussing expert testimony. The Harrells were both surprised and disappointed.

Both defense lawyers presented well-organized thoughtful arguments. Lee suggested a reasonable finding would equate to very little negligence assigned to Sunfun. Peter adamantly maintained the jury should not assign any negligence to Turbojet.

After the judge gave the jury its legal instructions, the jurors left the courtroom at eleven forty-five for deliberations. The six members worked while eating lunch and then indicated at 2:30 they had unanimously agreed on a decision.

The bailiff published the verdict. Breakdown of negligence: Sunfun 40%; Turbojet 10%; Paul 50%. Total damages: $3.2 million.

Although the Harrells were not pleased the defendants were only assigned 50% of the fault, they were elated with the damages award. Anderson explained a judgment would be entered in the amount of $1.6 million. He also told the Harrells he thought the trial was clean, meaning no error took place during the five days, which could have served as a basis for an appeal.

Beverly Harrell thanked Anderson for recovering enough money to assure her daughter would receive the medical care she so desperately needed. Anderson was relieved that his lackluster closing argument had been forgotten.

Teresa and Anderson packed up his car and headed back to the office. Anderson turned on his cell phone. Sixteen missed calls. Something was going on. The office was quiet. The usual crowd that met Anderson in the reception area after a trial was nowhere to be seen.

"There will be a $1.6 million judgment entered for the girl and her family. What do you think about that?" Anderson asked Kelly as he walked over to her desk.

"We need to talk right now. In your office," Kelly said without lifting her head. Kelly shut the door behind her. Her hands were trembling. She was holding a manila envelope.

With a quivering voice, Kelly said, "Mr. Parker, I have always respected you. You work hard, you're honest, and you're polite to every-body you work with. I don't know what happened between you and Ms. Babson, and I really don't care. It's not my business. But now your actions are going to affect the firm. This afternoon I received an en-velope addressed to me that contained these two pictures."

The photographs she dropped on his desk were different from the ones Anderson received the night before. But they were similar enough.

"Oh my God. I am so sorry. Please let me explain."

Kelly held up her hand. "Stop. There's no explanation you can give. You should know pictures just like these were also delivered to Gwen and two lawyers in the firm. Everybody's talking. But that's not your biggest problem. Ruth's been calling nonstop. She sounds like she's been crying. I'd guess she's received the pictures, too."

Anderson's heart sank.

"Okay, Kelly. Thank you for your honesty. We'll talk later. Please hold all my calls so I can call home."

Ruth answered on the second ring. As soon as she heard Ander-son's voice she said, "How could you do this? I have stuck by your side through thick and thin. We have two wonderful daughters and, I thought, a great relationship. I was even deluded enough to think our sex life was fairly decent and satisfying. Guess I was wrong about that. Lisa and Julie both came by to tell me they'd been sent these disgust-ing pictures of you. So I'm getting pictures...my friends are getting these pictures... Who else knows about this? Everyone in the world? What the hell is going on, Anderson?"

Anderson had no idea what to say. He didn't even know where to begin. "I'm coming home. Please, Ruth. Let me get home and we'll talk. I'll explain."

"I shouldn't let you in this house ever again. But, for the girls, I'll give you one chance to explain this disaster. Just one. If I don't be-lieve you, that's it. You're out."

Gwen and another firm lawyer Kevin were waiting outside his door. As Anderson hurried toward the elevator he said to them, "I promise we'll talk first thing Monday morning. But I must go to Ruth. Please just do the best you can to control the situation. Tell everyone this issue will go away and the firm will remain strong." As Anderson sped home, he hoped his words were true. But he had no idea what the future held for him.

CHAPTER 42

T he front door was unlocked. The house was silent as Anderson walked inside and hung his jacket on the hall coat rack. He wearily rubbed his face and his shoulders drooped dejectedly. He heard a soft noise and looked up. Ruth was in the living room waiting for him. Anderson sat in the chair across from her. The two pictures of Nicole and Anderson were placed side by side on the coffee table in front of Ruth. Anderson picked up the pictures and started to tear them into little pieces.

"Where are Emily and Beatrice?" he asked quietly.

"I had the babysitter come early," Ruth said, her tone bitter and formal. "I asked her to take them to the park. I didn't want the girls to overhear what I want to say to you."

"You obviously have the right to be upset. Before you speak your mind, I want to tell you the entire story. You said you'd give me one chance. I'm counting on that. You know I always tell you the truth."

"So I thought." Ruth's voice cracked.

"I'm so sorry," Anderson began, his tone sincere.

"Are you?" Ruth asked.

"I truly am," he said. "I just don't know what I'm apologizing for."

Anderson told her everything. He told Ruth about the celebratory drinking on Duval Street. He told her about going back to Nicole's room. He told her the last thing he remembered of the evening was sitting on her balcony, looking at the stars. He honestly did not remember anything after he finished his glass of champagne—until he woke up in Nicole's bed the next morning. Ruth had listened as patiently as possible while Anderson told his story. But she was so furious, she could hardly sit still. Everything he said sounded like a lousy excuse, and she couldn't believe he would think she would fall for it. Ruth was so mad she didn't know where to start.

"When I saw those pictures, my first thought was to clean out the savings accounts, cancel the credit cards, and tell you to get the hell out of my house. And I still want to do that. But I don't know what will happen to Emily and Beatrice. I need time to process this. And everybody in Tampa's gonna know about it. I'm sure somebody's gonna put it on the Internet. Aside from our own issues about how this happened, we're all going to suffer from the fallout of this, and I want to protect our girls from being hurt any way I can. So for their sake, you may stay in our house until I figure out what I'm going to do. But you'll stay out here. On the sofa. I'm not going to disrupt our daughters' lives so drastically by kicking you out of the house without any warning. But this doesn't mean I forgive you or that I understand what the hell is going on.

"Whether you are totally innocent or guilty as sin, you're still an idiot who went out of town with his female employee—and proceeded to drink yourself under the table and into a compromising situation. I'm not entirely sure you don't deserve whatever comes to you. But I'm not letting my little girls suffer because of your stupidity." Ruth leaned forward as she spoke, her hands gripping her knees tightly, her voice low and threatening. "And don't even think about getting anywhere near me. There's no telling what diseases you might have picked up from her. For your own sake, I'd suggest you go get tested."

Anderson sat silently, each word she spoke hitting him like a hammer. Giggling voices announced the arrival of the babysitter and children just as the front door slammed open.

Ruth got up from the chair. "I'm going to be with the girls. Maybe you should think about how to get all of us out of this mess."

CHAPTER 43

Anderson watched Ruth leave the room. He truly had no idea what to do next. He needed to get out of the house, away from her anger, away from the girls' laughter. He'd never be able to act as if nothing was wrong in front of them. They'd pick up on it right away. He had to get some breathing space. To think.

In the garage, Anderson found his racing bike hanging on its rack. He hadn't ridden it in weeks because of his workload, but there it was, waiting on him. He pulled it down along with the tire pump. Quickly he put air in the tires. He threw on a rumpled pair of shorts and an old T-shirt that he found in the basket of clean laundry sitting on top of the washer. His tennis shoes were by the back door as usual. He grabbed a cap off the hooks lining the wall and pulled it down tightly over his eyes. He rolled his bike out the door and jumped on. Picking up speed as he turned onto Bayshore, he lowered his head and began to pump as if the devil were chasing him.

Once he reached Davis Island's beach, Anderson coasted to a stop. He leaned his bike against a parking rail and walked toward the water. Sweat streamed down his face and his shirt was soaked. Whenever he was stressed or faced a problem, anytime something was bothering him, Anderson's solution was to run or ride his bike until he could barely stand. The focus of pushing himself as hard as he could took his mind off the problem and usually, while in his zone, the answer would come. Anderson's other solution was the water. Saltwater was best, but any open water would do.

He sat on the seawall and looked out over the gently lapping waves. The sailboats in the harbor rocked on their anchor lines as the wind softly dried the sweat from his face. Two boys in a small boat just past the marina cast their fishing lines out into the water. Anderson smiled. He remembered doing that for hours as a kid. He never tired of it either. There was always the possibility of catching the big one. Ah, the carefree life of being a kid.

Anderson wandered along the docks, thinking about Ruth. He hadn't been totally straightforward with her and he realized it now. He owed her an even greater apology than the one he'd given her. Even if nothing at all had happened with Nicole, he had allowed himself to be tempted by the idea of her. And he had been stupid to travel to Key West alone with Nicole, especially after she'd tried to seduce him at the Marriott. And despite turning her down, he'd entertained the idea in his head more than once since she'd offered herself to him. And all of that was a betrayal of Ruth.

He held his head in his hands and wondered how he'd ever allowed himself to get in this position. He loved Ruth and his girls and had no intention of hurting them. He'd been so caught up with what was going on at work that he'd not bothered to work things out with Ruth and find out why she seemed to be retreating from him. He held himself responsible for everything. Somehow he had to find a way to make it up to Ruth and his girls.

Anderson rode home slowly as the sun set behind the trees; orange and red streaked across the sky. He quietly let himself into the house. A pillow and quilt were folded on the end of the sofa.

CHAPTER 44

A
nderson tossed and turned on the couch all night. His mind kept whirling with everything that happened in the last few days. His life had been totally turned upside-down and he had no idea what to do to fix things—to get his old life back. Somehow he doubted that was ever going to happen. Despite his resolution on the beach to further confess to Ruth and admit to his own failure in their relationship, he still had to tackle the problem of his public humiliation—how to restore his reputation and redeem his honor. In the wee hours of the morning, he finally fell into a fitful sleep.

The loud jangling of the telephone jerked him awake. As Anderson struggled to untwist the blanket that had wrapped around his legs during the night, Emily yelled down the steps.

"Dad, pick up the phone!"

What now? Anderson thought as he reached over to answer.

"Boss." Anderson recognized Larry's gruff voice immediately. "I need to come by and talk to you immediately. There's been an important development you should know about."

"Thanks, Larry. I appreciate your concern, but everybody already knows about the photographs. And I mean everybody." Anderson laughed sardonically and laid his head back on the sofa, covering his eyes with his hand.

"You're right about that, Boss. The pictures are old news, but I think you'll be very interested in a phone call I received early this morning. I need to come over and talk to you about it now. And I mean now.

"By the way, you looked pretty studly in those pictures, Boss. How was that little tigress in the sack? What a filthy little paralegal she was! Although I'm sure Ruth doesn't appreciate your good taste, huh, Boss?"

"Larry, I don't think I can handle your humor this morning. I'm not quite up to it. And, if you want to know the truth, Ruth is not taking this very well—as I'm sure you could imagine. So I think I'd rather not talk about it. Okay?"

"Hey, I can sympathize, Boss. Haven't ever been caught without my clothes on camera before, but I've definitely been caught with my trousers down, if you know what I mean. But hey, let me come over and I think I can help. You need to hear what I just found out."

"Larry, what are you talking about?" Anderson grumbled. "You're wearing me out."

"I gotta tell you in person, Anderson. I'm coming over right now."

"Okay, Okay. Give me an hour. I need to shower and have a cup of coffee. Then I might be able to face the world a little better. Maybe even you, Larry, although that's debatable. All I gotta say is this better be good. I've got a lot going on right now."

"Trust me, Boss. This will definitely be worth your time." Larry laughed and hung up.

Anderson slowly stood and headed toward the kitchen for his first cup of coffee. He was going to need lots of it today, he was sure. Ruth was somewhere else in the house, avoiding him. Twenty minutes later, he heard the doorbell ring. Who's that? he wondered. With his luck, the media was probably all ready to bounce on him.

He heard Larry's distinctive growl through the door. "Good morning, Boss."

"It hasn't been an hour, Larry. Not even close."

"I know, Boss. Sorry, but I couldn't wait. And I brought doughnuts – does that help?"

"Okay," Anderson sighed. He knew there was no stopping Larry once he was on a tear. "Let's go into my study."

After the door to the study was closed, Larry said, "My phone rang early this morning. Woke me up, and I'm still recovering from last night. What a night. But, hey, I digress.... So my phone rang and, let me tell you, I wasn't happy. But once she told me who she was...boy, oh boy, I knew you'd flip...."

"Larry, would you please tell me what the heck you're talking about? Could we start back at the beginning, please?" Anderson said impatiently, rubbing his forehead. He was used to Larry's rambling way of getting to the point, but this morning he wasn't in the mood.

"Okay, Boss. But you gotta guess who was on the other line. Just guess. You'll never figure it out in a million years...."

"Larry." Anderson glared.

"Right. Okay. Catherine Cartwright. Justin's wife."

"What?" Anderson asked, amazed. "Why in the world would Catherine be calling you?"

"Well, that's what I'm trying to tell you, Boss, if you'd stop interrupting and let me tell my story." Larry rolled his eyes. "Of course, I have no idea how she got my number. I didn't ask her because once she started telling me her story, believe you me, I wasn't even thinking about that anymore."

"Larry, if you don't tell me what you're talking about, I'm going to strangle you. And today, I might really do it. Don't push me. Just get to the point."

"I am, Boss. I am. She told me she needed to talk to me in confidence and, of course, I agreed. I'm the best at keeping secrets. All my girlfriends know that. But I would've told her yes to just about anything, I was so shocked she'd called me. So she tells me Justin had left for work early this morning, as he usually did on Saturdays. She'd decided to do some fall cleaning and, of course, I'm wondering why she's called me to tell me about her cleaning schedule, but I don't interrupt. I'm good at that, too, unlike some people I know." Larry glared at Anderson.

"So she gets out her mop and dust cloth—you know, all the stuff to clean house—and begins her project. She said Justin has a firm house rule that no one, absolutely nobody, is allowed into his private sanctuary, but every now and then, she breaks the rule so she can dust a little and maybe sneak a peak into what's so secret about his hideaway. You know, just to make sure he isn't up to a little hanky-panky on the side and that her position as number one wife is still safe. More or less, that's what she said. I think I might be summarizing a bit since you're making me hurry. But you get the drift."

"Larry."

"Yes, Boss. I'm getting there. So, she's in the Holy of Holies, right? And she sort of, by accident, opens his top drawer. And there is a legal pad with his writing on it, so of course she casually glances over it to see what deep dark secrets it might hold. And holy crap, you won't believe what she found."

"Larry, why in the world would Catherine Cartwright be calling you about anything, much less what secrets Justin's drawers might hold? Would you kindly tell me that?"

Larry ignored the interruption and continued his tale, "She looks at the pad and sees notes with dollar amounts, your name, and Nicole Babson's name. Of course, she says she can't stop there so she reads further—she says it looks like he made notes about a conversation he had with Nicole. It seems that your buddy Justin has set you up big-time. He hired Nicole to get a job with your firm and to take pictures of the two of you engaged in a little playtime. Obviously, she did a great job. Justin paid her big bucks and she's now moved on. A little richer, I might add. Catherine also found a list of the people Justin planned to send your lovely mug shots to."

Anderson was speechless for a few moments. He stared at Larry in shock. "That bastard!" he shouted once he'd recovered his voice. "I should have guessed he was involved in this mess. Justin never could handle defeat."

Anderson paused. "But I still don't understand why Catherine would be telling you this."

"I think Catherine finally saw the light about ol' Justin and got sick and tired of his crap. She said that after he lost the Green 61 trial, things got really bad at home. Justin had become obsessed with getting back at you. You came up in every conversation as if he couldn't move on from his loss to you in the courtroom. He became even more abusive, treating her and the girls like dirt.

"She'd begun to realize she was going to have to make the decision to leave him, but she was afraid. And then she found this stuff. She couldn't believe he could be so evil, and it terrifies her to think she's living with someone this deplorable. She'd put up with his despicable behavior for years, but this was even too much for her. And she doesn't want her kids to be subject to his verbal tirades any longer. Or worse, when he treats them as if they're invisible and not worthy of his attention. She said that might be the most painful of all. She said she couldn't live with herself if she didn't let you know what she'd found. She didn't feel right calling you personally, so somehow she must have thought I'd be the best way to get this information to you."

"Wow," Anderson said, amazed. "So Catherine has finally had enough of her condescending, arrogant, self-centered husband. Unbelievable. I always thought she was in it for the money. But maybe she does have a breaking point. Everyone does, I guess."

"Yeah," agreed Larry. "But I haven't told you the best yet. It seems Nicole thought she might have a little trouble getting you to cooperate with her scheme, you know, getting into the sack with her. Can't imagine why, but hey, each to their own. So, guess what devious plan she concocted?"

"Larry, you're a good man and I love you like a brother, but I've warned you once and I won't do it again...."

"Just listen, my man. She drugged you."

"What?"

"You heard me. She put something in your drink and then had her own little movie filming session with you as the main star!"

"What?"

"Man, are you deaf? I told you...."

"I know what you said. I heard you. I'm just in total shock." Anderson shook his head. "I always thought I was a fairly good judge of character, but I must admit that I absolutely and totally screwed up with Nicole. I had no idea she could be so cruel—and devious. No idea at all." He stood up and walked over to the window. Looking out, he could see Emily and Beatrice playing on the swing set. He watched them in silence for a minute or two, processing everything he'd just heard.

He turned back toward Larry. "Thanks for telling me this. I need to think how I'm going to use it. And I need to talk to Ruth."

Larry nodded. "You sure do, buddy. And right away. You're going to be the headlines of the paper and you better figure out how to get Cartwright to 'fess up."

"I know, Larry. Believe me, I know."

"My God, I've got to get Ruth in here right now. She's gotta hear this. Man, oh man, I might be saved. Hold on." Anderson ran from the room calling her name.

Reluctantly, Ruth agreed to hear what Larry had to say even though she was still highly suspicious of any excuse Anderson had to offer. Larry repeated his story, in a more abbreviated fashion, as Ruth listened.

When he finished, Ruth said, "Larry, I've known you for many years, but you've known Anderson even longer. I think you'd do anything for my husband and I need you to swear on your life you didn't make this up so I'd forgive Anderson's little escapade."

"Ruth, I'll swear on anything you'd like, but I might be able to do better than that. I told Catherine the only way I could believe her tale would be if I had the proof in my hand. She told me she'd try to get the notes this afternoon when Justin plays his Saturday tennis game. She was afraid to go back in the study this morning because he could come home from work at any time. Catherine said she'd call me around 4:30 and let me know if she had any success." Ruth sat silently for a minute, processing everything Larry had just told her. She turned to Anderson.

"Honey," she began, "maybe I owe you an apology. I don't know. You told me you didn't do it, and I didn't believe you. I still think you're an idiot for putting yourself in the situation in the first place. But it sounds like maybe you got suckered—and set up. If that's true, I won't put up with this—from Justin or from Nicole. They've ruined your reputation and placed our family in a terrible situation. I'll fight with you to prove your innocence and do whatever it takes." She paused. "But only if what Larry is telling me is the truth."

Anderson breathed a sigh of relief and came over to Ruth's chair. He knelt in front of her and laid his head in her lap, wrapping his arms around her.

"Thank you," he whispered.

"Um, guys—" Larry coughed discreetly "—would you like a little privacy? I feel a little out of place here."

Anderson and Ruth laughed as they turned together toward Larry. "Don't you dare leave," Ruth said. "We have to make our own plan of attack. What can we do to prove to everyone those pictures were a lie? Should we go to the police? Should we confront Justin?"

"I'm not sure Justin has committed a crime," Anderson said. "It doesn't appear he wants blackmail money. He just wants to make me look bad."

"He sure has done a good job of that," Ruth said. "I can't believe that doing this isn't a crime."

"Challenging Justin would only give him what he wants. He would love nothing more than to have me accuse him. He'd just laugh. Because he knows there's no way I can undo the damage he's done. But I don't think we can sit back and do nothing either. By Monday, everybody will be talking about the pictures. I know I should have been smarter in Key West, but it's important to me that my friends and colleagues learn that Nicole was paid to get me drunk, drug me, and take those pictures. Maybe I'll file a lawsuit against Justin for tortuous interference with the business relationship I enjoy with my law firm members. Remember, he sent pictures to my staff and lawyers."

"Wouldn't a lawsuit just cause us more embarrassment?" Ruth asked.

"We're fooling ourselves if we don't think this isn't going to spread like wildfire no matter what we do. Let's take the offensive and show everybody I was a victim of sorts. The courtroom will be the perfect setting to prove what a bastard Justin really is.

"With his wife's testimony and the tangible evidence, it will be a slam dunk. Once my case is filed, I'll have someone in the office take Nicole's deposition in California. I'm sure as hell not interested in seeing her again. Most likely, she will stick to her lies since she is in so deep, but either way, I need to know what her trial testimony will be. Let's see what legal research I can dig up to make sure we can take this to court. Larry, why don't you go on home? As long as you're in this with us, you might as well get your rest. This is going to take a lot of work."

"I'm in and you know it." Larry grinned. "I can't wait to see Justin get his due."

"I will be at the office this afternoon and will have Doug with me. I want him to hear what Catherine has to say. So you will need to have her call the firm after the two of you talk."

"What do you think, Ruth?" Anderson said. "Should I take Justin to court over this?"

"I wish we weren't in this horrible situation is what I really think. But since we are, I agree. Everybody will be talking about the pictures anyway, so let's go ahead with the suit and make Justin pay for what he did. And it looks like you certainly have the legal right to sue him. I guess we've got to get through this mess somehow so we'd better hold our heads high and stick it out together. We need to think about how we're going to tell the girls. They'll be hearing about it at school, too, I hate to say."

"I know," Anderson muttered. "I've been thinking about that nonstop. I'm so sorry I've put you and the girls in this situation. But I want to be as honest as I can with them so they will know their dad isn't as bad as people will say. It won't be easy, but let's talk to them tonight. Okay?"

"I think if we try to explain it to the girls together, at least they'll know we're in this together and that I'm not mad at you. That will help," Ruth said. "But how are you planning to handle the case?" She continued. "Are you going to represent yourself?"

"Well, first things first. I need to call an emergency firm meeting and let everyone know the facts. I also need to get Doug to co-counsel with me. Hopefully, he can work with me on strategy this afternoon, then I'll have him talk with Catherine."

Ruth put her arms around his waist and squeezed him tightly. "I do love you, but you were a bit stupid. This isn't going to be easy. For either of us."

"I was stupid," Anderson said. "About as stupid as I've ever been in my whole life. But what Justin did was wrong and, I swear, he's going to pay for it."

CHAPTER 45

Doug, it's Anderson. I hate to bother you on a weekend again, but I need you to help me with a new matter. Can you meet me at the office at 4:00?"

"No problem. I was planning on working this afternoon anyway."

An hour later, Doug was typing notes on his laptop as the two of them sat in the main conference room. Anderson told him everything. Doug was shocked. He'd had no idea they were going to discuss a lawsuit in which the senior partner in his law firm was going to be the plaintiff. He couldn't believe Anderson was dumb enough to be tricked by Nicole, but he was not about to say as much.

As Doug studied the pictures, he pretended to be thinking about the complaint to be drafted. Actually, he was looking at Nicole's body and beating himself up for failing to use his charms on her and getting her into his own bed. He'd obviously lost out on a golden opportunity. On the other hand, he wasn't having to deal with an angry female out for revenge either.

Pursuant to their plan, when Larry spoke to Catherine, he asked her to call Doug at the office. Anderson and Doug wanted further confirmation of the information Catherine had given Larry. Doug took the call in his office, so that once in the courtroom, Anderson could maintain he never spoke directly to Catherine about Justin's actions. Thirty minutes later, Doug returned to the conference room.

"Catherine's really mad at Justin," Doug said. "She wants to nail his butt to the wall. But there's bad news. The legal pad with Justin's notes had been moved so she couldn't get it today. She's sure she'll be able to find it, though."

"Anything else?" Anderson asked, processing the information. "You guys were on the phone for a while."

"We talked some more about what her life with Justin has been like. I sort of let her use me as therapy, you know. I figured if I let her keep talking, she'd get more fired up and that would be to our advantage." Doug grinned. "I attempted to throw gasoline on the fire, too. I asked her if she was upset Justin had paid Nicole all that money from her family's savings. Man, did that get her going. She was livid. She went on and on about how she couldn't believe he would use their money, their children's college money, for something as pitiful as revenge—and especially to that bimbo, Nicole. She said it was time for Justin to pay for how he had treated her, and everyone else, in his life.

"I casually mentioned there could possibly be a civil lawsuit against Justin for what he had done. She said to bring it on and that she would be more than happy to help by giving her testimony. I have to tell you, she was one pissed lady. She said she dreamed of the day when her testimony could be used in court against the bastard. Her words exactly, not mine."

"Wow," Anderson responded.

Doug and Anderson continued to discuss their strategy, ultimately deciding to file a lawsuit on Monday. The complaint would contain one cause of action, a claim for tortuous interference with a business relationship, alleging Justin intentionally interfered with Anderson's relationship with his staff and lawyers in an attempt to seek revenge because of his loss in the Green 61 lawsuit. Doug typed up a summary of plaintiff's evidence—Catherine's testimony about what she'd seen in Justin's study, the legal pad with Justin's damning notes and Anderson's testimony regarding the Green 61 trial and Justin's threat to obtain revenge.

Although Doug was almost positive that the husband-wife privilege would not foreclose Catherine's testimony at trial, he researched section 90.504(1) of the Florida evidence code. As he recalled from prior cases, the law indicated that the privilege only applied to communications between a husband and wife made in confidence during a valid marriage. Accordingly, her testimony regarding what she saw and read would be admissible.

Anderson sat in his darkened office long after Doug had gone home. He reflected on how his life had changed so drastically in the last three days. He was both nervous and excited about the lawsuit. Now he would have his chance to vindicate himself— to prove to the world that he had not pursued Nicole, but that she and Justin had set him up.

To Anderson, the lawsuit was not about money. It was about right and wrong.

And about getting a little revenge of his own.

Anderson knew it was going to be a tough phone call with his office manager.

"Gwen, it's Anderson, I hate to bother you at home on a Sunday afternoon but we need to talk."

"I'm listening," Gwen said tersely.

"I know everyone in the firm is upset, but everything's going to be all right. Larry just found the evidence to prove this terrible situation is the work of Justin Cartwright. He paid Nicole to get me drunk, drug me and set up the situation to take those incriminating pictures."

Gwen interrupted. "You don't look like an unwilling victim in the shots, Anderson. Our employees are scared and they're wondering whether the firm can survive the adverse publicity. You didn't help the situation when you left without talking to anybody Friday afternoon.

"I'm sorry I didn't talk with you on Friday afternoon, but as you can imagine, I had to get home immediately to talk to Ruth. And I agree with you—I am going to show our firm members I'm in control. That's why I'm calling you. Please contact all of our employees and tell them there will be a meeting at 9:00 tomorrow morning. If anyone has court dates or depositions, have them reschedule. Attendance is mandatory. I'll explain everything and assure them the firm will continue to prosper."

"That's the attitude I had hoped to hear from you, Anderson. I'll let everyone know to be at the meeting in the morning. See you then."

Anderson dreaded making the next call.

"Randy, it's Anderson. Am I interrupting a pro football game?"

"As a matter of fact, you are. I am comfortably ensconced in my La-Z-Boy watching the Miami Dolphins. But doctors are used to being bothered on weekends, especially by good friends. By the way, Anderson, you were quite the topic of conversation at the Yacht Club last night. Apparently, your now-famous pictures are being circulated by the Junior League gang."

"Thanks for the great news, Randy," Anderson said, rolling his eyes. "That makes my day. Listen, let's get straight to business so you can return to your couch potato existence. Contrary to what you've heard, or maybe seen, I don't think I had intercourse with her. I know that sounds strange, and believe me, it gets even stranger. But it seems I was drugged and set up. And the scary thing about it is I really don't know what happened. I want to assure myself I didn't pick up anything in the heat of the moment, if you know what I mean."

Randy chuckled. "Don't blame you there, old boy. There are some bad bugs running around in the singles' world. I'm assuming this is your first time, so let me warn you. The blood test is a walk in the park, but the swab test is not so much fun. I won't spoil the surprise for you now. Just be at my office at one tomorrow and I'll have my lab personnel take you in first after lunch. And good luck, Anderson. Sounds like you might need it."

CHAPTER 46

M onday morning, 9:00. All 13 members of Anderson's firm had crowded into the main conference room. Four people stood against the wall at the back of the room. The rest sat in the leather chairs surrounding the large table. Anderson had practiced his speech for hours. He didn't want to use any notes when he stood before his firm. He knew he had to appear sincere and confident. Standing at the head of the table, Anderson signaled for silence.

"Thank you for adjusting your schedules to attend this meeting. I wouldn't have arranged it if I didn't think it was crucially important for the future of our firm. When I left the employment of Justin Cartwright and started my own group, I pledged to uphold three principles: honesty, integrity, and hard work. I have remained faithful to my commitments, but I have made a mistake. And yet, it is not the failing you probably think.

"Let me back up. Ms. Babson was a bright hardworking paralegal in our law firm. I had respect for her as a person and an employee. We had a good business relationship. After the firm was successful in the Benson case, I had a celebration with her just as I would have done with anybody here if asked. After a few drinks, Ms. Babson made a sexual advance, but I rejected her offer, explaining I was a happily married man who was not interested in any outside interests. Ms. Babson's actions were never referenced or discussed by either of us again after that night and I assumed the issue was resolved.

"When the Radis case was called into the firm, Ms. Babson arranged for the two of us to travel to Key West to investigate the accident. We had a long day in Key West, but were successful in locating a very important witness whose testimony will serve as the basis for the lawsuit. We went to dinner that night to celebrate. My mistake was consuming alcohol with Ms. Babson after dinner. I should have been cautious in light of her previous actions, but I wasn't. Of course, hindsight is always 20/20.

"When we walked back to our separate rooms at the hotel that night, she insisted I come to her room for one last celebratory drink. I should have politely declined but, again, I didn't. That drink is the last thing I remember of the evening.

"I know all of you have seen the pictures that were mailed to the firm. Although they speak for themselves, I believe they were staged. This past Saturday, Larry was able to provide answers to many of my questions. Without getting into details, I want everyone to know that Justin Cartwright paid Ms. Babson to get those photographs. Larry found evidence that proves Ms. Babson took the liberty of drugging me and setting the scene in which she took those pictures."

There were gasps and whispers from around the conference table. Anderson waited for order to be restored.

"As I stated earlier," he continued, "my integrity is everything. By his actions, Justin has placed my character at issue and, even more importantly to each of you, has attempted to hurt our law firm. He will not succeed. I hope the members of this fine organization will stand united against him. Since my reputation is crucial to the stability of our law practice, I have decided to file a lawsuit personally against Cartwright. Doug will be co-counsel with me on the case and it will be filed today.

"Most likely, there will be substantial publicity surrounding the matter and I would ask that all press inquiries be directed to me. This case will give me the opportunity to tell my side of the story and win back the respect of my fellow members of the Bar, which I have worked so hard to obtain. With the exception of this lawsuit, it will be business as usual around here and the firm will continue to prosper. Any questions?"

There was silence in the room as everyone looked at Anderson. Then one of the young lawyers started to clap. "We support you, Boss."

Everybody clapped and stood in a demonstration of unity. Anderson almost cried.

As Gwen left the conference room, she whispered, "Good job, Anderson. We're gonna be fine."

Just before lunch, Anderson and Doug made the final changes to the complaint. It was then signed and a runner took the pleading to the courthouse for filing. Anderson told Kelly he had a lunch appointment and would not be back until mid- afternoon.

The doctor's waiting room was full of irritated patients whose appointment times had come and gone. Anderson approached the large woman sitting at the scheduling desk and identified himself. Initially, she could not locate Anderson's name, but then she saw the note indicating he was a friend of the doctor's and the lab was to take him immediately.

"Must be nice," the assistant said as she motioned for Anderson to enter through the side door. She escorted him to a room and told him to wait. A young nurse entered the examination room a few minutes later. On her tray were needles, glass tubes, and other medical paraphernalia. She looked at her orders, stared at Anderson's wedding ring.

"My papers indicate you are to be tested for all sexually transmitted diseases. Is that correct?"

"I'm afraid you're right," Anderson admitted.

She took out a needle and asked Anderson to roll up the sleeve on his right arm. "I'm going to withdraw blood to test for HIV, syphilis, herpes, and hepatitis."

The nurse filled two separate test tubes with his blood, and then told him there was only the procedure remaining for the gonorrhea and chlamydia analysis. Anderson thought she was motioning for him to expose his left arm, so he started to unbutton his other shirtsleeve.

At first, she just stared at him. Then in a professional tone she said, "Sir, it appears you've never been through this before. This second procedure consists of the taking of a culture. It will be necessary for me to put this swab stick in your urethra, so please take off your pants."

Not only did the test physically hurt, Anderson felt demeaned and embarrassed. As he was leaving, the nurse told him the doctor had placed a note on the file expediting the analysis. His results would be ready Thursday.

CHAPTER 47

J ustin was in a good mood for a Tuesday. He had heard through the grapevine that people were talking about the pictures and Anderson's problems were mounting. Justin was proud of himself.

The officer arrived at the receptionist's desk at 11:00 and announced he had to see Mr. Cartwright immediately. As she had been trained, Suzie told the officer Mr. Cartwright was in a meeting, but she would be happy to schedule an appointment.

"Not acceptable. I am here on official court business. Have him come out here now or I will find him in his office," the sheriff said officiously. Suzie picked up the phone and whispered to Justin.

"Are you Justin Cartwright III?" the sheriff asked as Justin entered the room.

"I am."

"This is a complaint filed in the Circuit Court for Hillsborough County entitled Anderson Parker versus Justin Cartwright III. Sign here to verify proper service. You should read the instructions attached to the lawsuit because a responsive pleading must be filed within 20 days." The officer gave this standard spiel when he served all complaints.

Justin was furious. How dare a state worker tell him how to handle legal papers as if he didn't know what was required. Imbecile. Justin's hands shook as he read the allegations in the complaint. He could feel Anderson's pain deep in his bones. His dream had come true. Ever since the Green 61 trial, Justin had wanted to oppose Anderson in court again. Now the confrontation would even be better—not only would they fight as lawyers but also as opposing parties. The stakes would be high and Justin knew Anderson's legal team would never be able to prove he was involved with the photographs.

"Jenny, drop whatever you're working on and come to my office immediately. We have a new case and I want you to assist me with it," Justin barked into the phone.

Justin had his secretary make a copy of the complaint, and he and Jenny read through the paragraphs together.

"I would never have imagined Anderson would have an affair. He doesn't seem like the type," Jenny said as she finished the last page.

"Well, it just goes to show you can't judge a book by its cover. Apparently, good ol' Anderson couldn't resist temptation after all, got his dick in a ringer, and now wants to blame me for his problems. This lawsuit is crap and I'm going to make sure Anderson pays for filing this slanderous piece of shit." Justin glared at Jenny as if she were at fault. Jenny took off her reading glasses and looked straight at Justin.

"I will be honored to work on the defense of this case with you, but before we start I have to ask you something. Did you have anything to do with this woman taking the pictures?"

"Jenny, I should be pissed you felt the need to ask such a question. But so there will no doubt in your mind, I swear on my father's grave I had nothing to do with whatever this woman and Anderson did."

Justin decided the best defense was an offense, so he instructed Jenny to conduct legal research as to possible counterclaims.

On Wednesday, Justin and Jenny met again to review the proposed responsive pleadings, which had been prepared the night before. Jenny explained that she had considered numerous claims back against Anderson, including slander, but had ultimately decided to keep the suit simple by just bringing a cause of action for malicious prosecution.

"Anderson is going to try to prove to the jury you orchestrated the taking and distribution of the pictures. He must be assuming he can convince the jurors with his argument you were upset with the Green 61 trial result so you paid this lady to set him up. We know you were not involved. Our counterclaim is there was no probable cause for Anderson's baseless, tortuous interference cause of action, which is entirely speculative in nature. Your recoverable damages will be the attorneys' fees you expend in defense of the case and the damage to your reputation as a result of his allegations. Any additional counterclaims brought by you will not expand the damages a jury could award and could put additional burdens of proof upon us. As a result of my research, I recommend filing the answer and this malicious prosecution counterclaim that you are now reviewing."

Justin nodded his head in agreement. "File it today. And Jenny, please call our source at the Tampa Tribune and suggest he check this court file. This case is definitely sexy, no pun intended. It's worthy of an article that will further embarrass our new adversary, Mr. Parker." The door shut and Justin laughed out loud.

"Embarrassing Anderson and ruining his pristine reputation with those pictures was a work of art. But it's nothing compared to the sweet revenge I will be awarded at trial."

CHAPTER 48

As was his usual routine, Anderson read the paper early Thursday morning while nursing a cup of coffee in his kitchen. His eyes locked onto an article in the Metro section: Prominent Attorney Sues Former Boss. The article discussed the pictures and Anderson's lawsuit against Justin. Justin was quoted as saying the claim was baseless, and he had nothing to do with Mr. Parker's fling or the incriminating pictures. Justin also announced he was going to try his malicious prosecution counterclaim in front of a jury since there was absolutely no probable cause for Anderson's allegations. Anderson folded over the section of paper, wishing the article would disappear. But he knew there would be more press. It was Justin's style. Obviously Justin had leaked this first story, and now that the newspaper smelled blood, all significant filings and court proceedings would be covered.

The same receptionist was behind the desk at the doctor's office. As Anderson approached, she reached into a drawer to retrieve an envelope. "Mr. Parker, there's no need for you to see the doctor. Here are your test results. Have a good weekend."

Anderson waited until he was secure in the privacy of his car before he opened the envelope with trembling fingers. All results were negative. It had been a while since Anderson received good news and he breathed a sigh of relief. He couldn't wait to tell Ruth and relieve them both of the worry that had been lurking in the back of their minds.

CHAPTER 49

Judge Ginny Amsler always started her Monday mornings by reviewing her mail and interoffice memorandums. After she signed some proposed orders forwarded for consideration by counsel, she turned her attention to the clerk of court's printout of new cases assigned to her division. There were a few auto accidents and one breach of contract claim, but the new matter, which caught her attention, was number 8, Parker v. Cartwright.

Ginny knew both Anderson and Justin socially but had never been the judge on any of their cases. Judge Amsler had read the Tribune's article on the case from the week before so she appreciated it was a newsworthy matter that would require strict controls. Although Ginny had never issued a case management order without a motion filed by counsel, she decided it was necessary in this case.

Justin and Anderson both received the court's order the next day. Judge Amsler required all counsel of record to appear in her chambers on November 6 for the purpose of coordinating discovery and setting a trial date. The mandate further indicated the lawyers should be prepared to advise as to what depositions they wished to take. Finally, the court indicated the case management conference would be closed to the press, but all future proceedings would be open.

Anderson was pleased the judge was moving the case along so quickly. He wanted to get to trial as soon as possible so he could tell his side of the story. He called Doug into his office and they began to work on strategy decisions. The first issue they addressed was which depositions the plaintiff would schedule. Both lawyers agreed it was imperative that Doug travel to California to take the deposition of Nicole Babson. They knew she would maintain her deception, but a record of her testimony was necessary so impeachment could be planned. In addition, it was clear Justin would have to either bring her live to trial or read Nicole's deposition, so the hope was that he might opt for the less effective reading of her deposition if it was already taken.

The tougher issue was what to do with Catherine. If her deposition was taken, then Justin would not be surprised by her testimony at trial. Clearly, the damages aspect of the case would be elevated if Justin lied about his involvement and then his wife impeached her husband's sworn statements. Anderson suggested they wait to make the decision on Catherine's deposition until Doug contacted her again and discussed what she could talk about in court.

Two days later, Doug appeared at Anderson's office door with good news.

"Shut the door and let me have it."

"Last night I made contact with Catherine Cartwright. I truly believe she wants to see her husband go down in court even more than we do. She is a very angry woman. I brought up our concern of whether to take her deposition or not, and she was adamant that a video deposition of her testimony should be taken as soon as possible. After I explained that if her husband is unprepared and is then caught lying to the jury, the damages would be higher, she said she would do whatever we wanted. She wants this case to hurt Justin and, as we'd expect, hitting his bank account and his reputation are his most sensitive spots. Catherine even volunteered to meet with me the weekend before trial to practice her testimony. The only bad news is she still hasn't been able to locate the yellow legal pad, but she's confident she will find it when there is more time to search his office."

"That is good news," Anderson said, nodding. "So what do you think we should tell Judge Amsler about Catherine's deposition?"

"Clearly, Catherine's testimony will be helpful to our case, but I think maintaining the surprise element outweighs the risk of not taking her deposition before trial," Doug said.

"I agree. We'll tell Judge Amsler it's really a simple case that doesn't necessitate much discovery so the only deposition the plaintiff will take will be Nicole Babson,"

✧ ✧ ✧

The Channel Ten news crew waited outside Judge Amsler's chambers, but the bailiff instructed them the case management conference was closed to all except the parties and their lawyers. As the combatants opened the door to enter the room, the crew shouted threats about their First Amendment rights and their right to an open court system. The bailiff ignored them and shut the door on their noise.

For formality's sake, Judge Amsler wore her black robe. She was seated at the head of the table. On her left were Justin Cartwright and Jenny Connors. On her right were Anderson Parker and Doug Ellison. The bailiff secured the room and Judge Amsler began.

"As you have noted, our first meeting will be private so we can all speak freely. I have never served as a judge for any of you so I want to set strict rules for how this matter will proceed. Remember there will be a lot of press coverage of this trial. You are both prominent members of society and everyone is going to be drooling to hear the juicy tidbits. I realize this case is personal to all involved and contains sensitive issues, but the nature of the matter will not serve as an excuse for inappropriate gamesmanship. Before me is the best trial talent in this area of Florida. I will not tolerate dirty trial tactics, including but not limited to, speaking objections, improper references to documents not in evidence, irrelevant impeachment, or anything of the sort. Do we understand each other?"

All counsel nodded.

The judge continued. "I will not hesitate to hold anybody in contempt of court who I believe intentionally violates the rules of evidence or procedure. Now that we have solved all potential behavior problems, let's move on to how the case will proceed. Since I do not anticipate the parties will be able to agree on anything, I have made some decisions for you. The trial will start on Monday, June 5 for a period of one week. The pre-trial conference will take place on May 29."

Justin interrupted. "Your Honor, I too want to get in front of a jury as soon as possible, but I will have to check my calendar for availability."

The judge put her hand up, signaling for Justin to stop speaking. She continued. "Mr. Cartwright, you are not listening. I am making the rules. You simply have to follow them. The only conflict I care about would be if you or Mr. Parker were on the Federal Court docket for the first week in June. Last week, my judicial assistant called the Chief Judge's office for the Middle District, and neither of you has a trial scheduled in Federal Court that week. That is why I picked the date. As to any other conflicts, vacations, seminars... reschedule. No more comments.

"Now that we all agree on the trial date, let's move on. Witness and exhibit lists will be filed with the court on or before May 22. I don't anticipate there will be expert testimony in a factual dispute like this one, but if a witness is an expert, identify the person as such. Next on the agenda are depositions. My order stated that both sides should be prepared to list their depositions today. Plaintiff goes first. Mr. Parker, how many depositions and of whom?"

"The court is correct in its wisdom that this is a factual dispute that will require few witnesses and no experts."

Judge Amsler interrupted. "No need for suck up, Counselor. Just list your witnesses for depositions."

"I have just one. The deposition of Nicole Babson to be taken in California," Anderson continued.

The judge made a note and then turned to Justin. "What says the defense?"

"Three depositions. Ruth Parker, Mr. Parker's office manager, Gwen Hughes, and Mr. Doug Ellison."

Judge Amsler looked deep in thought, scratching her head with her pen. "You may take the first two, but I'm concerned about Mr. Ellison. He is co-counsel for the plaintiff so you cannot ask any questions that would invade the attorney-client or work-product privileges."

"Agreed, Your Honor. All areas of inquiry will solely focus on his role as a lawyer in the firm, not as a lawyer on the case."

The judge responded, "Okay for now. But proceed cautiously. Look how much we have accomplished today. We have identified depositions and secured a trial date. Most importantly, we have established how this case will proceed. I will make the rules and you will follow them. And, of course, our final agreement—you excellent lawyers will treat me with respect and never bullshit the judge. Unless there are additional matters, this hearing is over."

And with that, Judge Amsler left the room. The four lawyers stared after her in awe. Justin and Anderson glared at each other, like prizefighters at a weigh-in, and the parties packed up their bags and left the judge's chambers. The battle was on.

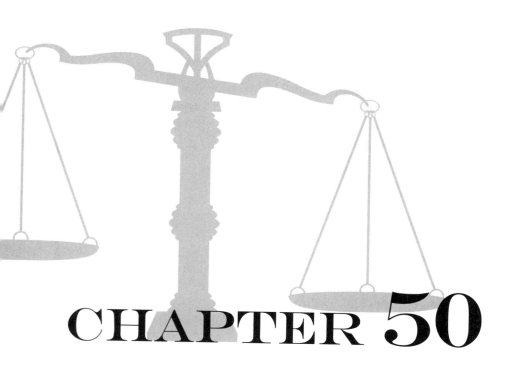

CHAPTER 50

There had only been one additional newspaper article since the first one. Anderson Parker, as the plaintiff, refused to comment for the story. Justin Cartwright was quoted as saying he was thrilled Judge Amsler granted his request for an expedited trial date in June and promised to prove at trial that Anderson had no basis for his claims.

Judge Amsler read the article with amusement. She started to summon counsel to her chambers to discuss Justin's statements, but instead made a mental note to cover the issue at the May 29 pre-trial conference. Even though the press was not spending an inordinate amount of time on the pictures and trial, the conflict was a frequent topic of conversation in social and legal circles. Ruth and Anderson had decided to ignore the comments and rumors surrounding the situation in an attempt to maintain a normal life. But even though Anderson was not going to let the Nicole Babson story rule his life, he was still dedicated to proving his innocence at trial.

Anderson and Doug made one last crucial decision—Anderson would accompany Doug to Nicole's deposition, the first to be taken in the case. If she was confronted with Anderson—and the reality of what she had done—she would be far more likely to tell the truth, the two attorneys decided. A week later, Doug and Anderson flew from Tampa to Los Angeles and then drove to Santa Barbara. That night they ensconced themselves in their hotel room and ordered room service so they could focus on preparing for the crucial deposition the next morning.

Anderson realized that the sight of Nicole would be sure to rekindle painful memories. He could not predict how Nicole would treat him in light of the litigation so he planned to stay as far away from her as possible. He'd arranged for Doug to do all the questioning so he'd have no need to engage her in conversation at all. This was the woman who, after all, had nearly destroyed his family, his marriage, his career, and his reputation.

Justin and Jenny were already present in the court reporter's conference room with Nicole when the plaintiff's team arrived. The witness was sworn and Doug started his questioning. Nicole was forthcoming in her responses to background information inquiries and seemed honest and willing to cooperate. After about two hours of questioning, Doug moved to the night at the Tampa Marriott, after the successful verdict in the Radis trial.

"Nicole, that night you and Anderson went to the Marriott bar to celebrate your win with a drink?"

"Yes, that's true."

"And then you invited Anderson to your room and implied that you were willing to sleep with him?"

"Yes, that's true also," she admitted candidly.

"And how did Anderson respond to your overture?"

"He told me that I had misunderstood our relationship—that he was a happily married man."

Listening to her answers, Anderson thought there might be an outside chance Nicole was going to tell the truth and admit to her involvement with Justin. Then came the first warning of catastrophe.

Before Doug could ask any additional questions Nicole volunteered, "As I just told you, Mr. Parker let me know that night that he was not interested in anything more than a business relationship. That's why I was so surprised by his aggressive behavior in Key West."

Doug was startled by her answer. Instead of sticking to his carefully crafted outline, he asked in surprise, "What did you mean by your last answer, Ms. Babson?"

Nicole took a deep breath and responded, "After our little incident at the Marriott, I was comfortable with having a strictly business relationship with Mr. Parker. His behavior toward me was courteous and respectful. I enjoyed learning from him and thought that we had a very healthy work relationship. All of that changed that night in Key West. After a few drinks, he seemed to develop an attitude of entitlement. When we returned to the Pier House, he insisted I allow him to come into my room. I knew it was a bad idea. But he was my boss and superior so I didn't want to say no for fear of later repercussions.

"At first I thought I was imagining his sexual advances, but then he became more obvious. At that point, he became so insistent I probably couldn't have stopped him even if I'd wanted to." Nicole paused. "But I didn't. Anderson was all I'd ever wanted, and I believed that he cared for me."

Anderson couldn't believe what he was hearing. Out of the corner of his eye, he saw Justin looking at him with a slight smirk on his face. Doug was shocked, thinking that Nicole was one of the most conniving females he had ever seen. And he had a lot of experience in this area.

Nicole continued. "I could feel our passion growing and things took off from there. Things started getting a little crazy and I joked we should take some pictures with my camera. Anderson thought that sounded pretty kinky and so we set up the camera in the corner of the room. He even showed me how to activate the timer and then we went back to our fun and began to assume sexual positions for the camera. I had never seen this side of him before and, I must admit, it was very exciting.

"The next morning was awkward. Anderson acted as if he wanted us to pretend like the night before never happened. My feelings were hurt, but it was acceptable to me. He was the married one. When we got back to the office he treated me differently. It seemed like he'd lost respect for me and that was when I knew we could no longer work together. I made the decision to come back to California. It was fine with me to keep our dirty little secret quiet but somebody intervened. For kicks I printed our playtime pictures, you know, for memories' sake. I'd put them in my office drawer. Somebody took the pictures. I don't know who and I don't know how, and I really don't care. All I know is that I've now been drawn into this stupid lawsuit and, according to my cousin in Tampa, everybody knows I slept with a married man."

Anderson wanted to jump up and ask her why she was making up this horrible story, but he knew it was fruitless. Nicole was way past the point of no return. Doug tried to ask a few more questions in an attempt to discredit her story, but Nicole denied any involvement with Justin Cartwright. She even went so far as to say that she had never even met Mr. Cartwright before the deposition.

To Anderson's surprise, Jenny Connors began the questioning on behalf of the defendant instead of Justin, as Anderson had expected. Nicole again confirmed Anderson was the aggressor in Key West. Nicole also testified that sexual intercourse had definitely taken place and a condom was not used. The deposition was a complete and total disaster.

On the return flight to Tampa, Doug turned to Anderson. "Boss, I want you to know I believe you totally. But as a lawyer I have to tell you, Nicole's testimony will hurt us at trial."

"Thanks for your vote of confidence. I agree with you."

"Keep your spirits up. Catherine's still our secret weapon."

"I can only hope," said a glum Anderson

CHAPTER 51

The notice indicated the video depositions would be taken two weeks later, on April 4, as follows: Gwen Hughes at 9:00, Ruth Parker at 10:00, and Doug Ellison at 11:00. The subpoena served on Gwen Hughes was duces tecum, which meant that she was required to bring referenced documents to her deposition. Specifically, the subpoena commanded that she bring the firm employee handbook and the two photographs she received in the mail. Doug and Anderson met for preparation on the Monday before the depositions.

"Why would Justin want to take our depositions? We don't know anything about Key West or those pictures," Doug said.

"I don't understand either," Anderson said. "Knowing Justin, he's up to something. And I'm baffled by his request for the employee handbook and the photographs."

Justin brought Jenny to the depositions and the two of them sat across from Doug and Anderson. Justin started Gwen's questioning angrily.

"Locate in the firm's employee handbook," he practically shouted, "the section that prohibits a firm owner from having sex with a salaried employee and read the language out loud."

Gwen was confused. Depositions usually began with a request for the deponent to state his or her name. Justin's approach was highly unusual, making Gwen even more nervous than she already was. Flustered, she flipped through the handbook erratically even though she knew it inside and out.

Gwen found the page she was looking for and read, "I guess you mean section II.A., which states, 'Unwelcome conduct based on gender, which interferes with an employee's job performance or creates an intimidating, hostile or offensive working environment, is prohibited. Such harassment may include sexual propositions or physical conduct.' Is that what you mean?"

"So, in your expert opinion, would Anderson fucking Nicole have been prohibited by section II.A?"

Anderson objected and put his hand out instructing a shocked Gwen not to answer the question. "Mr. Cartwright, please conduct yourself in a professional manner and refrain from improper questions that are asked solely for harassment purposes."

Refusing to look directly at Anderson, Justin yelled, "Don't ever tell me what to do. Nobody asked you to sue me, but now that you have, I'm going to take everything you have by way of my counterclaim. You have made serious mistakes and now you will pay. Don't ever address me directly again. Make your stupid objections and I will continue with my questioning."

Everybody in the room was frightened by Justin's behavior. The anger in his eyes was clear for all to see. Anderson suddenly realized why Justin was taking the three depositions. It was strictly for harassment purposes. Justin had no plans to call these people as witnesses at trial. He only wanted to take advantage of the opportunity to add to Anderson's suffering. The plaintiff's team knew it was going to be a long day. If they objected, the verbal fighting would extend the depositions. Doug and Anderson decided they would sit back and let Justin have his pound of flesh.

"Ms. Hughes, please answer the question."

"I don't know for a fact that Mr. Parker and Ms. Babson engaged in sexual activities."

Justin pointed to the two photographs on the table, "Do these pictures depict your boss, the president of your law firm, lying naked with an employee?"

"It appears so," she answered uncomfortably.

"Ms. Hughes, tell me if the following behavior is what you would expect of the president of your firm. He takes a paralegal to Key West, gets drunk with her, takes her clothes off, and then engages in wild sex while taking pictures of all the fun. Does that sound like activity that is approved in your employee handbook?"

Justin was getting to Gwen.

Tearfully, she whispered, "I don't know."

"Maybe you should get a new boss. No more questions," Justin concluded.

The room was quiet as Gwen exited.

"Are you proud of yourself?" Anderson asked Justin.

"Screw yourself, Anderson. Go get your wife. We're going to have some real fun now. That was just the warm-up."

Anderson went down the hall to another conference room in the court reporter's office, where Ruth was waiting to be called in for her deposition. Ruth looked extremely nervous—she had never given a deposition before or testified in court. And now she had to answer intimate questions about her husband that could alter his life. Anderson's gloomy expression obviously didn't help her feel any more secure.

"Honey," Anderson began quietly, putting his arm around his wife, "Justin is in a foul mood today and he is going to ask mean, disgusting questions. If we object, the deposition will last longer. Just stay calm, answer to the best of your ability, and let's get this over with."

Doug added, "One additional suggestion. Keep your answers as short as possible and don't let him engage you. He'll do the best he can to provoke you and try to make you angry. Don't let him succeed."

"Don't worry. I'm ready. I can handle anything he can dish out— he's obviously never seen a mama bear protecting her family and has no idea what he's in for," Ruth said calmly, as the three of them walked toward the deposition room.

✧ ✧ ✧

Before he even asked his first question, Justin placed a picture of Nicole and Anderson directly in front of Ruth.

"Is this your husband, and if so, who is the other naked person on the bed?"

Coolly, she answered, "It appears to be Anderson, and I believe the other person is Ms. Babson."

"Do you know if your husband has been screwing other employees of his law firm?"

Doug looked to Anderson to see if he was going to intervene, but his boss just stared at his opposing counsel in disbelief.

Ruth looked at Justin with pity. "Why are you doing this?" she asked, shaking her head. "Remember when our families used to be friends?"

"Times have changed, haven't they?" Justin snapped. "Back then, your husband wasn't suing me. Don't ask me any more questions. I make the rules. You give the answers. If you don't do what I say, the court will hold you in contempt of court. Understand?"

"Fine, if that's how you're going to be about it. And to answer to your last question, I don't know," Ruth replied curtly.

"Let me ask you this. Since your husband has been engaging in wild sex down in Key West, are you concerned that he's brought home some lovely diseases you get to share with him?"

"Not at all. Anderson wanted to make sure of that so he went to get tested. Everything came back negative."

"Now, isn't that convenient," Justin retorted.

He continued to ask questions designed to anger and insult Ruth, but she kept her composure.

"So, Mrs. Parker," Justin concluded, "after all that you have found out about your husband recently, I have one more question. Are you planning on leaving him for his shameful and humiliating behavior?"

Ruth looked at Anderson. "I love him very much and we are a team. I'm not going anywhere."

"We will see about that," Justin said sarcastically.

He turned toward Doug. "Are you ready for your deposition? It will be short and sweet. Just like your present employment."

After a few background questions, Justin asked, "Mr. Ellison, you went to California and heard Nicole Babson's deposition. You know your boss is in trouble in this case and will lose everything. Are you considering moving to another job? Or are you going to go down with the ship? Would you like to interview with me and work for an honest lawyer who doesn't sleep with his staff?"

Doug scratched his head, acting as if he had to think about the questions. Then he responded clearly and deliberately, "Sir, you just asked me a lot of questions at one time, but I will respond to all of them with one answer. I respect and admire Anderson Parker. You, on the other hand, are a snake in the grass. With no class—if you'll forgive the improper metaphor. I would rather be unemployed than work with you."

Justin turned to the court reporter. "That's it. This deposition is over." He then leaned towards Doug and whispered so that the court reporter was unable to hear, "Fuck off, you little shit. You will see firsthand how I demolish people in court."

CHAPTER 52

D oug kept in touch with Catherine frequently via cell phone to make sure she was holding up under the pressure and still willing to go to trial. Justin was growing meaner and more irrational every day, she told him. In tears, Catherine said that she was only able to survive Justin's behavior toward her and the children because she knew she would have her chance to get back at him in court.

On April 18, an additional order arrived from Judge Amsler's office, which confirmed the pre-trial conference for May 29 at 11:00. The new order also indicated that the press would be kept out of the pre-trial conference just as they had been for the case management conference. Counsel was again instructed to file their witness and exhibit lists one week before the pretrial. The next paragraph indicated that both plaintiff and defendant should be prepared to discuss what witnesses they anticipated calling to prove their claims.

Drafts of plaintiff's witness and exhibit lists were given to Anderson two hours before their meeting. Doug followed the general rule that a party should identify as many potential witnesses as possible so they will not be foreclosed at trial. If a witness wasn't listed, he or she could not take the stand. The flip side was there was no rule limiting the number of listed witnesses.

Plaintiff's list included everybody who received pictures, all employees of Anderson's firm, all employees in Justin's law firm, all members of Anderson's family, all members of Justin's family, everybody who was present at the Green 61 trial, and of course, Anderson, Justin, and Nicole. Catherine was cleverly concealed in the large listing. The proposed exhibit list was equally broad, and there was a category that would encompass the yellow pad found by Catherine. The lists were finalized and filed on May 21.

Doug and Anderson developed a strategy for the pretrial conference. Anderson would do the talking and answer Judge Amsler's questions. He planned on telling the judge that the plaintiff was going to prove Justin had threatened him at the conclusion of the Green 61 trial, and he was the only person who would have had a motive to interfere with Anderson's business by forwarding pictures. The game plan was not to discuss all of plaintiff's witnesses because they didn't want to alert Justin that his wife was going to be called to testify to the jury.

To no one's surprise, the media jammed the entryway to the courthouse on the day of the pre-trial conference. This would be the most salacious trial in Tampa in recent memory, and every news outlet wanted a piece of it.

"Gentlemen and Ms. Connors, it appears we will have one more get-together without members of the media watching our every move," Judge Amsler first stated. "My first topic of conversation is the media. I understand there was quite the crush outside this morning. After our last hearing there was an article in the local paper in which Mr. Cartwright was quoted as saying he was thrilled I granted his request for a June trial date."

The judge turned toward the defense team and stated, "Sir, that was a blatant lie. You never asked for a trial date. I assigned one on my own. What do you have to say for yourself?"

Justin thought for a second and replied, "I should not have said that. I'm sorry."

"Probably the best answer you could have given. Counselor, I don't want to get off on the wrong foot with you. Don't push me again. Understand?"

Justin did not like a woman dictating to him and he wanted to lecture her back. But he knew better than to further antagonize the judge. So he simply responded, "Yes, ma'am."

Judge Amsler continued. "As a precaution, I'm entering a gag order as to this case. I don't want any members of your firms or families talking to reporters. Very simple, you open your mouth, you are held in contempt of court, and you go to jail. This matter will not become a circus. Now let's get to work.

"I have reviewed both parties' witness and exhibit lists and it is obvious that both sides are playing 'hide the ball,' and I don't like that one bit. Mr. Parker, can you be more specific as to your case for tortuous interference?"

"It's pretty straightforward," Anderson replied. "We will put on testimony about how Mr. Cartwright threatened me at the Green 61 trial, as well as other witnesses."

"Enough. It is clear to me that you two do not intend on laying out your cases. Fine. Just make sure you stay within your pretrial lists. We will reconvene at 8:30 on Monday, June 5. Jury selection will start at 9:00. Last comment to all. The world will be watching so behave and play fair."

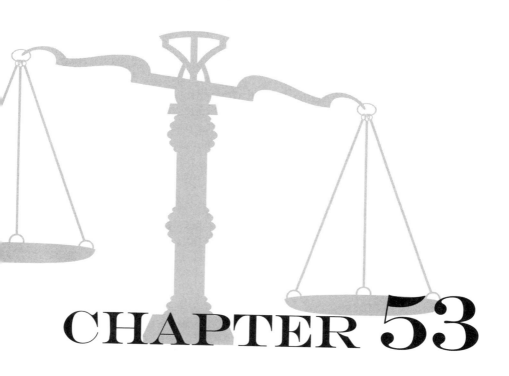

CHAPTER 53

Anderson and Doug arrived at courtroom 4B at 7:30 so they could be the first people allowed into the room to set up. In keeping with their custom, they wanted to position themselves at the counsel table closest to the jury. Between 7:30 and 8:00, members of the local media arrived, but Justin and Jenny still were not there when the bailiff unlocked the two large mahogany doors promptly at eight. It took fifteen minutes for the plaintiff's team to unpack and organize their table. Justin and Jenny arrived with ten minutes to spare, the mark of highly confident litigators. Anderson immediately noticed there was something different about Justin.

Anderson leaned toward Doug and whispered, "Justin looks relaxed this morning. Did you notice how casually he's dressed? What do you think he's up to?"

Before Doug could respond, Justin appeared in front of them, extending his right hand, "Good morning, gentlemen. If you need any professional courtesies from me during the trial, just ask."

Anderson shook his hand, but he did not reply. After sitting second chair with Justin in proceedings over the years, Anderson knew Justin always had an angle—anything he felt gave him an advantage. What was his plan for this trial? Maybe Justin was going to play the role of the victim, the average guy on the street who was falsely accused. A visual came to Anderson's mind of a slimy lizard that could change its color to blend into a new environment. That was Justin.

Judge Amsler was late to arrive to the courtroom. After making her apologies, she exchanged pleasantries with the lawyers and welcomed the spectators to her courtroom. Then she announced that the bailiff was going to bring 24 potential jurors to the courtroom.

Doug and Anderson eyed the pool as they assembled in four rows of six uncomfortable chairs. The plaintiff's team had decided they would prefer to have male jurors, as women might not forgive Anderson for apparently cheating on his wife. Or even for being dumb enough to travel with an attractive female paralegal and have drinks with her.

As plaintiff, Anderson was allowed to speak first. He spent a considerable amount of time talking with each potential juror in an attempt to establish a bond. Anderson's likable demeanor and inquisitive nature almost always led to a connection with other people. He was a natural at making friends and he used that to his advantage in the courtroom.

As he began asking questions involving the facts of the case, he wanted to know if anyone had read or heard anything about the case. Four individuals answered in the affirmative that they had read at least one newspaper article regarding the case. Judge Amsler excused the entire jury pool to the deliberations room and brought the individuals back to their chairs one at a time. When the four indicated they were biased as a result of what the newspapers had printed, the judge dismissed all of them on the basis of cause. As the ultimate decision maker on legal matters, a trial judge had the right to strike any potential jurors when he or she felt they couldn't serve as unbiased factual decision makers as a result of outside influences. Thus Judge Amsler had the ability to make juror strikes for cause.

"Mr. Cartwright, do you now see the danger in speaking to the media while a case is pending?"

Justin answered calmly, "Your Honor, I apologize to all present if my actions had any bearing on losing four potential jurors for cause."

Anderson was concerned that Justin's response seemed sincere. The plaintiff's team had been hoping the judge and Justin would fight with each other during the trial, so the last thing they wanted was for Justin to appear reasonable.

Anderson moved into specific issues he wanted to cover.

Revenge was the first concept he discussed with the jurors. Anderson found a friend in juror number eight. Mr. Eric Carmichael told the panel he had been the victim of revenge by his brother Brian when their mother died and left almost all of her estate to him instead of the children evenly. Eric described how Brian became possessed with settling the score and did crazy things, which made life for him and his family miserable.

After letting Mr. Carmichael vent for a few minutes, Anderson asked a question in an attempt to bring his point home. "Sir, if you knew there was a legal claim you could bring called Tortuous Interference with a Business Relationship, which would make your brother pay for his irrational acts, would you consider filing such a lawsuit?"

"Absolutely. Brian scared me and my family to death. We never knew what he was going to do next. If for no other reason, I would have sued him just to make him stop."

Anderson then asked the panel if somebody would volunteer to define the word "meddle." Juror number sixteen, a young lady in her mid-twenties, raised her hand and stated, "Funny enough, when I was playing Scrabble last night with my cousin I used that word and she challenged my spelling. We looked the term up in the official Scrabble dictionary and if I recall correctly, it means 'to interest oneself in what is not one's concern.'"

"Do you think it is proper for a person to meddle in another individual's business?" Anderson asked.

Already proud of herself for demonstrating her vocabulary to the other panel members, the young lady continued, "No, definitely not. I remember what my mother would tell my sister and me when we fought as teenagers. 'The world would be a better place if people would just mind their own business.'"

Anderson then covered the importance of being truthful in a court of law. As usual, all potential jurors unanimously agreed it was totally unacceptable for a witness or party to not tell the entire truth when on the witness stand.

Finally, Anderson prepared to cover his last topic, which was extremely sensitive. He came out from behind the podium so there was no physical barrier between him and the twenty. "Ladies and gentlemen, it is important that you keep in mind that this trial is about how photographs were used improperly. The issue is not the pictures themselves.

"I anticipate Mr. Cartwright will try to further demean me with photographs. There will be an explanation for the photographs, but for now I need to make sure all of you can decide the issues in the case based on the evidence only, in light of the pictures. So consistent with my practice of not hiding anything from you, I want you to know there will be exhibits of me naked with a woman who is not my wife. If that fact alone would make you want to find against me without hearing the rest of the evidence, please raise your hand."

The potential jurors looked at each other. Two women and one man raised their hands. When asked to explain why she raised a concern, the first woman explained that her first husband cheated on her. She would find it impossible to treat somebody fairly who was caught with a woman.

Anderson asked the judge to rule that the juror candidate be dismissed for cause based on her answer, since it was apparent she was biased and could not decide the case on only the evidence.

Justin did not want to lose the three for cause strikes. He wanted them on the jury or at least at a minimum he wanted to force Anderson to use his preemptory strikes on them. Justin asked for permission to inquire.

"Ma'am," Justin began, addressing the juror, "we all have feelings and opinions. But the real issue is whether you can decide the case on the evidence, not on preconceived notions. Wouldn't it be fair to say that you can listen to all the evidence and then make an educated decision?" Justin asked.

She thought for a second. "No. I can't be fair if there are incriminating pictures. I would think of my first husband and be unable to look past those memories."

Judge Amsler dismissed the challenged juror despite Justin's best efforts.

The second woman's story was similar to the first with the exception that it was her current husband who was seeing another woman. Despite Justin's well-thought-out questions and objections, the potential juror was also dismissed on a cause basis.

The male juror's story was different. He was very active in his church and read the Bible every night before he went to bed. It was his opinion that a person who engaged in adultery was a sinner who was destined to go to hell and therefore did not even deserve a trial as he had already been judged in the eyes of God.

Justin attempted to rehabilitate him but it wasn't even a close call.

The three were dismissed and the panel was down to seventeen. Anderson announced he had no more voir dire questions.

An hour lunch break was ordered by the court. Before they left for the cafeteria, Anderson and Doug huddled in the back corner of the courtroom out of the hearing of the media.

"I hated to discuss the substance of the photographs so early in the trial but we had to weed out bad jurors," Anderson said.

Doug replied, "I agree. It was a brilliant idea. Obviously those three would have hammered us and we're going to need our three preemptory challenges to get rid of some of the women."

After lunch, Justin approached the jury in an "Aw, shucks" manner.

"I'm Justin, folks," he said, in an approach approximating downhome folksiness. "I don't particularly want to be here. I would rather be at my job or with my family just as you would like to be, I'm sure. But I don't have a choice as these two lawyers have served legal papers on me and forced me into court. I don't understand why they have chosen to sue me, so I am here to defend myself against their baseless allegations.

"Let me ask you this. Is there anybody on this panel who feels it is a serious matter to sue somebody without probable cause?"

Numerous people raised their hands. Justin directed his next question to a thirty-something white male who looked like he might drive a truck for a living.

"Share your thoughts with me, sir."

Angrily, he said, "I once owned a gas station. My partner claimed I took money out of the cash register and sued me. It was a crock. The judge should have thrown it out, but he had no balls, I mean guts. I paid a few bucks just to get out of a trial. I wish I'd stood up to him like you're doing."

Justin loved his answer, so he pretended to fumble through his notes, giving the panel time to reflect on the man's anger. Justin asked additional questions to establish that a person should never bring a lawsuit unless there were sound, undisputable facts to support the serious allegations. Justin had the jurors in the palm of his hand, acknowledging that if a baseless lawsuit was brought, the party suing should be punished.

Justin entered into his last area of inquiry.

"Who on the panel has had the challenge of raising children?"

Ninety percent of the group raised their hands.

"Bless you. Since there are so many of you patient people I will direct the next question to all of you. In raising your children, was there ever an occasion when you caught your child doing something awful and their response was to blame someone else?"

A young black woman waved her hand and, without even waiting to be acknowledged, said, "My daughter would always blame everything on the boy who lived in her closet. Problem was, he would always disappear when I came into the room."

Everyone laughed.

Justin smiled. "Seriously, wouldn't you all agree a person should accept responsibility for his or her actions and should not try to divert attention from himself or herself by baselessly blaming others?"

Almost everyone on the panel nodded their heads.

Once they were finally chosen, the jury was given an extended break and the lawyers and Judge Amsler met in her chambers to announce their preemptory challenges to potential jurors. When the process was completed, a jury was announced. Four males, two women, and a female alternate juror.

The trial was about to begin.

CHAPTER 54

J udge Amsler gave the jury introductory instructions and advised that
they would now hear the opening statements of the parties. She told
the panel the opening arguments were not evidence, but were to assist the jury in understanding what each side thought the testimony
and exhibits would prove.

Since the plaintiff had the burden of proof on the initial claim, Anderson addressed the jury first. After he thanked the seven for their
service, he told them he wasn't going to attempt to summarize what
each witness was going to say. He wanted them to decide the sum and
substance of the testimony themselves. But the real reason Anderson
was not addressing specific witness testimony was because he wanted
Catherine's appearance to remain a surprise. Anderson leaned against
the side of the podium and spoke softly to the jury.

"In order," he began, "for you to decide what weight to give to
each witness's sworn testimony, it is important for you to understand the history of Justin Cartwright and me.

"After law school at the University of North Carolina, I accepted
a job with the trial department of a large firm here in Tampa. I was
the associate of the senior trial lawyer, Justin Cartwright. For five
years I worked long hours and progressed through the ranks. At the
end of my fifth year, Justin told me in confidence that he was leaving to set up his own firm. I resigned from our firm and joined Mr.

Cartwright's new organization.

"I continued to work very hard, but after three years his aggressive attitude wore me down. We clearly had philosophical differences as to legal ethics, so I knew my only choice was to leave. I had hoped to find a position with another firm, but I found Justin had called ahead and poisoned the well everywhere I went. My only real option was to open my own practice.

"As chance would have it, Justin was the opposing counsel in my first trial. I represented a mother and father who'd lost two children in a boating accident. Mr. Cartwright was the lawyer for the marine company and its driver who were the adversaries in this case. After an extensive trial, the jury returned a large verdict in favor of my client. As we were leaving the courtroom, Justin told that one day he would even the score with me. I should have taken his threat more seriously." Anderson glanced at Justin, who barely appeared to be paying attention.

"Months later," Anderson continued, "a paralegal named Nicole Babson came to our firm seeking employment. We were looking for a new paralegal to assist with a big case and her resume and qualifications fit the bill. After she signed on with us, she first worked with an associate and then she assisted me.

"We were successful with the trial, and in the excitement of victory, Ms. Babson made a sexual advance toward me. I assumed it was just that, the thrill of victory, that kind of thing. So I told her, as kindly as I could, I was not interested. She's young, and again I assumed it was her enthusiasm and youth and decided to put it behind us. We never spoke of it again.

"A few weeks later, a horrible accident took place in Key West in which a young man injured his leg during a snorkeling trip. The situation required immediate attention so Ms. Babson and I traveled to the accident location on an expedited basis to preserve the evidence and follow through on the necessary investigation. We were successful in our work, but now I realize Ms. Babson used the opportunity to make sure I drank a lot of alcohol. Somehow that night, she took pictures of the two of us naked.

"The photographs themselves are not the issue in this case. Your decisions should be based upon what was done with the pictures. Ms. Babson testified she did not mail the photographs to my family and friends or the members of my firm. The evidence and common sense will lead you to the proper conclusion in this case. Only one person had the motive to interfere with my business and family. Justin Cartwright made good on his threat to get back at me. After you have heard from the witnesses and reviewed the evidence, you will return a verdict telling Mr. Cartwright he was wrong to inter-fere in order to extract revenge. Thank you."

After a short recess, Justin stood behind the podium and ad-dressed the jury, "Ladies and gentlemen, in the next few days you will be faced with some factual disputes, but there will be one piece of evidence that is not subject to interpretation. It speaks for itself."

Justin walked over to the corner of the courtroom and pulled up a poster-size enlargement of a photograph. He intentionally kept it turned away from the jury as he walked back toward the podium. The jury gasped as he placed the picture of Nicole and Anderson on the easel. Nicole was sitting on Anderson as he lay on the bed. Al-though they were both naked, her back was toward the camera.

"Pictured here are Nicole Babson and Anderson Parker. Both without their clothes, in a hotel room in Key West. You will note that I am not in this picture. In fact, I have never been to this city. For reasons unknown to me, this married man decided to cheat on his wife. Now that he has been caught and is in trouble he wants to blame everything on me. He thinks the best defense is offense. "Ms. Babson's deposition will be read for you. She will testify she has no idea who stole her pictures. You will hear, however, that the last time she had possession of the photos was in her office at Anderson Parker's firm. Ms. Babson will also tell you the first time she met me was on the day of her deposition in California."

Justin then explained to the members of the jury that there were two different and distinct claims in the case. He suggested the evidence, not speculation, would support a yes finding on his malicious prosecu-tion cause of action and a no finding on Anderson's tortuous interfer-ence suit. Justin turned to return to his table, but then he placed his hand on his chin as if he had just remembered an important fact.

"Originally, I wasn't going to talk about why Anderson left my law firm, but since he brought up the issue, I feel it would be only fair to set the story straight. Like many of you, I have children so I work very hard to feed and clothe my family. Although I am not proud of this fact, I have to admit I commonly work many nighttime hours.

"When Anderson and I were working together, we had a tragic case involving a young man who had been shot and injured. As we prepared for trial, we had to work late many nights to get ready. One night when we were working on trial exhibits, Anderson indicated he was tired of working long hours at measly hourly rates. I was shocked. He told me he wanted more. He wanted to be rich. He planned to quit working for me so he could start his own firm doing only plaintiffs' work and make big money off dead and paralyzed clients."

Anderson's jaw dropped. He couldn't believe what he was hearing. "Objection, Your Honor," he said, rising to his feet. "Can we approach the bench?"

"Counsel, come up for a side bar," Judge Amsler responded.

Anderson and Justin stood beneath the judge, out of earshot of the jury. Anderson spoke first.

"Judge, we are officers of the court who have taken an oath to tell the truth. Mr. Cartwright knows his last slanderous comments are total lies. He is intentionally misleading the jury."

"What do you have to say for yourself, Mr. Cartwright?"

Justin looked hurt. "I find it interesting that a man who cheats on his wife accuses me of being dishonest. I am merely representing to the jury what the evidence will be. When I testify, these exact facts will become part of the record."

"Based upon the representations of counsel, objection overruled," Judge Amsler said, as she motioned for the lawyers to return to their prior positions.

Justin went back to the podium and continued. "I'm sorry. I forgot where I was before Mr. Parker interrupted me. Let's see. Now I remember. I was telling you how Anderson decided he wanted to make easy money as an ambulance chaser. It was no big deal to me. Lawyers commonly come and go at firms. I was willing to forgive him for departing even though clients needed him. But I cannot overlook this frivolous lawsuit he is bringing against me. It hurts me and my family. By your verdict, you will send a message to Mr. Parker to stop engaging in dishonest behavior like this." Justin pointed at the blown-up picture and then slowly sat down.

Judge Amsler instructed the jury the court would recess for the day and the plaintiff would start his case the next morning.

CHAPTER 55

A nderson, Ruth, and Doug sat in the main conference room with file materials spread out around them. Ruth dropped her pad on the table.

"He is such an evil liar. When he said you left his firm because you wanted to make easy money, I almost jumped over the railing and punched him."

Anderson put his arm on her shoulder. "Well, darling," he said ruefully, "that would have been exciting but not productive. Just remember, tomorrow Justin's true character will be revealed."

"I just got off the phone with Catherine," Doug said. "Larry's going to serve a trial subpoena on her tomorrow at 2:30 and then drive her to the courthouse. When you're ready for her testimony, Larry will escort her to the courtroom. And she thinks she knows where the missing legal pad is. She's almost positive she'll be able to get to it tomorrow while Justin's in court and bring it with her."

"Fantastic. Did she tell you anything else?"

"Just for you not to worry because she remembers everything exactly."

"Great," Anderson said. "Then Tuesday should be our big day. Let me summarize one last time what's going to happen tomorrow, so we're all on the same page. I will take the stand first, and Doug you will follow our outline. Remember we want to take our time and consume the entire morning with my testimony. After lunch, I will call Justin as a witness and give him the opportunity to deny everything. We will ask for a brief break after Justin, and then we will parade Catherine into the courtroom. I will try to take up the rest of the day with her testimony so the jury can think about what Nicole and Justin did."

"Great plan, Boss," Doug said. "As you have taught me—preparation, preparation, and more preparation. See you guys in the morning."

Doug departed and the two of them went into Anderson's office. Ruth motioned for Anderson to join her on the client couch. She started to massage her husband's neck.

"I know this entire ordeal has been very stressful for you," she said. "But I believe in my heart you were right to bring the lawsuit. Somebody had to stand up to Justin and teach him that he can't cheat his way through life."

Anderson turned around and kissed his wife gently.

"Thank you for supporting me. Tomorrow I will let everyone see that I am a loving husband who is only guilty of bad judgment. The day will end with Catherine finally bringing the truth to light about this horrible situation. It's too bad it's come to this."

"With someone like Justin," Ruth replied, "it was only a matter of time."

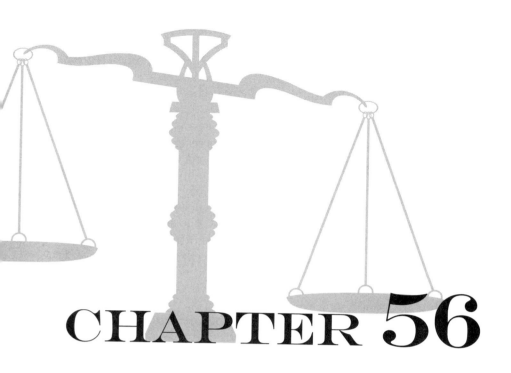

CHAPTER 56

J udge Amsler called the court to order, and Doug announced that the first witness to be called on behalf of the plaintiff was Anderson Parker. Anderson looked tired but determined as he raised his right hand and took the oath to tell the truth. The predicate, or "get acquainted" questions, took an extended period of time. The jury learned about Anderson's upbringing in rural North Carolina and his education at Chapel Hill. Anderson told the panel how his father's work-ending hand injury influenced his perception of the legal system. Ruth watched proudly as her husband testified from the spectator section of the courtroom.

Eventually, Doug moved to the issue of the relationship between Justin and his client. Anderson told the jury he did not agree with his ex-boss's philosophy of doing whatever was necessary to protect a client from paying, even if it meant "bending" the rules. Anderson described Justin's anger when he told Justin he'd finally had enough of his demands to conceal information. Doug made sure Anderson had plenty of opportunity to discuss the details of the night he resigned from Justin's law firm.

Doug then questioned Anderson about the details of the Green 61 trial. Anderson testified about each time that Justin threatened him in court. Doug asked him to repeat Justin's exact words at the close of the trial.

Anderson looked straight at the jury as he answered, "'Go fuck yourself. I will even the score with you someday.'"

Justin remained alarmingly unperturbed.

After a brief morning break, Anderson's testimony resumed. He was asked to describe how he met and worked with Nicole Babson. But the crucial issue everyone was waiting to hear about came next.

"Mr. Parker, could you please tell the jury in your own words what happened on your trip to Key West with Ms. Babson?" Doug asked politely.

"Looking back, I realize now I exercised bad judgment going there with her. At the same time, we had a client whose future depended upon emergency investigation and preservation of evidence. We had to act quickly before the evidence was gone."

"What happened that night?"

"To be totally honest, I don't remember. It had been a long day and I drank too much. The last thing I remember was feeling ill when I was sitting on Ms. Babson's balcony. I've seen the pictures and I know what they show. But I have no idea how I ended up in her bed without my clothes. And I really don't believe I did anything with Ms. Babson that night. I was in bad shape. I don't think it was even physically possible."

The comment drew titters from the audience. Ruth looked over to the jury box and noticed three male jurors raising their eyebrows doubtfully.

"I had absolutely no idea any pictures were taken," Anderson continued. "The first time I learned of the photos was when they were hand-delivered to my office. Then the next day, my secretary, my office manager, lawyers in my firm, lawyers in my old firm, my wife, and a few of our friends received pictures, too."

Doug then spent a while having Anderson set forth how the mailing of the pictures had caused him damages, both emotional and monetary. Time management was an important consideration in the direct examination. Doug noted he was approaching the time for a lunch break, and he wanted Anderson's testimony to conclude in the morning. He decided to cut his questioning short to fit his planned timeframe.

"Mr. Parker, let me ask you one last question, which is in great part based upon common sense. Can you think of anybody besides Justin Cartwright who would have had any motivation to hurt you and your law practice?"

"Absolutely not," Anderson said adamantly.

"Please explain your answer."

Anderson turned toward the jury. "I have never been threatened seriously by anybody except for Mr. Cartwright. He was angry at me for leaving him, forming my own law firm, and then winning the Green 61 trial against him. I hurt his pride in more ways than one. Justin warned me he was going to get revenge, and he certainly made good on his threat. It's clearly a matter of simple logic. Nobody else had any reason to send the pictures. Justin Cartwright warned me he was going to do something despicable, and he did it."

"No additional questions at this time," Doug announced as he sat down. Justin approached the jury with a single legal pad.

"I tried to write down all of your theories this morning," he said, facing Anderson, "but I couldn't keep up with your speculations. I noted you are sure about only a few facts. For instance, you testified under the threat of perjury that you didn't believe you had sex with Ms. Babson."

"That is correct," Anderson confirmed.

Justin continued, "You seem to like the words 'common sense' and 'logic.' I guess it would be a logical conclusion that you didn't get tested for sexually transmitted diseases after your little tête-à-tête in Key West since there was no consummation, am I right?"

Anderson realized he was going to look bad no matter how he answered.

"It probably wasn't necessary, but just to be safe, I was tested."

Justin paused a moment before commenting sarcastically, "I see, or more accurately should I say, the jury sees. Now, I was wondering. In addition to your conjectures, do you have one single document to mark as an exhibit for the jury, which supports your theory that I was involved with the pictures in any way?"

"Not at this time," Anderson said.

"Judge, I have no more questions for Mr. Parker."

What was that all about? Anderson wondered. The judge announced a lunch break and both sides quickly filed out of the courtroom to discuss their next bit of strategy.

Anderson, Ruth, and Doug sat in the back corner of the courthouse cafeteria. Jurors were eating close by, so the group kept their voices down.

"I didn't like the question about the testing," Anderson said. "I simply told the truth, and I hope the jury will understand I went through those just to be extra cautious. How did Justin find out about the tests anyway?"

"Remember, the subject came up in Ruth's deposition," Doug said.

"Well, I don't think it's that big a deal. The important thing is for us to make Justin look like a calculating liar with Catherine's testimony. Doug, are we still organized for this afternoon?"

"Absolutely. I spoke to Mrs. Cartwright this morning. We talked about how she should dress. She's excited, but at the same time she's nervous about how Justin will react after her testimony. She's afraid of him and I can't say I blame her."

"Okay. It looks like our preparation is going to pay off. At 1:15 I'll put Justin on the stand. My goal is to conclude his testimony just before 3:00, so you should plan on having her in the hallway at 2:45."

Justin looked relaxed in the stand. He did a good job of maintaining his composure as he answered the questions Anderson asked him. Anderson and Justin's working days together were again discussed thoroughly. Justin repeated his opinion that Anderson left to make easy money.

"Were you angry when I decided to no longer be associated with you?" Anderson asked.

"I wouldn't say I was angry. Lawyers leave firms all the time. It is a fact of life in the legal community. What I felt was disappointment in you. Anderson, you had progressed nicely as a litigator, but then you decided you didn't want to pay your dues. Apparently, you determined you could work less hours and make more money if you took 40% of the compensation paid to seriously injured people."

Anderson tried not to show his anger as he progressed with his questioning. "Isn't it true I resigned from your firm because you wanted me to hide evidence?"

Justin replied with a dramatic sigh. "Counselor, I have no idea what you are talking about."

It was apparent to Anderson that Justin was not going to lose his cool and he would lie to the bitter end. Anderson moved on to the Green 61 trial. Although Justin candidly admitted the verdict was a loss, which had adverse consequences for his career, he denied he threatened Anderson or indicated he desired any form of revenge.

"I have lost trials in the past and will lose some in the future. It's part of life as a courtroom attorney."

Anderson concluded his direct examination at 2:40. Jenny indicated there would be no cross-examination of Justin in the plaintiff's case, but Justin would testify when the counterclaim for malicious prosecution was presented.

At the same time, Larry was picking up Catherine and driving her to the courthouse. The car ride was quiet except for Catherine asking for her trial subpoena. Larry noticed that she seemed extremely nervous. Larry kept Catherine hidden away in the witness conference room until Doug joined them shortly before 3:00.

"Are you ready?" Doug asked.

"I have been looking forward to this moment for a long time," she told him. "I am prepared."

Doug continued. "Do you have the legal pad with you? We want to mark it as an exhibit."

"Unfortunately, I could never find it. But don't worry. My testimony will carry the day."

Their conference was interrupted by the bailiff calling Catherine Cartwright to the courtroom. When Anderson announced that the plaintiff's third witness was Catherine Cartwright, Justin became visibly upset. He stood up at counsel table and made a speaking objection.

"This is ridiculous!" he shouted. "She is my wife! When will Anderson Parker's harassment end? Catherine doesn't know anything about Mr. Parker's exploits in Key West."

"Counsel, approach the bench." Judge Amsler's anger was obvious.

Since it was apparent to Judge Amsler there would be heated argument regarding the next witness, she excused the jury for a mid-afternoon recess and instructed the panel to return to the courtroom at 3:30. First she spoke to her bailiff.

"Although Ms. Cartwright has not yet been sworn in, she has been identified as the next witness in front of the jury. Please take her to the witness room and stay with her until we reconvene. I do not want any lawyers talking to her before she testifies."

Judge Amsler then turned to Justin. "I warned you about speaking objections in front of the jury. Do not push me, Mr. Cartwright. What is your problem?"

"Your Honor, the plaintiff's intrusion into my personal life is wearing me down. It is bad enough I have to miss work to defend this baseless lawsuit. Now he drags my wife into this matter for no reason at all. Catherine has to take care of our children. She doesn't have time to tell Anderson she has no knowledge of his drunken orgy."

The Judge raised her hand. "Mr. Cartwright, watch your mouth. Mr. Parker, I assume you have good cause to call Mrs. Cartwright as a witness."

"Yes, I do. We believe she has relevant information surrounding the elements of our cause of action."

"She'd better. Based upon the representations of Mr. Parker, Mrs. Cartwright will start her testimony at 3:30. I am taking a break. I suggest counsel take a few minutes to calm down."

The developments pleased Anderson. All present in the courtroom appreciated Justin was slowly becoming unraveled. Anderson could not wait for the fireworks to start. With the anticipation of redemption, Anderson started his direct examination of Catherine. He carefully covered background information. Catherine talked about the eight years Justin and Anderson were business partners. She candidly admitted her husband was disappointed when Anderson left the firm and then again when he won the Green 61 trial.

At approximately 4:15 Anderson was ready for his big moment. It was time for the jury and the world to learn he was a victim of Justin's calculated scheme.

"Mrs. Cartwright, please tell the jury in your own words what you know about your husband's involvement with Nicole Babson and the pictures."

Catherine looked confused. After a pause she said, "I really don't know anything. I have read the allegations in your lawsuit but don't have any firsthand knowledge. The name Nicole Babson means nothing to me."

Anderson felt as if he were standing naked in front of everybody. His mind raced. The first thing he thought of was Doug's comment to him on Monday night. Catherine had told Doug she remembered everything exactly. A memory came flooding back. It was back when Anderson had been practicing law for about two years. Justin, then his boss, told him when a witness says that he or she remembers everything exactly, the person is lying.

The whole situation became clear. Justin could only obtain total revenge if he defeated Anderson in court. The son of a bitch had used his wife to bait him into filing a lawsuit. Stunned, Anderson turned around to look at Justin. His ex-boss's wink confirmed his nightmare.

"Mr. Parker, do you have any additional questions for this witness?" Judge Amsler asked.

Anderson realized he had been staring at Catherine.

"Do you by chance know of a legal pad that contains notes made by your husband involving Nicole Babson?" Anderson asked, just to confirm what he already knew.

"I really have no idea what you are asking me," Catherine replied impatiently. To Anderson's eye, she was hiding a smirk. She knew exactly what she had done to him. "I wish I could help you, but I haven't a clue as to what you are talking about."

It was clear to Anderson she had been coached by the best. He knew every additional question was going to make the situation worse, if that was even possible.

"No further questions, Your Honor."

Justin had only one question.

"Honey, why are you in this courtroom today?"

Holding up a piece of paper Catherine said, "I am only here because Mr. Parker's office served this trial subpoena upon me. I was supposed to be at our daughter's school for a teacher's conference this afternoon."

Catherine was released and she left the courtroom.

The jury was left to wonder why Anderson had called her as a witness. Anderson was devastated. Judge Amsler looked at her wristwatch and advised the jury the trial would break for the day due to the late hour. Before Judge Amsler left through the back door, she told Anderson to be ready with his next witness first thing tomorrow morning. Anderson and Doug leaned back in the counsel chairs and attempted to collect their thoughts.

With Jenny at his side, Justin appeared in front of the two lawyers. "Anderson, I thought I trained you better. Remember my rule? Never call a witness unless you know what he or she will say. Maybe you should have taken her deposition or at least made sure you had an exhibit to document her testimony. Such as...a yellow legal pad." Justin's tone dripped with sarcasm. "Now you are in quite a unique legal position," he said. "I believe the Latin term is 'deep shit.'"

Justin laughed as he walked away.

CHAPTER 57

Justin was on cloud nine as he and Jenny headed back to the office. "Do you need me to help with trial preparation tonight?" Jenny asked as she removed her briefcase from the back seat.

"No, this trial is basically over. We don't need to do anything else. You can head on home. I'm just going in to check my mail and return some calls."

After working for a while, Justin leaned back in his leather chair. He was thrilled with the courtroom proceedings that day and wanted to share his excitement with somebody. He thought of calling Catherine, but she had been a pain in the ass lately. Even after he'd been so generous and agreed to void their prenuptial agreement if she helped with his Anderson scheme, she started having second thoughts. She felt guilty about setting up dear Mr. Parker and tried to weasel out of the deal. Nah, he wasn't going to let his wife's sympathy dampen his celebration. He could think of only one person who would want to hear every detail of Anderson's destruction, but he certainly couldn't make that phone call with anyone around to hear.

Justin roamed the halls, looking into offices, confirming that everyone had gone home for the day. After assuring himself that the office was empty of all employees, even cleaning people, Justin returned to his office and allowed himself the pleasure of reveling in his certain victory. He punched in the number, flipped on his speakerphone, and leaned back in his chair with his feet on his desk.

"Nicole? It's Justin."

"Hold on. Call me back on this number. I don't want to talk on my cell."

Justin dialed again.

"Nicole?"

"Yeah, it's me. Do you have a verdict yet?"

"No, but it was a great day."

"You haven't forgotten I get 25% of your recovery money for giving that deposition, right?"

"Of course I remember. And trust me. It's gonna be a big verdict. But the best part was Anderson's distress today. He had no idea what was coming and he got clobbered. He really thought Catherine was going to turn on me and be his star witness. What a sap. He thinks everyone is just like him and wants the whole world to be goodness and light. Sickening. Hey, but at least it worked for me. I knew exactly how to get Anderson to fall into our little trap. And it was perfect. I wish you could have been there to see his face when Catherine denied knowing what the heck he was talking about. He was so screwed and he knew it. Oh, man, I love it. It was beautiful."

"Poor little Mr. Goody Two-Shoes," Nicole responded. "First I put him in his coffin and then Catherine nailed it shut."

Justin laughed. "Exactly. We tag-teamed the poor son of a bitch. Just what he deserved."

"Is the jury getting pissed?" Nicole continued.

"I can't tell for sure, but I think so. I sure would be if I were in their situation. Anderson has offered no real proof of my involvement and now he's out of witnesses."

"Be careful. We both know Anderson's very resourceful. Is it possible he has something that ties you to the pictures?"

"No way. I always wore gloves and I mailed them from a neutral location."

"Good. So, what happens tomorrow?"

"I plan to read your deposition first thing in the morning. Then I'll present my own testimony on damages. I think the jury's gonna throw him out on his ass, and I think they'll give me a crock-load for my counterclaim. You'll be sitting pretty, young lady, when we finish with Mr. Parker. I'll call you tomorrow with our good news. How's that sound?"

"Serves him right. I can't stand a man who thinks he's so high and mighty. And I won't mind spending his money either. It'll bring me great pleasure. But you wanna hear the greatest irony of all? We never even did the deed. Anderson got his panties all in a wad for nothing. I swear that man is an idiot. I couldn't do anything to get him interested in me so I finally had to resort to slipping a roofie in his drink so I could set the entire thing up. Man, that was a chore. I never knew a doped man could be so heavy. I definitely earned my money."

"Nicole, you're wonderful! So Anderson really didn't sleep with you—but he thinks he might have. And so does Ruth. What torture. Ahh, now that's true justice, my lady."

Justin pushed off the speakerphone and laughed out loud. "What a woman. I'm glad I didn't cross her."

CHAPTER 58

Larry paced the conference room floor, trying to control his anger. "That woman lied to me. Can't I be called as a witness to tell the jury about our conversations?"

"Unfortunately, Catherine is not a party to the lawsuit so her statements would be hearsay and not admissible," Anderson said. "We could try to argue that Catherine's statements are exceptions to the rule since her words will be offered solely as prior inconsistent statements to impeach her credibility. We would probably lose this argument and if we did win it, Judge Amsler would allow Justin to recall Catherine as a witness so she could deny the statements. It would be a bad strategy call by us unless we had a written document to impeach her with. Justin thought out this entire situation carefully." Anderson frowned. "That's why the so-called legal pad was never produced. We took his bait, but we must not panic." Anderson stood and addressed Doug and Larry further. He looked like a leader rallying his troops after a defeat but both Doug and Larry knew that Anderson was about to break.

"Justin set this whole thing up so we must ask ourselves, Who would know about the scheme? We'll get nowhere with Catherine, but his plan was complex. Somebody else must know about Nicole or have some clue as to what Justin was up to. Even if they don't realize exactly what it is they know. We've got to find that person." Anderson sat back down in his chair and began to rub his forehead. All pretenses were gone.

"What about Jenny?" Larry asked as he scribbled on his notepad.

"No, that wouldn't be Justin's style. He would never confide in an associate, especially not a woman. He treats his associates like they're his slaves—and he thinks women are a lower level of creation than men—so he would never trust a female associate with his darkest secrets."

Larry stopped writing, "I just thought the two of them might have talked since they've spent so much time together on the case. Or maybe he gave something away without realizing it."

Anderson stood again and started to walk around the table, pacing as he thought about the situation.

"Any ideas, boss?" Doug asked. Doug had never seen Anderson looking desperate in any setting, but Anderson's demeanor on this day certainly came close.

"On second thought, I think Larry might have a good idea—but Jenny isn't the one. Justin's other associate, Josh, could be our answer. When we all worked together at the old firm, there would be many times I would go home when the two of them would stay and talk late into the night in Justin's office. Justin seemed to confide in Josh more than he did with any of the other associates. I assume they're still close. Maybe Josh has some clue as to what's been going on. Of course, getting him to admit that to me will be the trick. He's not going to give up his boss easily. But I'm going to see what I can do about that. He lives just over the bridge on Davis Island so I'm going to head over to his house now and see if I can convince him to help me.

"Larry, keep your cell phone close in case I need you to serve a trial subpoena on him. And Doug, I'll call you if I need you for any trial preparation. Thank, guys. I'll let you know what I find out." And with that, Anderson headed out the door.

Once in his car, Anderson headed straight through downtown and over the bridge to Davis Island, following part of the route he and Josh used to jog together back in the early days of their legal careers. They'd both been young attorneys at the large firm where Justin headed the trial department.

To release stress, they'd often run on Bayshore after work or meet at Josh's apartment and run from Davis Island. Anderson and Josh had parted ways for a brief time—Anderson left the firm when Justin began his own firm and Josh decided to stay put. But after a short while, Josh couldn't resist the pay increase and joined Anderson in the torture chamber known as The Law Offices of Justin Cartwright. Josh and Anderson had worked side by side under Justin's dictatorship, but when Anderson left to start his own firm, they'd lost contact. Anderson did receive a baby announcement from Josh and his wife, Kimberly, when they had a little boy, but other than that, they never spoke again.

Anderson pulled his SUV in front of the familiar house. He remembered how jealous he'd been when Josh and Kimberly had bought this house. He'd had so much debt from his law school loan that he couldn't even think about buying a house early in his career. That had always slightly irked Anderson—he had wanted to provide good things for his wife, too. Now he had the house, an even bigger one, but he was afraid he was going to lose it all. He needed Josh's help to keep that from happening.

Anderson could hear a baby crying as he walked up the front steps and knocked. Kimberly opened the door, wrestling with a screaming child who was kicking wildly, trying to pull off a wet, soggy diaper.

"Somehow I was expecting we might be hearing from you," Kimberly said as her toddler continued to cry relentlessly. "I'd like to assume you're here to offer your babysitting services, but something tells me you'd rather talk to my husband about your lawsuit against his boss—who you're trying to destroy and who, in case you've forgotten, provides our one and only source of income. Which we need. Despite the noise level, we do love our kids and would like to be able to feed and clothe them." Without waiting for a response, Kimberly yelled up the stairs, "Josh, guess who's here to see you." Turning back to Anderson, she said softly, "And I bet I know what he wants to talk about, too."

Kimberly stomped away with her fussy child, abandoning Anderson at the door. The look of surprise on Josh's face as he came down the steps warned Anderson right away that Josh didn't know anything that would help him. He didn't have that guilty look. He just looked astonished that Anderson would appear out of nowhere expecting help when he was the one who'd left their relationship behind. Josh broke the silence.

"This is a bit awkward, Anderson. You're in the middle of suing my boss and here you are, at my house, obviously wanting something from me."

"I need your help." Anderson was desperate. "Justin has set me up and I need a witness who can prove it. I know that Justin worked with Nicole to get those pictures. I was hoping you could shed some light on the situation for old time's sake—maybe you might know something about it?"

"My good buddy, from what I've heard—and seen—you brought this little problem on yourself. In fact, I'm surprised Ruth has stuck it out with you. If Kimberly had seen me in pictures like yours, she would have kicked my butt out of the house so fast my head would still be spinning. Oh, but not before she found time to sever an extremely important part of my body." Josh grimaced at the thought.

"Truth be told, Anderson, no one in our law firm understands why you filed this lawsuit against Justin. You fucked up, no pun intended, and now you want to blame your roll in the hay on him. And he ain't going down easy. Personally, I don't appreciate your lawsuit, which is costing my firm time and money—which none of us can afford. So, to answer your question? I can't believe you have the balls to come here and ask me for anything. And to be a witness for you? What a joke! Please, get your betraying ass off my property. And don't come back again."

Anderson felt like a horse had kicked him in the chest. He could barely catch his breath as he drove over the bridge back toward home. He had no idea Josh's resentment had been so strong. Not only had he lost a friend, but he also had no hope of redeeming himself. He was totally out of ideas.

Ruth was in the kitchen when he walked in the house. He could smell the soup she was cooking and hear her humming to herself as she often did when no one else was around. He smiled despite his troubles. Just what he needed—a good dinner and a sympathetic wife. He realized he was extremely lucky to have either right now. She turned when she heard him enter the room.

"Today was awful. What are we going to do?"

Anderson leaned back against the counter. "To tell you the truth, I don't have the slightest idea. We need a witness to Justin's plan, but we are running out of possibilities."

"What do you mean?" Ruth asked as she lifted the lid from the pot to stir the soup.

Anderson told her about his visit with Josh.

"Well, I think you were on the right track. There must be somebody who's heard or seen something—what I mean is, it doesn't have to necessarily be someone Justin spoke to. I don't think he would have talked about this plan to anyone anyway— it's just too devious. They could betray him too easily, and I bet he didn't trust anyone with the details, except for Nicole, of course, but then she was paid well to stick to her story and disappear." Ruth's face reflected her intense concentration. "Surely someone saw him with Nicole or noticed something odd going on. We just need to think who that someone might be. What about his secretary? She'd certainly be around enough to notice anything unusual?"

Anderson frowned. "She's new, I think. Justin's secretaries don't stick around very long. He's too rough on them. Between his hours and his attitude toward them, they usually don't last longer than a year, if he's lucky. So this one wouldn't have had time to know what was usual or unusual about Justin's behavior. She'd be too busy trying to keep up with his orders and keep out of the way of his temper." Anderson walked over to the kitchen table and sat down. He picked up a fork from one of the table settings and began twisting it between his fingers.

"But that does give me another idea! Eleanor! He's always treated her like crap, but she's stuck around. I don't think Justin would have trusted her with any information that could come back to haunt him. But then again, he thinks he owns Eleanor, so he might have been a little careless around her. It's worth a try. We don't have any other great ideas."

Ruth rested her hand on Anderson's shoulder. "You won't know unless you try, but this time why don't you approach her a little differently than you did Josh? Don't ask her if she knows anything—that gives her too easy of an out. She'll immediately deny that she does and then you're up against a brick wall. Just tell her that you already know she knows. If you can scare her more than Justin does, maybe you just might get her to tell you something."

Anderson looked at Ruth with a slight glimmer of hope on his face. "It might just work," he said.

"I've often wondered why she stayed with him all these years. He must have some sort of hold over her for her to have stuck it out for so long. She's obviously learned how to deflect his anger and keep out of his way, so she's a smart lady. She's not going to give anything away too easily. But between fear of breaking the law and maybe a promise for help in getting another job somewhere else, hopefully she'll be willing to talk to me."

Anderson jumped to his feet. "We don't have any time to waste—I need to call her now!" He flipped through the phone book and found her number. Dialing, he looked at Ruth. "Maybe we do have a chance after all! Keep your fingers crossed."

The phone rang and rang. No one answered and Anderson was about to give up when a young voice answered the phone. "MacDonald residence."

"May I speak with your mom, please?" Anderson asked.

After a brief wait, during which Anderson paced across the kitchen three or four times in anticipation, Eleanor answered the phone.

"Eleanor? It's Anderson Parker. Don't hang up—I have something very important to talk to you about, something that might affect you and your kids for a very long time." Anderson hoped that by getting in his warning early, he could keep her on the phone long enough to hear the rest of what he had to say.

"What are you talking about, Anderson? You have no business calling me. You and Mr. Cartwright are in the middle of a lawsuit against each other and I do not want to be mixed up in this. Justin would fire me if he even knew I answered your call, much less talked to you longer than it takes to tell you where to stick it—although you know I, personally, would never use such language. But that's exactly what Justin has said to me many times in the office. You know you're on his hit list, don't you?" Eleanor rambled nervously, talking faster and faster with each word she spoke. She was clearly terrified of something and that's what Anderson was hoping. Maybe he could help Eleanor while she was helping him. "Please, please don't call me again, Anderson. I have my twins to protect and I've got to keep this job."

"Eleanor, just listen to me for a second. I think we can help each other so that you don't have to live in terror of Justin threatening you with losing your job. You know about Justin and Nicole's plan to set me up so I'm serving you with a trial subpoena tonight and calling you as a witness tomorrow. Now, I know that sounds like a threat and I guess it is. But it doesn't have to be. You can use this as your opportunity to escape Justin. You can choose to stick with him and lie, in which case you will ultimately be prosecuted for perjury, as will Justin. Or you can choose to tell the truth. Then you and I can work together to get you out of this mess you're in so you and your family can have a better life."

Anderson held his breath, hoping his bluff would prove successful. By the tone of her voice, he was sure she knew something. He just hoped that his threat, as well as his promise of help, would convince her to tell him.

"I'm begging you. Please leave me out of this. Justin will ruin me. I'll lose my job with him and he'll guarantee that I never find another. I can't lose this job!" Eleanor's voice was frantic with fear.

"I don't have a choice and neither do you. This is a serious matter. We need to meet to discuss this tonight. Now." Anderson continued to push.

There was a slight pause and then Eleanor said, "Okay, Anderson. I'll meet you at the Starbucks on Howard in 20 minutes." Her voice wavered. He was afraid she'd never show.

"I'll pick you up, Eleanor. We can talk in my car. You don't have to go anywhere. I'll be right over." Anderson hung up the phone before Eleanor could protest.

Anderson immediately picked up the phone again and called Larry to tell him to meet him at Eleanor's house as quickly as he could get there. He prepared a trial subpoena in his home office and printed it.

As he headed out the door, Anderson kissed Ruth on her cheek. "You may have been right about Eleanor. Wish me luck!"

Anderson pulled up to Eleanor's house. He could see her waiting on the front porch. As soon as she recognized his car, she walked out to the street, opened the car, door and slid inside.

"I can't believe you're doing this to me, Anderson."

Anderson could see her hands trembling as she twisted a ring around and around her finger. "I'm sorry I have to do this, too, but you're my only hope. And I really do think this will make things better for you in the long run if you just tell the truth. Once it's all out in the open, we'll find you a good job and you won't have to deal with Justin ever again."

As they spoke, Anderson saw Larry's truck pull into her driveway. Larry walked over to the car and Anderson handed him the trial subpoena. Larry then turned and presented it to Eleanor in his capacity as a licensed process server. Eleanor and Anderson talked long into the night. On the way home, Anderson called Doug and they discussed what needed to be done for the following day. Anderson finally returned home after midnight. Ruth was wide awake.

CHAPTER 59

Anderson, Doug, and Ruth arrived at the courtroom early the next morning. Anderson leaned over and whispered to Doug, "Be calm and don't act excited. We still have to look like we're about to have our asses handed to us."

Court was called to order and Judge Amsler asked Anderson to announce his lineup of witnesses before the jury was brought in. Slowly, Anderson rose.

"At this time the plaintiff has no additional witnesses in support of the tortuous interference with a business relationship claim."

"Interesting. Well, I guess that means it is your turn, Mr. Cartwright. What do you have for us in defense of Mr. Parker's claim against you?"

Justin jumped to his feet. "The defendant/counterclaimant will first read the deposition of Nicole Babson taken in California and then will present my testimony as to the damages suffered as a result of Mr. Parker's baseless lawsuit. These two items should take us to about 11:00 and then we will be ready for closing arguments."

Doug pretended to cough and excused himself to get some water. Once in the hall, he called Larry and told him to have Eleanor at the courtroom at 11:00.

Justin had Jenny read the deposition of Nicole Babson for the jury. It seemed to strengthen his argument that he had played no role in the chain of events. Jenny then announced to the jury that Mr. Cartwright's defense was concluded, but Justin would now be called back to the stand in support of his malicious prosecution counterclaim. As Jenny questioned him, Justin calmly described how the lawsuit disrupted his personal life, his business revenue, and had cost him just under $100,000 in legal time and bills, including costs. Doug handled his cross-examination.

"Mr. Cartwright, you are asking this jury to award you money, is that correct?"

"Yes, it is."

"I assume you are telling the absolute truth to these members of the panel?" Larry pointed to the jury box.

"I am."

"You want them to believe you had nothing to do with the Nicole Babson situation?"

"I want them to find I was not involved because that is the truth."

Justin's testimony concluded at 10:45. Jenny told the court there were no additional witnesses and they were ready to present closing arguments. Anderson raised his hand as he stood.

"Yes, Mr. Anderson," Judge Amsler said.

"Your Honor, members of the jury, the plaintiff has one witness to call in defense of the counterclaim for malicious prosecution."

"I see. And who would that person be?"

"We call Eleanor MacDonald to the stand."

Justin, ashen, rose to his feet. Had Anderson found something out? Had she gone over to the other side?

"Your Honor," he argued forcefully, "this is additional unnecessary harassment, just as when he forced my wife into the courtroom."

Judge Amsler instructed the bailiff to take the jury out so once again the courtroom was clear. "Mr. Cartwright, you are starting to get on my nerves. I already warned you about your speaking objections in front of the jury. What is your excuse now?"

In a calmer voice Justin answered, "Judge, I'm sorry. But for them to call my office manager is absurd. She knows nothing about the situation."

"Mr. Parker, why are you calling this witness?"

"Fair enough, Judge," Anderson replied, rising. "Ms. MacDonald will tell us about a phone call between Nicole Babson and Justin Cartwright that took place last night. In that conversation, Justin admitted he paid Nicole to set me up and—"

Justin bellowed, "What the hell! No way! This is ridiculous. She can't testify. Judge, you must stop this charade." Justin no longer spoke with the calm confidence he had maintained throughout the trial.

"Mr. Cartwright, please do not interrupt Mr. Parker. Please continue, Mr. Parker."

Justin jumped up, raving, "This is bullshit, and Judge, you will stop it now."

"Counselor, don't tell me what to do or not to do. I am going to allow the witness to address the jury."

Justin totally lost control.

"Jesus, obey the law, woman."

The judge did not speak for a moment, her face red, glaring down at Justin. She turned to the court reporter. "Ms. Buckley, were you able to clearly transcribe Mr. Cartwright's last statement in its entirety?"

"Every word, Your Honor," she said.

"Counselor, I am going to keep my composure, but I want you to know that never has a lawyer spoken to me in such a disgusting manner as you just did."

With his head down, Justin returned to his chair. Jenny looked at him with an expression of pure disgust. Without a word, she picked up her trial bag and walked out of the courtroom. The jury was brought back in and seated. Eleanor was escorted to the witness chair, where she took the oath.

"Good morning, Ms. MacDonald. As you know, my name is Anderson Parker. Have you ever testified before?"

"No," Eleanor said, glancing around the courtroom. She had worked with attorneys for many years, but this was her first visit to a courthouse.

"There are basically just two rules. Relax and tell the truth."

"Okay."

"Yesterday evening you overheard a phone conversation between Ms. Nicole Babson and Mr. Justin Cartwright. Please tell the jury where you were at the time of the phone call."

"Next to the doorway of his office," she began. "I had been working late in the firm computer room when I heard loud voices. I went to Justin's office to see if he needed me. Our procedure is that I wait at the doorway until he finishes a conversation, and then we speak. When I overheard the conversation on his speakerphone, I was so shocked that I quietly stepped back. I didn't think Mr. Cartwright would appreciate that I had heard what he was saying."

"Please tell the members of the jury in your own words what you heard."

Justin spoke up. "Objection. Hearsay."

Judge Amsler turned to Anderson. "Response."

Anderson picked up three copies of a ten-page memorandum of law Doug had drafted late the night before at Anderson's request. He asked for permission to approach the bench and the request was granted. He handed the memo of law to Judge Amsler and a courtesy copy to Justin.

"As is set forth in plaintiff's memorandum, there are four separate and distinct exceptions to the hearsay rule, which allow the entire phone conversation to come into evidence through the testimony of Ms. MacDonald. First, the statements by Justin are admissions against interest made by a party. Second, the remarks of Nicole are the statements of a person who is a conspirator with a party. Third, the conversation is a reflection of the character of a party. And fourth, the entire conversation should be allowed at the discretion of the court so all admissions can be put in context."

The judge indicated she wanted a few minutes to read the law she'd just been presented with. Everybody maintained their positions in the courtroom.

"I am going to allow Ms. MacDonald to be questioned regarding the entire conversation. Counselor, please continue."

Anderson returned to his notes. "Please tell the jury what Ms. Babson and Mr. Cartwright said."

Justin rose and shouted, "Don't do it. You don't have to!"

"Sir, do not coach witnesses in my courtroom. Sit down and no more outbursts." Judge Amsler turned toward Eleanor and said, "Please continue with your testimony."

Anderson repeated his question and Eleanor relayed her account of the conversation between Nicole and Justin.

"Ms. MacDonald, could you tell the jury exactly what you heard Ms. Babson say about what happened with regard to consummation of the sex act?" Anderson boldly asked.

Eleanor blushed slightly but spoke out clearly. "She said that you wouldn't cooperate and she had to drug you to get those pictures. Once you'd passed out in her bed, she arranged everything to make those pictures look like you were having sex. But you didn't."

The members of the jury gasped, glaring at Justin. Anderson asked Eleanor a few more questions to highlight portions of her testimony and then concluded with a question about Nicole's comment about her California deposition.

"What did Nicole say about her sworn testimony in this case?"

"She told Mr. Cartwright, 'You haven't forgotten I get 25% of your recovery money for giving that deposition, right?'"

The witness was tendered to Justin for cross-examination.

Softly, Justin asked, "Eleanor, you have become angry with me on many occasions in the past, true?"

"Yes, I have."

"There have been times when you thought about quitting, right?"

"Yes."

"And now you are testifying falsely to punish me. Why?"

Eleanor did not answer. She just cried as her head fell into her hands.

Judge Amsler told Eleanor she could step down from the witness stand. Eleanor did not look at her employer as she passed him on the way out of the courtroom.

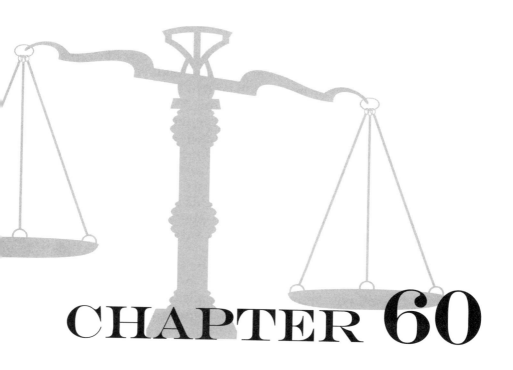

CHAPTER 60

Judge Amsler said, "Ladies and gentlemen, we are approaching the lunchtime hour. Here is what I propose. Since this has been a relatively brief trial, I do not anticipate, nor will I allow, extended closing arguments. I suggest we go straight into final arguments. Then I will take about ten minutes to instruct you on the applicable law. You can have lunch brought in and eat while you deliberate. Does that game plan work for you?" All seven nodded their heads.

Judge Amsler did not ask the lawyers for their input because she didn't care what they wanted.

"Mr. Parker, I want you to give one closing argument that will encompass both your direct claim and the defense of the counterclaim. Same rule for you, Mr. Cartwright. Finally, I see no reason for either side's argument to exceed 30 minutes."

Anderson stood in front of the jury, looking directly at the seven, as he spoke. "I apologize," he began, "because you had to take time from your employment and family to referee this distasteful dispute between lawyers. The subject matter is repulsive and the behavior of the attorneys involved has not been exemplary. But please keep in mind that you are here because of the calculated scheme masterminded and paid for by Justin Cartwright. When he sent those pictures in an act of revenge, I was seriously damaged. As you can imagine, my marriage was put to the test and my law firm almost fell apart.

"The first question you must answer is in regard to the tortuous interference claim. If you believe the answer should be yes, you will be sending a message to my wife, Ruth, and to the fellow members of my firm that Justin wrongfully caused this situation. Why is the answer to the first question clearly yes? Common sense tells you why. Not only is Mr. Cartwright the only person who had motive to damage me, he even announced his intentions after the verdict in the Green 61 trial. It is ironic that the strongest statements in support of my case came out of Mr. Cartwright's own mouth. Mr. Cartwright was so excited by the success of his scheme, he couldn't resist calling Ms. Babson to brag.

"Let's review a few highlights from the conversation. 'Anderson fell into our little trap.' 'I always wore gloves and mailed the envelopes from a neutral location.' 'You will be sitting pretty, young lady, when we finish with Mr. Parker.' 'I haven't forgotten you get 25% of my recovery in payment for your deposition testimony.'

"Mr. Cartwright will more than likely raise the question of Eleanor's truthfulness. You saw her up here on the stand. There's no way she was faking her fear of her employer. You know she was honestly recalling the conversation she heard with her very own ears. It would have been impossible for her to make up such a story. The Court will want to know what your finding will be with regard to Mr. Cartwright's cause of action against me. As you've seen, there was clearly probable cause for my lawsuit so it's impossible for me to be guilty of malicious prosecution.

"Let's now talk about the second question. This is where you will have the opportunity to decide if Justin's actions caused enough harm to me, to my family, and to my law firm to be worthy of awarding damages. My lawsuit was never about money. When you check yes on Question One, I will be vindicated and justice will have been served. If you want to send a message to Mr. Cartwright that you do not approve of his actions, award money. I will leave the decision to you as to what is a fair number. Thank you for your time and consideration."

Justin stood behind the lectern, looking calm and cool. He thanked the jurors for their service, then began speaking authoritatively.

"Members of the jury, the bringing of a lawsuit is an important decision that one should make only if there is clear evidence and probable cause to support all allegations. Mr. Parker does not have evidence for his claim. He made a mistake with a woman and now he wishes to be absolved for his sins by having you say it was all my fault.

"Let's review the evidence together. First, let us talk about the exhibits. Mr. Parker did not introduce one single item into evidence for you to review. Where is the check I supposedly gave Ms. Babson?

It could have been easily subpoenaed. Was there a receipt for the development of the pictures? How about any phone records showing I talked on the phone with Ms. Babson? They could have been located in discovery if they existed. Was there any documentation presented on how I supposedly met Ms. Babson? Mr. Parker wants to talk about common sense. Well, wouldn't it be logical to conclude there would be at least one piece of paper that would connect me to this lady from California?

"Next, let's talk about witnesses. I presented the sworn testimony of Ms. Babson by deposition. She candidly discussed how she had sex with Mr. Parker and told us the details of the evening. Despite numerous attempts by Mr. Parker to get her to admit otherwise, she steadfastly denied I was involved with her in any shape, form, or fashion. Mr. Parker doesn't want you to think back to her testimony. And what about the testimony of my wife, Catherine? She knew absolutely nothing about this lady. Sound judgment would dictate that if I had been involved in this elaborate scheme with Ms. Babson, somehow my wife would have had some clue as to its existence.

"What is the only shred of evidence he brings in front of you? The statements of an employee who obviously has an ax to grind. As I told you in my opening argument, I admit I have made mistakes and am not perfect. One of my shortcomings has been that I have worked too many hours to support my family. As a result, I am not always in the greatest mood in the office. Maybe I'm not the best boss. But don't reward Mr. Parker for using the presentation of a disgruntled employee who is reaching out for attention. Remember, it would have been very easy for her to fabricate her story."

Justin took a step closer to the jury. "Follow the greater weight of the evidence and ignore my obviously disgruntled employee, who clearly has a vendetta against me that I find hard to understand. The correct decision is 'no' as to Question One, 'zero damages' on line two, 'yes' as to malicious prosecution, and then whatever damage number you think is fair and just on the last line. Thank you for upholding justice."

Anderson couldn't believe Justin turned the case and tried to make it about Eleanor's integrity. Justin always had the talent of being able to twist anything to his favor. And it might just work this time, too.

✧ ✧ ✧

Judge Amsler excused the alternate juror and read the instructions to the remaining six, then they left the courtroom for deliberations. She told the lawyers not to leave the courthouse and to keep their cell phones with them at all times.

Anderson was cleaning up his table when he heard Justin approach. Thinking maybe Justin was going to apologize, he turned. Justin leaned his head close to Anderson and whispered, "I will make sure I collect every goddamn cent from you, and if the verdict is high enough, I will try to bankrupt you."

Anderson did not give Justin the dignity of a response. He stared briefly at Justin before he turned his back and left the courtroom.

Less than an hour later, Anderson, Doug, and Ruth had just placed their trays on the courtroom cafeteria table when Anderson's cell phone began to vibrate.

Anderson listened, then said, "We'll be right there."

"So much for lunch. The jury already has a verdict. It's been only 48 minutes."

After the jury was brought back into the courtroom and seated, the judge asked the jury foreman, "Have you reached a verdict?"

"Yes, Your Honor."

"Please hand the verdict form to the bailiff for publication."

The courtroom waited in anticipation as the bailiff unfolded the paper and began to read the verdict out loud.

"Did Justin Cartwright tortuously interfere with Anderson Parker's business relationship?"

"Yes," the bailiff continued, and a gasp went up from the courtroom.

"What damages, if any, accrue as a result of the interference?"

"Two hundred thousand dollars."

Justin slumped in his chair.

"Does Anderson Parker's lawsuit constitute malicious prosecution?"

"No," the bailiff concluded, and then he shrugged.

Judge Amsler looked up from her notes and turned to the jury, "Thank you for your service. You are dismissed." As the jurors filed out of the courtroom, she continued. "Counsel, I want you to remain."

After the courtroom was cleared, Judge Amsler said, "We now have a verdict, but there are other issues remaining. Mr. Cartwright, I advise you that you have been held in contempt of court. My secretary will be calling tomorrow to coordinate a hearing on contempt issues. I am personally calling the Florida Bar and requesting that a representative of the disciplinary division attend the proceeding. I will also be making a written request to the Bar that you be disbarred from the practice of law in Florida immediately, and that criminal proceedings be brought against you for your actions in regard to this matter. Court dismissed."

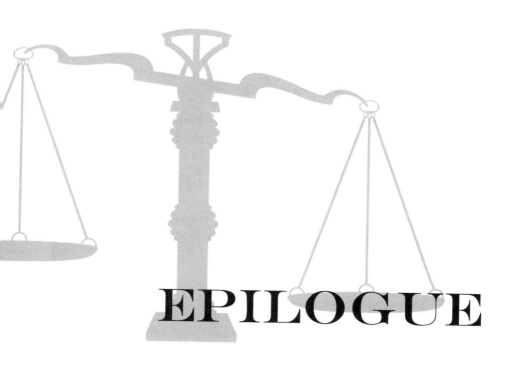

EPILOGUE

J
ustin's problems continued to grow. He hired ethics counsel the day after the conclusion of the trial. The $325 per hour pained him dearly. His lawyer told him there was a good chance he could lose his license to practice law because of three factors: his language to Judge Amsler in the courtroom, the possibility the Bar representatives found he perjured himself to further a lawsuit, and his prior problems with the Florida Bar. Criminal proceedings were also a distinct possibility.

Matters were no better at the office and at home. After both Eleanor and Jenny resigned, five additional employees took off and the firm was a mere shell of its former prosperous existence. Numerous clients had left as a result of trial publicity and new file intake had all but dried up.

Catherine was furious about the drop in income. She had worked hard to have the prenuptial agreement voided and now the family business was not going to be worth as much as she had banked on. At night Justin would retreat to his home study, lock the door, sit at his desk, and try to formulate a strategy to put his challenges behind him.

So far, the only complication he had taken care of was the judgment entered on the jury verdict. Although he was surprised to receive Anderson's offer to settle, he was glad to accept it. He mailed a check for $150,000 to Stetson Law School, as Anderson requested. Justin thought the $50,000 reduction in the amount of the judgment was a prime example of why Anderson would never be the trial lawyer he was. Anderson displayed kindness and sympathy, two weak traits that would stop him from reaching the top of his profession.

Justin sat at his desk and admitted to himself for the first time ever he was in trouble. He had never been scared before and he didn't like the feeling. As he worked on his outline for the quickly approaching contempt hearing, he wished his father were still alive so he could help him. To Justin, his father had been the perfect lawyer. A man who never felt sorry for anyone. A litigator who could formulate strategy to make witnesses say anything. And most importantly, a technician who could find a way out of any bad situation. No matter the cost.

It had been a long, tough haul for the Parker family, but life was beginning to return to normal. Both Emily and Beatrice had won their soccer matches that morning in the hot Florida sun. They had celebrated their wins by eating lunch at Steak n Shake and then coming home for a swim in their pool. The girls had fallen asleep early from exhaustion after a full day.

Anderson and Ruth cuddled in bed. As she hugged her husband, Ruth said, "I'm glad you thought of having Justin donate the money to Stetson. I hope that will get him out of our lives permanently."

"Yeah, he never gives up, so he probably would've appealed. But I knew he couldn't resist saving $50,000 off the judgment, even if it meant endowing a chair for an ethics professor at Stetson Law School."

"Well, I'm glad he took the deal. I never want to see him again."

"The ironic thing of it all is that Justin destroyed himself. I really didn't have anything to do with it. It was his own ego and big mouth that sunk him in the end. Life will be a little easier for us now that he's gone. I hear through the legal grapevine he will lose his law license and may be charged by the State Attorney's Office for perjury. I could almost feel sorry for him. But I don't. He deserved everything he got. I just hope I never meet another defense lawyer as devious and unethical as Justin."

Ruth pulled Anderson closer in her arms and responded, "That...would be impossible."

ORDER INFORMATION

Visit
www.impliedconsentbook.com
to order online.